Kate was a believer

Her friends considered Kate to be the most brilliant and the most reserved of their group. A good friend to have in a crisis, for Kate never lost her head....

There was another side to Kate, who'd never forgotten one soft summer day when she'd felt joyously alive in the arms of a handsome young man.

Kate had been searching all her life for something she'd briefly glimpsed. She believed it was as beautiful, as thrilling as the first spring flowers blooming on the Rockies, and that when she found it, it would complete her.

So when Kate slipped the topaz ring on her finger and understood how past, present and future live in each of us, she yearned with all her being to know once again the passion of living—of loving.

ABOUT THE AUTHOR

Emma Merritt tells us how she came to write *Return to Summer*: "When I first arrived in Estes Park, Colorado, and stood on the side of the mountain staring into the distance at The Stanley Hotel, I felt as if I had stepped back in time. Arcing through the fine mist that hovered about the pristine white building with its red gabled roof and cupola was a rainbow, so delicate as to seem unreal. The snow-capped peaks of the surrounding mountains majestically spired into the sky, reaching for the sun, each a prism turning the golden rays into a profusion of colored splendor. It was so easy for me to imagine that the mist, touched by the sunbeams, was a delicate golden veil behind which lay a magical land; it was as easy for me to cross over. As you read *Return to Summer* may you find the same romance and magic at The Stanley Hotel that I did. After all, you can go anywhere you wish through books and stories."

Books by Emma Merritt
HARLEQUIN AMERICAN ROMANCE
276–WISH UPON A STAR

RETURN
TO
SUMMER

EMMA MERRITT

Harlequin Books

TORONTO • NEW YORK • LONDON
AMSTERDAM • PARIS • SYDNEY • HAMBURG
STOCKHOLM • ATHENS • TOKYO • MILAN

I dedicate *Return to Summer* to the Grand Old Lady of the Colorado Rockies—The Stanley Hotel.

I owe a debt of gratitude to the following people:

- Christine Pacheco and Kathy Clark for conceiving the idea of the series set at The Stanley Hotel and for including me;

- Evan Marshall, my agent;

- Jan Milella, Kathy and Julie, my partners and good friends.

Very special thanks go to Tahti Carter, my editor, for believing in the magic of The Stanley and for sharing my vision of a time-travel story, and to Frank Normali, Patricia Maher and all the people at The Stanley for introducing me to the Grand Old Lady herself.

Published April 1990

First printing February 1990

ISBN 0-373-16337-1

Prologue

"1910!" the ten-year-old exclaimed incredulously and quickly raised her head, settling a shiny copper braid over each shoulder. Suspicious blue-gray eyes stared into her grandfather's face. "That was a *long, long* time ago, Grandpapa."

"Aye, that it was." Patrick O'Grady chuckled softly and dropped the picnic basket to the ground. Huffing slightly from the climb up the mountain, he sat down on the huge boulder that lay to one side of the narrow path.

The child gazed at her grandfather a while longer, then turned her head and scrutinized the cabin in the clearing in front of them. Ravaged by time, its timbers were now a weatherworn gray. The door had fallen off its rusted hinges, and the windowpanes had long since been broken; the casements hung precariously. The porch columns were rotten, the roof sagged. The only part of the structure that defied time was the stone fireplace.

"Did you really know the people who lived here, or is this another one of your stories, Grandpapa?" the girl asked as she lifted her long, slender fingers to brush a strand of hair from her face. No sooner was the tendril tucked behind her ear than the gentle spring breeze tugged it loose again.

"'Tis another of my stories," he answered, taking no umbrage at the child's question and allowing an indulgent smile to curve his lips.

Her pigtails flying behind her, the child raced across the path to the clearing and began to investigate the remains of the cabin. Just as quickly she twirled and ran back to her grandfather to lift her solemn face, her eyes bright with question and discovery. "May I walk inside, Grandpapa?"

"No," he answered, "the boards have rotted with age, Katie, and there's a deep cellar in there. I'm afraid that you might fall through."

"Why doesn't someone fix the cabin up, Grandpapa?"

"They might just do that one of these days," he said.

She smiled at him. "That way it won't be lonely."

Holding her hands behind her, Kate stood in the middle of the path and stared at the cabin. Patrick shoved back his hat, then planted his cane on the ground between his legs. Both hands crossed over the grip, he gazed at the child, who had recently come to live with him permanently and who was quickly becoming more like a daughter than a granddaughter.

Patrick was sure that Kate's parents loved her, but their love for each other and their dedication to archaeology was greater. For the first ten years of Kate's life they had taken her with them, always placing her in the keeping of a nanny. While some children adapted to such circumstances, Patrick quickly realized that little Katie could not. Surrounded by people, she withdrew into a shell of loneliness and blossomed into life only when she was with him during the summer. And yet although he knew she adored him, it was clear that she still loved her parents and wanted to be with them.

Last year when vacation was over, Caitlin and her husband George had explained to Patrick that Kate was socially immature, a state they blamed on themselves. So deciding that she needed a stable home life and to be with children her own age, they asked him to keep Kate in Estes Park and to provide her with a home. Patrick had agreed with his daughter; he wanted nothing more than to keep Kate all the time. He wanted to teach her to laugh and play; he wanted her to have the opportunity to be a child. In asking him to take Kate, Caitlin and George had shirked their parental duty, and it hurt him deeply that his daughter had done such a thing. It hurt Kate more.

No matter how long he might live, Patrick would never forget last August, when the time had come for Caitlin and George to leave. Kate had cried and pleaded with them to take her with them, but they, thinking they were making the right choice, had remained adamant in their decision to leave her with Patrick. Looking back now on the past nine months, Patrick knew from little things Kate had said that she felt as if they had abandoned her.

Running back to her grandfather, Kate lifted her solemn little face, her eyes bright with expectation. "Tell me a story, Grandpapa."

"That I will, lassie." Patrick shifted his weight slightly and patted the boulder on which he sat. "Come sit beside me, and I'll tell you all about the people who owned this cabin, Mr. Blaze Callaghan and Miss Caitlin McDonald."

Her face lighting up, Kate skipped across the path. "Oh, goodie, Grandpapa. This is my favorite story. Did

you really name Mama after Miss Caitlin Mc-
Donald?''

"That I did, lassie. Your grandmother, God rest her
soul, and I named her after the grand lady. We named
her Caitlin.''

"And she named me Kate after the same grand lady,"
the child said.

"Aye."

"I'm not going to be an archaeologist, Grandpapa," she announced quietly. "I'm going to stay home
with my children and tell them stories like you do."

"Ah, Katie, me darlin'," Patrick sighed, still grieving over his daughter and son-in-law's action, "you're
the joy of my life."

Kate's haunted face glowed with one of those rare
smiles that came from the depth of her little soul to
transform her from pretty into beautiful. Patrick's
breath caught in his throat and his chest contracted in
pain. At times Kate looked too ethereal to belong to this
world, and he feared losing her, as he had lost his beloved wife. He laid aside his cane and with both hands
clasped her slim waist to swing her through the air. Settling her tiny frame next to his own, he looped an arm
about her body and hugged her closely and protec-
tively. Saints above, he could not stand the thought of
losing little Katie. With her mother traveling all over the
world, she was all the family he had left now. Her
coming to live with him had given his life new perspec-
tive and focus. Determined to be a good parent, he had
compensated in every possible way for Katie's parents'
absence and had tried to teach her to laugh again. Aye,
more than anything else he wanted to teach Katie to
smile.

Although it was spring, the mountain breeze was cool. When Patrick felt Kate shiver, he buttoned her sweater and pulled her closer. Again she swatted the errant curl out of her face, but the silky strand, seemingly with a mind of its own, quickly slid back across her forehead. Smiling, Patrick reached down and secured it behind her barrette. Against Katie's fragile beauty, his hands looked big and clumsy, he thought. For a minute the two of them sat in silent communion, gazing about.

Eventually he sighed in breathless wonder. "Look at the valley, Katie. Nowhere else can a person see such beauty."

Arcing through the fine mist that hovered over the small town of Estes Park was a rainbow, so delicate as to seem unreal. The snow-capped peaks of the surrounding mountains majestically spired into the sky, reaching for the sun, each a prism turning the golden rays into a profusion of colored splendor.

"Like Rip Van Winkle," he said, his big hand gesturing to the alpine mountain bowl below, "the valley is impatiently awakening and casting aside its coverlet of snow and draping around its shoulders the vibrant green cloak of May. And over there—" His hand waved through the air, then stopped, and he saw the child's head turn to follow his indication.

Ensconced on a south-facing slope overlooking the valley was an imposing four-storied building, pristine white with a red-gabled roof and cupola. Stretching before it were open meadows, the lush green splashed with the brilliant colors of scattered wildflowers. Rising behind the building were great rock outcroppings.

"'Tis The Stanley Hotel, the Grand Old Lady of the Colorado Rockies." She's as elegant and royal as she was the day she opened in June 1909, and has reigned imperial potentate ever since," he said.

"What's elegant, Grandpapa? And regal? And what's a po-ten-tate?" came the barrage of questions as Kate snuggled closer to her grandfather's warmth.

Laughing softly—something Patrick did more now that Kate was with him—he patiently defined each of the terms. "Indeed she rules over the entire area, lassie. The Stanley's domain consists of the valley, the village, Longs Peak." With a sweep of his arm, he exclaimed, "Why, the entire surrounding range of mountains. And many are the distinguished guests that she has been host to: John Philip Sousa. The Unsinkable Molly Brown. And Miss Caitlin McDonald."

Kate grinned in delight. Her grandfather's voice was becoming softer, and his eyes were taking on that faraway look. She knew that he was going to weave again the magical tale . . . the one about her favorite person in the entire world, Miss Caitlin. Closing her eyes, she could see the faded brown photograph of the Irish performer in Grandpapa's album on the coffee table in the living room of their mountain home.

Pulling up her feet and planting them on the boulder, Kate hugged her legs, a shiver of anticipation running along her spine. Although she knew this story by heart—in fact, she knew every story that Grandpapa told by heart—she still loved to hear them again and again, especially the one about Miss Caitlin, as Grandpapa always called her. Each time Kate heard the story, she felt as if she were hearing it for the very first time.

"The June morning was beautiful, lassie, and I, a wee lad of nine, was waiting on the front lawn of The Stanley for the arrival of Miss Caitlin McDonald, famed Irish singer and pianist, hired by Freelan O. Stanley himself to celebrate the first anniversary of the hotel's opening. People came from everywhere—all over Europe and America—to hear her. Old F.O. and his wife Flora had the piano tuned especially for Miss Caitlin.''

"Just like me, Grandpapa," Kate asked excitedly, "she played the piano and sang?"

"Aye, lassie, that she did," Patrick answered. "A voice like a nightingale she had."

"Do I sing like a nightingale?" The blue-gray eyes stared at him earnestly, almost wistfully.

"Better than that, my Katie darlin'."

Kate sat quietly for a few minutes, then said in a soft voice, "Mother sings better than a nightingale, Grandpapa."

"Aye," the old man replied sadly, "that she does, lass."

"And she plays the piano better than anyone else in the whole wide world, doesn't she?"

"Aye, Katie. Your mother has a talent for the piano."

"Me, too, Grandpapa?" she asked, lifting her face to his.

"You, too." He bent and planted a light kiss up on her forehead.

Laughing with happiness, Kate said, "I'm going to practice the piano for hours everyday, Grandpapa, until I can play just like Mother and Miss Caitlin. You wait and see. And Mother and Daddy will be proud of me, Grandpapa." She raised an earnest face to his. "You'll see. They will."

"Aye, my darling," he said, his voice thick with emotion, "that they will. But I'd like for you to make me a promise."

"What's that, Grandpapa?"

"I love Miss Caitlin and her memory very much, and equally as much I enjoy telling her story. And I love your mother, but I want you to promise that you'll practice the piano so that you can play just like Kate Douglass."

Kate threw her arms around the big man and rubbed her cheek against his massive chest. She loved her grandfather and felt so secure with him. "I will, Grandpapa."

"Now, lassie, I'll tell you about Miss Caitlin." Patrick began his tale.

Engrossed in the story, Kate leaned her head against her grandfather and listened in rapt silence. Her gaze fixed on the old building on the side of the mountain, she pretended that the mist, touched by the sunbeams, was a delicate golden veil behind which hid a magical land, one into which she crossed as she listened to Patrick O'Grady's deep, mellow voice.

Chapter One

The afternoon sun cast a softening hue on the rugged terrain as Brent Carlton leaned his shoulder against the porch column of the log cabin nestled in a copse. While Brent loved the scenery, he also appreciated the serenity of his mountain retreat. He loved the aspens, whose leaves rustled gently in the wind, and the small stream that rushed behind the house.

"She's a classic," a voice called from the yard, and Brent turned to look at his younger brother, who gave the brass trimming of an antique automobile one last swat with the polishing cloth before he moved to the mahogany steering wheel.

"Yes, she is." Brent's gaze shifted from Caleb to the 1910 Stanley Steamer.

"Are you going to enter her in the car show at The Stanley?" Caleb asked.

Brent straightened and walked to the car, his boots crunching on the loose pebbles of the driveway. "I was thinking about it, but the timing isn't right. That's one of the busiest weekends at the resort."

Caleb glanced at his brother and chuckled disbelievingly. "You're going to have to tell another lie, Brent Carlton, to back that one up. You may own Elk Ridge

Resort, but I've worked there long enough to know
when we have peak season, and this certainly isn't it.''

"It's peak season for summer tourists," Brent answered, playfully reaching out to tousle his brother's
hair. "You've worked there long enough to know that."

Caleb tossed his head, a swath of straight blond hair
flying back, only to resettle on his forehead. "You could
spare one weekend, Brent. For the past two years since
your divorce you've become a workaholic. You can afford to take the time off, and—" he held up his hand
for silence "—you have a qualified staff to run the
place. You have absolutely no reason for not going to
the Caitlin McDonald Musicale Celebration at The
Stanley Hotel.''

Without answering, Brent picked up an extra polishing cloth and began to rub the wooden fender; for a
long time neither he nor Caleb spoke.

"Kate's going to be there," Caleb finally said. Brent
looked up and grinned. "Aren't you even curious to see
her again after all these years?"

"Not curious enough to go."

Brent lowered his head and rubbed the fender harder.
He refused to let Caleb know how much he did want to
see Kate, how much he longed to be with her again. He
had never forgotten her: the special smile that completely transformed her from pretty into beautiful; those
startling blue-gray eyes; that rich, long and thick auburn
hair. Through the years she had haunted him, always a
shadow on whatever he did, and he had always known
that for some inexplicable reason he loved her.

"I wonder what she's like now," Caleb mused, ap-
plying a little more polish to his rag.

Knowing the game his brother was playing and determined not to show any curiosity, Brent said nothing and rubbed the fender even harder.

"How old would she be, Brent, about thirty-five or -six?"

Sighing, Brent said, "Thirty-four. She was eight years younger than me."

Brent's hand stopped moving, and he stared blankly at the fender. Strange how time could erase any and all barriers, he thought. When Kate was seventeen and he twenty-five, the age difference had been what had effectively separated them. Now that she was thirty-four and he forty-two, the difference in their ages was a moot point. Still, they were apart, and ironically it was the years that had done it again. This time the gulf was even greater—seventeen years and one marriage each. His had finally dissolved into divorce; the last he had heard, Kate was happily married.

His thoughts going back through time, Brent lifted his head and gazed at the log cabin he and Caleb had built; then he looked down at the valley below. The breeze riffled his hair and blew the collar of his shirt against his neck. He remembered that summer day seventeen years ago when he had first met Kate. Wearing costumes of the era, she had posed as Caitlin McDonald, famed Irish singer and pianist who had performed at The Stanley in honor of the hotel's first anniversary in 1910. It was, in fact, Kate who had first introduced him to the legend of Caitlin McDonald and Blaze Callaghan.

On assignment from the university in preparation for his master's thesis, Caleb had taken the photographs for a portfolio on the legendary Irish performer, whose life had tragically ended at her husband's cabin in the mountains above The Stanley. Rumor had it that her husband Blaze Callaghan had killed her in a jealous rage.

Caleb moved to the front of the automobile, and it seemed as if his voice came from a great distance. "Isn't she beautiful, Brent?"

"Yes," Brent murmured, his mind not on the Stanley Steamer but on Kate. She had been more than simply beautiful, Brent thought. She had been a vision of exquisite loveliness, a picture of womanly perfection.

"Do you remember the way she looked when I took that first photograph of her?" Caleb asked.

Brent would never forget the way Kate had looked as she climbed out of the Stanley Steamer in that outlandish 1910 costume. Even without the photograph, her image was indelibly imprinted upon his mind. The austerity of the simple, straight lines of the navy-blue traveling costume she had worn were softened by the high collar of her white linen blouse and matching lace jabot, which hung in thick, deep ruffles from neck to waist. She wore an enormous navy-blue hat with large ostrich feathers in different shades of blue swirling over the crown. The sun at her back cast a golden nimbus around her, and the tendrils of her auburn hair shone like polished copper. He had thought her too ethereal to belong to this world.

Later in the day, when the photographing had taken them to a cabin on the side of a mountain behind The Stanley, Brent had accompanied Caleb. To add authenticity to the scene, he had agreed to pose as the infamous Blaze Callaghan. Kate had worn a pastel gray riding skirt and white blouse, the front of which had been doused with coloring, so that it looked as if she had been shot and was bleeding. Brent had knelt on the ground and cradled her in his arms.

Waiting for Caleb to take the photograph, Brent had stared deeply into her startling blue eyes, lost in their shimmering depths. Smiling, she had lifted a hand to cradle his face and had whispered:

> I have been here before,
> But when or how I cannot tell:
> . . . .
> You have been mine before,—
> How long ago I may not know:

All those years had passed, yet the words continued to haunt him and the desire to be with Kate, to make her his own had never truly left him.

STANDING on the log bridge that crossed the rushing mountain stream, Kate stared at the cabin. Ravaged by time, its timbers were now a weatherworn gray. The door had fallen off its rusted hinges, and the windowpanes had long since been broken; the casements hung precariously. The porch columns were rotten, the roof sagged. The only parts of the structure that defied time were the stone fireplace and the root cellar beneath the cabin floor.

Although it was spring, the cool mountain breeze made Kate draw her beige cashmere sweater around her shoulders and brush tendrils of hair from her face. Listening to the rustling leaves, she turned her head and gazed about. A delicate, fine mist hovered over Estes Park, and in the distance the mountains soared into the sky. On the south-facing slope overlooking the valley sat her favorite building, The Stanley Hotel, and before it

were spread lush meadows filled with the color of spring
flowers.

From the far-distant past Kate could hear her grandfather's voice as if it were yesterday and she were again
a child of ten. "'Tis The Stanley Hotel, the Grand Old
Lady of the Colorado Rockies," Patrick O'Grady had
told her. "She's as elegant and royal as she was the day
she opened in June 1909, and has reigned imperial potentate ever since."

Thinking of her grandfather brought back fond
memories, and Kate smiled to herself. As a child she
had been fascinated by the legend of Caitlin Mc-
Donald, famed Irish singer who had come to The Stanley Hotel in June 1910 to celebrate its first anniversary,
and who had fallen swiftly and irrevocably in love with
a race car driver, Blaze Callaghan. The romance between them had been short and tragic, ending in Caitlin's murder and Blaze's death three days later in an
automobile accident.

Many were the times that Kate had stood in this same
spot and listened to her grandfather tell her the tale.
Now she would tell their story in her own way. For the
past five years she had been so totally engrossed in her
research that her friends had accused her of being almost obsessed. Well, now that was all coming to an end,
she reflected.

Today, however, neither memories of Patrick
O'Grady nor of Caitlin McDonald had compelled Kate
to come to her favorite retreat. It was memories of a
man—Brent Carlton—who had appeared in her life,
then disappeared so quickly that she sometimes wondered if she had imagined him. She had only known him
briefly, but felt as if she had known him all her life.
Paradoxically, she felt as if she had been in love with

him for even longer than that, yet they had never even shared a date, let alone a kiss! There had not been the barest hint of intimacy between them, in spite of the deep bond she had felt then. And, of course, he had been twenty-five and she seventeen—at the time an insuperable barrier.

Leaning back against a tree trunk, Kate remembered the dream she'd had last night. Wearing a white lace dress over a gray chemise in the 1910 style, her long auburn hair hanging loose down her back, she had stood across the clearing outside this same cabin, the early sunlight breaking through the morning mist to cast a golden haze around her. In the dream she had looked like herself, but she had somehow known that she was Caitlin McDonald and that the cabin was newly built.

She had heard someone call her name and turned her head to see a man running up the mountain path toward her. Strangely enough it was Brent Carlton—more mature than the Brent she had known, but Brent, nonetheless. Yet he was also Blaze Callaghan. Wearing a white shirt, unbuttoned at the neck to reveal a V of dark hair, striped suspenders and navy-blue slacks, his handsome face was dark with worry. He looked all around and when he saw her standing there, he rushed toward her and she toward him, running as fast as her white satin, high-heeled slippers would allow, but no matter how fast she ran, she could not reach him. Someone yelled from the shelter of a large clump of bushes. Kate looked up to see a stranger standing there, his face contorted in anger.

"I'll get even with you, Blaze Callaghan, if it's the last thing I do!" The man raised a rifle to his shoulder and aimed at Blaze. Screaming, Kate rushed forward to pull Blaze aside, and the bullet pierced her heart instead. She clutched at her chest, which was afire.

"Kate!" She heard the anguished cry and the sound of footsteps as he ran to where she had fallen. Kneeling, he cradled her body in his arms, clearly not caring that her blood was no doubt staining his clothes. She felt his tears drop gently against her forehead.

"I'm not going to let you die this time, love," he murmured.

In the dream the man who was both Brent and Blaze scooped her into his arms and carried her down the mountain to the place where he had parked his Stanley Steamer Runabout. In the far distance maniacal laughter echoed through the mountain forest.

In a deep sweat, Kate had awakened crying and unable to sleep. She had dressed and driven up here to the cabin where she had met Brent Carlton almost seventeen years ago to the day. Through the years Kate's thoughts of Brent had grown fewer and fewer, and she could not imagine why she had dreamed about him now—on the eve of the Caitlin McDonald Musicale.

Pushing away from the tree, she moved closer to the porch, gingerly laying her palm against one of the sagging columns. She gazed proudly at the cabin. Now it belonged to her. After many years of wanting and trying, she had finally succeeded in purchasing it and had already hired an architect to renovate it.

She thought of another cabin, the one Brent and his younger brother Caleb had been building, and wondered if they had ever completed it. Closing her eyes, she remembered Brent as clearly as if he were standing in front of her at this very moment, as if it were that day so long ago. . . .

A GIRL OF SEVENTEEN, she had run down the stairs of The Stanley to greet the stranger who had just arrived in the antique 1910 Stanley Steamer. "Hi. I'm Kate Douglass," she called, brushing a strand of hair from her face and blinking against the glare of the morning sun. "You must be Mark. Linda's told me all about you."

"Hello, Kate," the driver said, a friendly smile curling his lips as he opened the door and stepped out of the antique automobile. Of medium height, he wore a blue short-sleeved casual shirt and faded jeans that hugged lean, muscular legs. He lifted a hand and ran it through his short, velvet-brown hair. He was one of the most devastatingly handsome men Kate had ever seen in all her seventeen years. But it was his eyes that compelled her attention—blue eyes, warm and friendly, and as pure as the sky above—beneath thick brows and framed by long, curling lashes. "Sorry, but I'm not Mark. I'm Brent Carlton."

"Oh." Kate was confused. "I'm sorry. Linda said that Mark would be bringing the antique automobile, and...I thought you were he...." Her voice trailed into an embarrassed silence.

"Understandable misunderstanding," he said easily. "I guess Linda never thought to tell you that my brother or I would deliver the car. I decided to do it, because no one drives this baby except me."

Kate's confusion was growing. According to Linda Barrett, only three graduate students were involved with the Caitlin McDonald thesis project: Linda herself, the drama major who was designing the costumes; Mark Sutton, the photojournalist, and Jim Herrington, the historian. Now a total stranger, who seemed to know more about the affair than she did, had appeared and was in some way connected to the assignment.

As if he'd read her mind, Brent said, "My brother is Caleb Carlton, a friend of Mark's. Both of them are getting their degrees in photojournalism. That's how Mark knew about the Runabout."

"Is Mark coming?" Kate asked.

"No, he had to withdraw from the project. Although he thought the photograph portfolio of Caitlin McDonald was a good idea, he didn't think it was for him. Being Caleb's best friend and knowing that I had an antique car, he told Caleb about it, and Caleb was immediately hooked."

"So Mark's out of the project altogether and Caleb has taken his place?" Kate inquired, a little irritated that Linda had forgotten to tell her about the substitution; since she was a part of the project, she felt as if she should have been informed.

"That's right." His smile widened as he answered her questions. "In fact, you'll be meeting Caleb shortly. He'll be up later with Jim Herrington. They had to stop in Boulder to pick up some supplies."

"And what role are you playing in this?" Kate wanted to know.

Brent chuckled softly. "At present, Kate Douglass, I'm merely the chauffeur. And who are you?"

"I'm playing Caitlin," she answered and gazed into those beautiful blue eyes. A moment passed and Brent's smile widened still further. Only then was Kate aware that she was staring; she felt the heat of embarrassment flood her cheeks. Turning, she quickly shifted her attention to the car. "Your Runabout is beautiful," she said. "I don't blame you for not letting anyone else drive it. You've made it look brand-new."

"She's a classic," Brent said proudly, seeming not the least perturbed by the abrupt shift in topic. "A 1906 Model EX Runabout. She has a ten-horsepower motor with thirteen moving parts. The two-cylinder double-acting engine is the kind they use in locomotives. Run by a direct-drive spur gear, it doesn't have a transmission." He broke off and grinned. "Once I get started talking about my automobile, I don't know when to stop."

"I enjoy hearing about it. You've done an excellent job of restoring it." Kate walked around the old car and brushed her fingers lightly over the glossy wooden fenders, the leather upholstery and the solid brass trimmings. Then she touched the steering wheel.

"Mahogany," he said.

Kate moved to stand directly in front of the car. "Where did you get it?"

"Through a friend."

She pointed at the headlights. "Do they still work?"

He nodded. "The steam boiler, fueled by kerosene, powers the car and illuminates them."

"Is this one still good for traveling in the mountains?" she asked.

"Indeed." He patted the car. "She's an excellent mountain car. That's why I bought her, so we can take plenty of photographs up in the mountains. If I understand Caleb's project correctly, it's to be a photograph portfolio on Caitlin McDonald, is it not?"

Kate nodded. "It's interdisciplinary: drama, home economics and journalism. Linda, representing drama and home economics, has designed the costumes. Jim will do the documentary, and now Caleb is to do the photographing."

"That's what I thought," Brent said. "Caleb hopes that we can take some shots around the site of the old cabin where Blaze shot Caitlin."

"Where Caitlin was shot," Kate corrected automatically. "No one knows for sure that Blaze shot her."

Brent chuckled softly. "General consensus has it—"

"I don't care what the general consensus says, it's wrong," Kate declared. "Blaze did not murder Caitlin in a fit of jealous rage, and someday I'll have the evidence to prove it."

"You don't think they were star-crossed lovers?"

Kate slowly shook her head. "I believe they're soul mates, traversing time and the universe together. Caitlin loved no other man but Blaze, and he loved no other woman."

"You sound as if you're as caught up in the romance of this legend as Linda is," he said dryly.

"Probably more so," Kate replied, totally unashamed of her love for the story. "I've grown up with it. My grandfather knew Caitlin personally, and at times I feel like she's a member of my family rather than a historic figure. Are you a history buff?"

"Not in general," he answered, "but in particular. I'm looking for information on the Stanley Steamer."

"Hence your personal interest in this project?"

"Well, it's rather twofold. I'm interested in it because of Caleb and for myself. I understand that Stanley Steamer Mountain Wagons were used to transport people from the railhead in Lyons and Loveland to The Stanley Hotel."

"You're right," Kate answered. "Did you know F. O. Stanley furnished Blaze with his own personal Runabout, while he was out here working in the summer of 1910?"

"No, I didn't, but I do know Blaze worked for and studied under F. O., and by the time he was twenty-five, he had already established himself as a race car driver and a car designer. His death—suicide caused by your legend—cut short a brilliant career."

"'My legend,' as you put it, did not cut short his life," Kate snapped indignantly. "She had nothing to do with his dying in that car crash."

"Blaze Callaghan was an experienced steam jockey and an ace driver. His car didn't go out of control for no reason at all. He deliberately crashed into that tree."

"He did not!" Kate planted her hands on her hips and glared at him. She could take personal attacks easier than she could accept any criticism about Blaze and Caitlin.

Grinning, Brent shrugged. "Whatever. His untimely death cut short a brilliant career. He had already made discoveries that revolutionized the automobile industry at the time, and would have made more. His name would have ranked alongside Henry Ford's."

"Probably so," Kate agreed, the heat of her argument having evaporated. "He worked for the Stanley brothers, who designed and built the Stanley Mountain Wagons, and came out here in the spring of 1910 to organize and to supervise their fleet."

"It would be nice if we could find a Stanley Steamer Mountain Wagon," Brent said. "It would add even more authenticity to this portfolio."

"I don't think it matters," Kate said. "The only time Caitlin rode in a Mountain Wagon was when she arrived at The Stanley. She and Blaze did their touring of the countryside in his Runabout."

"Since I own such an automobile and shall be *touring* Miss Kate Douglass about the countryside, am I a

likely candidate for Blaze Callaghan?'' he teased, his
blue eyes twinkling.

Kate caught her breath, then slowly exhaled. ''Since
you own the Stanley Steamer, I would imagine that you
dictate your own terms,'' she said, suddenly shy at the
idea of him posing as Blaze. ''Linda would be willing to
do almost anything to have it in the photographs.''

Brent chuckled. ''Not quite. She only promised me
sandwiches and a cold drink for lunch, which I think is
gross underpayment, when you consider that I had to
take a day off from work and I'm furnishing the automobile and specialized equipment for the photographer.''

''You're also a photographer?''

''Hobbyist,'' he answered.

''Well, you're getting paid more than I am,'' Kate
said, surprised at the ease with which they were talking
and teasing one another. ''I haven't been invited to
lunch.''

''Then it's my pleasure, Kate Douglass, to invite you
to have lunch with me. I think perhaps you and I could
rustle up something more palatable than sandwiches,
and we'll most certainly want to, if Caleb is the one responsible for providing the food.''

''I'd love to,'' Kate replied, pulling her gaze away
from the magnetic blue eyes. Curious to learn as much
about Brent as possible, she said, ''You mentioned
earlier that you had taken the day off from work. What
kind of work do you do?''

''I manage the Elk Ridge Resort,'' he told her.

''I'm impressed!'' she exclaimed, turning her face to
his again. ''That's the real fancy one, where all the
wealthy women—''

"Yeah," he drawled dryly, a hint of disinterest in his voice, "that's Elk Ridge, all right."

"Does Caleb work there, too?"

"No, he doesn't have time to work. He's a full-time university student. He's a sheer genius when it comes to photography," Brent said with pride. "He's intelligent and dedicated. At sixteen he graduated from high school summa cum laude and that summer he entered the University of Colorado. By carrying heavy loads, he managed to complete his B.A. in record time and graduated magna cum laude. Now he's working on his graduate degree with the same purpose and intensity. No, he doesn't have time for anything else but school."

"You sound more like a father than a brother," Kate said thoughtfully. "Yet you can't be that much older than him."

"I'm twenty-five, and that many years older than him. As the old saying goes, it's not the years but the mileage that counts. I feel like I've lived several lifetimes during the past twenty-five years. And I guess I do sound like his father. Ever since Dad died, I've been the father figure in the house. With five kids to take care of and no formal education of which to speak, Mother had a hard time. Someone had to help her, and since I was the oldest, I was the logical choice." He smiled. "But enough about me. What about you, Kate Douglass?"

"I'm seventeen years old and a senior in high school. I'm graduating this year and have a full scholarship to the University of Colorado for a degree in music and history," she answered. "Because my parents are archaeologists who are in the field in out-of-the-way places most of the time, I live here in Estes Park with my grandfather, Patrick O'Grady."

"Archaeologists?" Brent said, his interest in her parents obvious. "You must be proud of them."

"I am."

"Do you ever accompany them on their digs?"

"Often during the summer," Kate replied and described two such archaeological excursions, one in the South American jungle, another in Egypt.

"You have no desire to follow in their footsteps?" he asked.

"No, I'm rather a homebody and enjoy the quiet life with Grandpapa."

"Patrick O'Grady, the famous storyteller," he said, and Kate nodded. "He's a good one to have in your corner. People claim your grandfather is the man who immortalized Caitlin and Blaze."

"Probably so," Kate said. "He's truly in love with Caitlin, and so am I."

"How did you get involved in this thesis project?"

"Linda. I met her when she came to the house to interview Grandpapa about Caitlin. Later she explained the interdisciplinary thesis project and asked me to pose as Caitlin for the photographs. In fact, she almost insisted."

"I can see why she would," Brent said, and Kate felt the intensity of his scrutiny. "You're the perfect choice. Your hair. The bone structure of your face. Your eyes. They're so reminiscent of hers."

Embarrassed, Kate laughed nervously. "Really, I don't look that much like her."

"No, you don't." He reached out to brush her hair from her face and continued to study her. "You're reminiscent of Caitlin. That's more important than looking like her."

"Why?" Kate asked, fascinated by what he was saying.

"Because you capture the essence of what the woman was, and that's what comes across in photographs."

"I hope so. Linda explained how important this portfolio is, not only for her master's degree, but also for her future career opportunities," Kate said and turned, breaking the momentary intimacy. "And speaking of photography, would you like to see the inside of the hotel?"

"I would."

"It's one of Colorado's most beautiful memorials," Kate said. "People around here refer to her as the Grand Dame of the Rockies."

"The Grand Dame has been here a long time, hasn't she?" Brent said, his eyes quickly skimming the building. "She needs a lot of love and care."

"I agree," Kate conceded. Quickly ascending the flight of steps that led to the veranda, Kate led Brent into the spacious lobby. "Here it is," she breathed.

Kate saw none of The Stanley's imperfections. Her love transformed it into the elegant building it had been at the turn of the century when F. O. Stanley had first built it. For Kate, time and its ravages could never take away from its stateliness. The Stanley was still the potentate of the alpine mountain bowl.

"Mark was right. These shots are going to be fantastic," Brent commented, moving to stand beside Kate. He rocked on his heels and slid the tips of his fingers into his back hip pockets. After studying the scene in front of him for a while, he pointed to the landing. "He suggested to Caleb that a photograph be taken of you coming down those stairs, and one of you sitting on the bench, and another one in the Music Room." He looked around. "Where's that?"

"Over here." Kate led him across the lobby into an adjoining room. Sunshine poured in warmly and freely through wide, arched windows that offered breathtaking views of the rugged Colorado mountains. "When the hotel first opened," Kate said, "this room served as a ladies' parlor and writing area in the morning. In the afternoon chamber ensembles or orchestras performed in the stage alcove."

"The piano," Brent murmured and walked to the alcove on the other side of the room, Kate trailing along. "We'll have to take a photograph of you here. She was an accomplished pianist as well as a singer, wasn't she?"

Nodding, Kate stared at the carved Steinway concert grand piano.

"You play?" he asked, slowly turning as he studied the huge room.

"Yes," she answered, then said, "the piano was a gift from F. O. to his wife Flora upon the opening of the hotel, and the one that Caitlin played at the first anniversary of The Stanley. On numerous occasions it was personally serviced and tuned by John Philip Sousa."

He turned and looked at her blankly. "What?"

"Nothing," she said, aware that her tone reflected her disappointment in his lack of interest. She should be accustomed to being ignored by now, but she was not! She turned to walk away.

Brent caught her shoulder and stopped her. "I'm sorry, Kate," he apologized, a half smile tugging endearingly at one corner of his mouth. "Although photography is only a hobby with me, I get caught up in it to the exclusion of everything else. I'm interested in everything about your Caitlin. I promise. Please repeat what you just said. I'm listening this time.''

Grateful that he cared enough to apologize, Kate smiled, unable to stay irritated with him. They talked longer, then lapsed into a comfortable silence. Eventually Kate returned to the lobby and left Brent to wander around the room. Moments later, Brent reappeared, walking briskly to catch up with her.

"I'm worried about Linda," she said. "She was supposed to be here at nine with the costumes."

Brent lifted his wrist and looked at his watch. "She's only thirty minutes late. Let's give her a little more time. While we're waiting, why don't you tell me more about your Caitlin McDonald?"

Kate cast him an incredulous look. "You don't know Caitlin?"

"I've heard bits and pieces," he confessed, "but never the complete story."

"Surely you studied about her in Colorado history?" Kate was still unable to believe that anyone would not know the story.

Brent grinned. "I'm sure it was taught, but I was probably too immature at the time to recognize the importance of the lady's beauty and charm. My interest only perked when I became the owner of the Runabout, and even then I was more interested in the history of the Stanley Steamers than in Caitlin. Now that I've met and talked with you and have seen the hotel, I want to know more about her life. For instance, what about Blaze? I've only seen one photograph of him. Do you have any more?"

"Yes, but only one of him exists in which he's not wearing his racing gear. He was evidently camera shy, and physical descriptions of him are sketchy, at best."

As she talked, Kate and Brent strolled in leisurely fashion through the ground floor of the hotel.

"Nearly every journalist reported that Blaze was about six feet tall with dark hair, sparkling green eyes and a zest for life that was contagious. As you already know, Blaze organized and supervised the Mountain Wagon fleet, and at F. O.'s request, he personally drove to Loveland to meet Caitlin's train. The newspapers had a field day with her arrival. They reported that he was angry when he learned that she and her maid and her luggage would fill up an entire mountain wagon. That meant eight other passengers had to be squeezed into another vehicle or wait for a return wagon. He hardly spoke a civil word to her during the entire ride from Loveland to The Stanley.

"But Blaze's anger didn't last," Kate continued. "In about a month they were married at The Stanley in a lovely but private ceremony. Less than three weeks later, both were dead: Caitlin murdered, Blaze killed in an automobile accident."

"The stuff that legends are made of." Brent walked to the window and gazed at the peaceful valley below. "If both of them had lived, they would be lost in the dusty volumes of history and forgotten."

"That's true," Kate admitted and joined him to look at the view. "But they did die, and under suspicious circumstances. Rumor has it that Blaze and Caitlin had a heated argument on the sweeping staircase of the hotel, the morning Blaze was to depart for Boulder in preparation for the coming Fourth of July race tournament. Fearing for his life, Caitlin followed and begged him not to enter the race with his Stanley Steamer. Blaze declared that his life was racing and automobile design, and she had known that when she married him. Caitlin issued an ultimatum: if he raced, she would leave him. In answer Blaze quietly announced that he fully intended to race, and without another word walked out of the hotel and left for Boulder."

"And while the good husband was gone, his wife became infatuated with another guest at the hotel and had an affair with him," Brent said, his fingers lightly touching Kate's arm to steer her to the front door. "Blaze Callaghan burst in on a cozy scene in a mountain cabin and shot both of them."

"You only remember the bad parts and make them sound worse when you repeat them," Kate snapped. "That's not the way it happened at all!"

"Oh!" Brent arched a brow and grinned at her. "You remind me of a mama cat protecting her babies. Tell me, Miss Douglass, since you happened to be there, exactly how did it happen?"

Her cheeks burning, Kate had the grace to smile, but she was undaunted in her defense of Blaze and Caitlin. "To be fair," she said, "one school of thought is that while Blaze was gone, Caitlin did spend a great deal of time with Sam Donovan, another guest at The Stanley, who arrived shortly before Blaze left for Boulder. When Blaze returned and found Caitlin gone, he inquired where she was. The desk clerk told him that she had given orders earlier that day to have a horse saddled, so that she could go horseback riding. More investigation on Blaze's part revealed that she had ridden away from the stables with Sam Donovan, and the kitchen staff reported that they had prepared, at Donovan's request, a picnic lunch for two."

"Since this only happened about eighty years ago," Brent said, "surely you have evidence of some kind? Letters? A diary or journal? Newspaper clippings?"

"A few of her letters, her trunks, valises and clothes are on display at the museum," Kate explained, "but her diary was never located. Neither she nor Blaze allowed the newspaper reporters to get close enough to obtain intimate stories about them. So, no, we don't have evidence to back up either claim, only a legend."

Brent grinned. "Since I've been properly put in my place, Miss Douglass, please proceed with your story."

Kate grinned back at him and continued. "As I was saying, one group of scholars claim that Blaze exploded into a jealous rage when he returned and was told that Caitlin and Donovan had gone riding. Determined to find Caitlin, he hopped into his Stanley Steamer and headed up the perilous road into the mountains. No one knows exactly what happened during the time Blaze searched for Caitlin and Donovan. Late that afternoon a wounded and dying Sam Donovan rode into the livery stable at Estes Park and fell out of the saddle."

As she talked they descended the front steps and wandered toward the Runabout. "He told local authorities that he and Caitlin had gone horseback riding and had stopped to picnic at a small cabin in the mountains. Blaze, in a fit of raging jealousy, had burst in on them with his hunting rifle and had begun shooting at them. Caitlin was dead, Sam fatally wounded. But before he was shot, he claimed that he had managed to grab the rifle and fire at Blaze, but was not sure if he had hit him. Thinking Blaze to be a maniac, Donovan fled the cabin."

"You know, the more you tell me, the more potential I can see in this story. Caleb was right: Cait . . . lin's story—" He stopped in midsentence and stared at her. "Is it mere coincidence that you're named Kate and she's named Caitlin?"

"A rather deliberate decision, I'm happy to say. Both my mother and I are named after Caitlin McDonald. You see, my grandfather, who met the famed performer when he was 'a wee lad of nine,' has had a lifetime love affair with her."

Brent nodded his head. "No wonder you're so reminiscent of her. You must know everything about her life."

Kate grinned and said lightly, though seriously, "I know quite a bit about her. After all, I am her namesake. And what were you going to say about Caleb's being right?"

"I can understand his and Linda's insistence on the Stanley Steamer and on my being Blaze."

"You're really going to pose as Blaze?" Kate asked.

"I had already told him and Linda no, but today, after meeting you, seeing the hotel, and from the little bit I've heard of the story, I think I am. Caitlin's story is incomplete without both of them."

"Very much so," Kate answered and glanced down, not wanting him to see the pleasure that surely shone in her eyes. Somehow it felt right to her that Brent should play the part of Blaze; he reminded her of the steam jockey. Her gaze settled on the license plate. When she saw the name in large, bold print, a shiver ran down her spine, and she felt the blood drain from her face. He had thought her name coincidental, but if he really were ignorant about the Runabout that F. O. Stanley had provided Blaze, this was downright eerie.

"Brent," Kate finally murmured, her voice sounding unnatural to her ears, "I think Providence has had a hand in getting you involved in this project."

Grinning broadly, he said, "Absolutely not, unless Providence is named Caleb Carlton. Whatever would make you think that?"

She pointed to the license plate. "Your Stanley Steamer is named *la dama de suerte*."

"So?" Moving closer to her, he cocked a brow, his blue eyes twinkling with gentle laughter. "No matter what the language, Lady Luck is not that unique a name. And after all, the Runabout indeed is a lucky lady to have survived all these years and remain in such terrific condition."

"Did you know that Blaze's racing car was really named *la dama de suerte*?" Kate stared into those liquid eyes and felt as if she were drowning in their crystal depths. "Don't you see?"

"No, I don't, and Miss Expert-on-Caitlin-and-Blaze," he said with a teasing grin, "you're mistaken. I've done enough research to know that his car was named the Siren, because of the burners' inclination to howl when the fuel pressure rises above the usual 50 psi."

"He officially named all of his cars—" Kate grinned back at him "—but he always gave each of them a nickname that meant something to him. This one was in the final stages of production when he met and fell in love with Caitlin. Because he always thought of her as *la dama de suerte*, he named his car after her. He was rather superstitious when it came to his race cars, and thinking it would bring him luck, he always named his car after a special woman in his life. However, Caitlin was the only one whom he ever called *la dama de suerte.*"

"It's a good story, Kate, and quite romantic," Brent conceded. "Still, I find it hard to swallow. I wish I were a believer or at least a romantic, so that I could suspend credibility, but I'm not. I don't think Providence has had anything to do with today or with any part of my life. If she did, up to this point she's pulled some pretty sorry punches."

"It does, Brent," Kate said, "and someday you'll know it."

"What happened after Donovan returned to Estes Park and told his story?" Brent asked abruptly.

Kate circled the Steamer to stand on the opposite side from him. "Not long after he rode into town, Blaze arrived in his Runabout, not stopping until he was at The Stanley. He lifted Caitlin's body from the back seat and carried it to their second-story suite. When questioned by the authorities, Blaze told a different story. According to him, Donovan had kidnapped Caitlin and held her hostage in Blaze's mountain cabin, knowing Blaze would come looking for her. He claimed that Donovan was a crazed man, determined to kill him out of revenge."

"That being?" Brent asked.

Kate shrugged. "Blaze said that when he arrived at the cabin, Donovan accused him of running off with his wife and leaving her after she became pregnant. She returned to Donovan, but died in childbirth."

"If that's true," Brent said, "Caitlin's lover is not so heroic, is he?"

"The only part of the story that can be verified," Kate said stiffly, "is that Sam Donovan's wife did leave him for a period of six months, returned pregnant and died in childbirth. There is absolutely no evidence to prove that Blaze Callaghan was the man with whom she had been living, and Blaze swore that he was not her lover. And I believe him," Kate added. "Caitlin was not the kind of woman to have fallen in love with a man who would lure a woman away from her husband, get her pregnant and abandon her. And Blaze was not the kind of man to do something like that."

"But that is only your opinion," Brent said.

"Yes." Kate was quiet for a few minutes, then said, "According to Blaze, Donovan had intended to kill him, but knowing the man's intention, Caitlin had thrown herself in front of him. Blaze claimed to have shot Donovan in self-defense and did not chase him because he wanted to stay with Caitlin, who died in his arms. That's the kind of people Caitlin and Blaze were," Kate concluded softly, resting her gaze on Brent. "Some people are destined to love only once in their life, and I believe that's the way it was with Caitlin and Blaze. I believe that's the way it's going to be for me."

"Yes," Brent murmured, "I believe so, too."

"Do you believe it's true for you?" she asked. "Or for me?"

Brent never answered the question. The fragile moment was shattered, first by the repeated blast of a car horn, then by the squeal of brakes badly in need of repair. Kate turned to see a faded red Volkswagen pulling to a halt in the driveway. The door swung open, and Linda Barrett hit the ground running. Her round face was a huge smile, her eyes glowing, her short, curly hair bouncing against her cheeks.

"Hello, Kate. Nice to see you." Then Linda's gaze fell upon the man. "Brent, I knew you'd join us, once you thought about the story. I just knew you would. And maybe now you'll agree to play Blaze."

Brent's eyes lingered on Kate's face.

"Didn't I tell you Kate was a natural for Caitlin?"

"Yes," he said, "she is."

HAVING A MARVELOUS TIME that day, Kate posed and Caleb shot picture after picture.

"Okay," Caleb announced at midafternoon, his blond hair gleaming like spun gold in the sunlight, "I'm ready to do the wedding scene. Brent, you and Kate go change clothes. By the time you're dressed, we'll have the arch set up."

"Kate," Linda said, "I'll be there in a sec to help you with your dress. Let me show Jim and Caleb how I want the props."

Opening the door to the theater building, Brent waited for Kate. "Where do I dress?" he asked.

"On the other side. Here, I'll show you." Kate led him to one of the back rooms, then entered hers, and was joined by Linda a little later. Quickly Kate combed her hair into the legendary Gibson Girl coiffure, then with Linda's assistance stepped into the wedding dress. Gowned in satin, lace and tulle with accents of faux pearls, Kate stood in front of the full mirror that Linda had propped against the wall and gazed in rapt silence at herself. Linda fitted the veil over the top of her chignon, the ecru silk rosebuds gleaming richly against her auburn hair.

"This will do it." Linda handed Kate a bouquet of opened roses identical in material and color to the buds that held the veil in place, then stepped back and surveyed her work with obvious pride. "Kate, even if I must say so myself, you look beautiful. Now, I'm going to run back to see if Caleb and Jim have that archway fixed. You and Brent get out there as quick as you can. We need to go up to the cabin, and I want to eat lunch. I'm so hungry I could eat a bear, and I can't work much longer today. Okay?" She bounced toward the door.

"Okay," Kate said softly, still looking at the gown. A few seconds later she heard a faint knock on the door.

"Kate," Brent called, "are you ready?"

"Yes," she answered.

The door opened, and she saw Brent standing there staring at her. She fleetingly wondered if she were looking at him with the same wonder on her face. She had been aware of his height and massive shoulders from the moment she first saw him, but the doorway seemed to accent them. The tuxedo looked as if it had been made for him. While the formal attire gave him an air of sophistication, it also added an element of mystery—something that both excited and frightened Kate.

"You . . . look most handsome, Mr. Callaghan," she whispered.

A slow smile appeared on his lips. "And so do you, Miss Caitlin. Shall we join the others?"

"Yes," she whispered and wondered if she were indeed going crazy. For the moment she felt as if she were Caitlin and Brent were Blaze. She was glad when the sunlight hit her squarely in the face. This was reality; this was her world.

Caleb took numerous photographs of Brent and Kate, up the stairs, down the stairs, on the landing at the door to the Caitlin McDonald suite, then under the flowered archway.

"Kate, look up into Blaze's face!" Caleb shouted. "You're in love for the first time in your life."

Obeying the command, Kate pressed herself against Brent and his arms closed about her. Her palms slid up his chest and over his shoulders; she lifted her face and gazed at Brent. The look she saw there swept her breath away.

"That's great!" Caleb cried and after taking several more photographs, ran up the steps to the arch where his brother and Kate stood. He slapped Brent on the shoulder. "That's it, Brent. Damn, but you really know how to do things the right way. I'm so glad you came today."

"No, Little Bro—" he smiled and pulled away from Kate "—this is the one who knew how to do things the right way. I told her earlier today that she was the soul and spirit of Caitlin McDonald, and she is. What's next, Caleb?"

"The shots at the cabin. How about our driving up there and eating lunch before we shoot?"

"Kate. Hello, Kate!"

Hearing the greeting, Kate turned to see two little girls, no more than nine or ten years old, scampering up the hill toward the Stanley Steamer. One, her hand over her eyes to shield them from the afternoon glare, hung back; the other ran forward, grinning and waving at Kate. The only words Kate could think of to describe her were sunshine and laughter.

"You sure look pretty in that dress, Kate," the child said. "One day I'm going to wear a dress like that."

"Not me." The other moved closer, her face screwed up in disgust, her dark lashes framing large, chocolate-colored eyes. "There's no way you could ride a horse in that dress."

"You can't ride that dumb horse all your life, Nicki Chandler," the first child said. "Someday you're gonna have to wear something besides those old blue jeans and shirts."

"I'll ride Major all my life, if I want to." The brown eyes flashed angrily; she clamped her hands to her waist and tossed her head, flicking a saucy black ponytail over her shoulder. "You're just jealous 'cause you can't ride, Hayley Austin."

"I'm not, either." Hayley's little chin angled stubbornly and trembled slightly. "I could ride a horse if I wanted to, but I don't. I could be good in sports like you and my brother, but I don't want to. There now!"

Kate moved to where the girls stood and knelt between them, looping her arms over their shoulders. "What are you two doing up here?"

"Playing," Hayley answered, the twinkle quickly returning to her eyes. She looked up at Brent. "Who's he?"

"Your husband?" Nicki asked, a grubby little hand gently touching the lace inset on the bodice of the gown, only to be knocked away by Hayley.

"You're gonna get the dress dirty," she explained quite haughtily.

"I'll touch it if I want to." Nicki made a face at Hayley, but caught her hands behind her back, turned to Kate and asked, "Are you getting married?"

Kate laughed gently. "No, this is a friend of mine, Brent Carlton. We're posing as Caitlin McDonald and Blaze Callaghan for those three university students over there, so they can take some photographs. We were playing pretend."

"I'll be glad when I get to university," Nicki said, turning her head to look at Caleb as he repacked the equipment. "It's easier than school. I'd rather take pictures than study."

"Believe me," Linda said, her voice brimming with laughter, "we do our share of studying."

"I like to take pictures better," Nicki said and wandered over to Caleb, while Hayley migrated toward Linda. Kate and Brent hurried to change out of their costumes.

Later when Kate emerged from the theater, wearing her own clothes once again, the girls were gone. Gales of laughter came from the red VW, where Linda, Caleb and Jim sat waiting for her. Smiling at Brent, Kate crossed the lawn with him and allowed him to help her into the Steamer, then settled back to enjoy the ride. Soon they reached the sheltered spot high on the mountain that overlooked The Stanley.

As they unpacked their equipment, Kate walked down to a narrow log bridge that spanned a rushing mountain stream. Placing her hands lightly on the railing, she lowered her head and stared into the crystal-clear water.

Then she saw the reflection of Brent's face next to hers. He crossed his arms over the railing and leaned forward. "Tell me how Caitlin's story ended, Kate."

She was quiet for a long time. This was the part of the story that she did not like to tell. Eventually she said, "Needless to say, the townspeople were quite upset when they learned that Caitlin was dead. They were also angry that she had betrayed Blaze. In betraying him, they felt that she had betrayed them, too. Although the local authorities accepted Blaze's story, they had to go through some semblance of an investigation. Much to their surprise, they found a letter in Caitlin's desk, supposedly written by her. In it she claimed to be infatuated with Sam Donovan. She went on to describe Blaze's violent jealousy and her fear of his angry outbursts. She confessed that her hasty marriage to him was a mistake and that she was contemplating leaving him, because she feared that one day he would physically abuse her."

She paused, then said, "Blaze vehemently denied that the note was written by Caitlin. F. O. Stanley stood staunchly by Blaze's side, his belief in the younger man's integrity never wavering. Because of Stanley's influence, the authorities placed Blaze under house arrest, pending the results of a full investigation into Caitlin's death and the verification of her handwriting on the note."

The other three joined them on the bridge and listened in silence as Kate finished the tragic tale. "Fate, in her whimsical way, stepped into the picture. Three days later Blaze drove the Stanley Steamer in the Fourth of July race. He was speeding along in front of the pack when his car went out of control, swerved into a huge tree and crashed. Blaze died only minutes after they pulled him from the wreckage."

"Suicide?" Brent asked.

"No one knows," Kate answered. "At the time, many thought it was a death wish come true. After Blaze's death the investigation ceased and the note was lost . . . or destroyed. In fact, none of Caitlin's personal records survived."

"And human nature being what it is, from that day forward Estes Park had itself a legend," Brent said, "its parameters growing by leaps and bounds during the next eighty years."

"Come on, you two!" Caleb shouted. "I'm ready for the final shot."

This was the most painful photograph for Kate. The pastel gray riding skirt and white batiste blouse were lovely, and she cringed when Linda covered her with coloring, so that it looked as if she were wounded and bleeding. Brent, clad in dark trousers with red and blue suspenders, a white shirt and striped tie, looking very much like a technicolor Blaze, who had stepped out of the old sepia photograph, knelt on the ground and cradled her in his arms.

"If I were Blaze Callaghan," Brent said, "I would never have let Caitlin McDonald die like this."

"I don't know that you could have kept her from it," Kate murmured.

"I would have tried." Brent lowered his head and pressed his lips softly against her forehead, his warm breath moving over her face. The kiss was sweet, warm and friendly. Kate lifted a hand to cradle his cheek and whispered the words from Dante Gabriel Rossetti's poem:

> I have been here before,
> But when or how I cannot tell:
> . . . .
> You have been mine before,—
> How long ago I may not know:

Chapter Two

Glad that she had worn loafers and was in excellent physical condition from jogging two miles every day, Kate easily covered the distance down the mountain to The Stanley, but did not as easily push aside her memories of Brent Carlton. She rushed up the flight of stairs into the lobby, grateful for its warmth. As always, she stood for a moment when she entered the hotel and gazed about, never tiring of its timeless beauty. Then her eyes landed on the Stanley Steamer, and she again felt Brent's presence as greatly as she had felt it last night in her dream.

Leaning against the wall, she did not move until she heard the bustle of a tourist group move through the lobby and heard Hayley Austin, the assistant manager of the hotel, say, "F. O. Stanley designed the hotel himself and began construction in 1906. He had the supplies and materials transported twenty-two miles by horse teams over roads constructed for this project."

When Hayley saw Kate, she smiled and waved to her, but kept on walking with the group and talking. "Three years later, the hotel opened in June, 1909, and equaled any European resort in services and amenities. This is the dining room. The kitchen, also designed by F. O.

Stanley himself, was perhaps the first all-electric kitchen in the country. F. O. also designed the hydroelectric plant necessary to supply power to the kitchen."

The group moved away and Hayley's voice faded into the distance. Kate slowly rounded the Stanley Steamer on exhibit and walked through the Music Room to the stage, where the Steinway piano sat. She stood for a long while, yet did not sit down. Instead she idly flipped through the sheets of music she laid on top of the piano when she had arrived earlier. She was procrastinating and knew it. She could play all these songs by heart: she had memorized them as a young girl and played them many times during the years for Grandpapa. From the inception of the Caitlin McDonald Musicale in 1979, Kate had played the role of the leading lady, except for last year, the year that her husband Martin Norris died. Less than a year later Grandpapa also died.

Kate had played the piano after Martin's death; in fact, she had taken solace in it. But when Grandpapa died, so did her desire to play. She had not played—really played—since then. When she played, she was closest to him. Now, knowing that her dearest friend was dead, that she would never see or hear him again, it was more than she could bear. Still, she knew that she could not put off the inevitable any longer.

Closing the sheets of music, she finally sat down, her hands curling around the smooth mahogany bench on either side of her. Slowly she lifted her hands, the tips of her fingers tentatively touching the ivory keys. Of their own volition Kate's trembling hands began to move over the keyboard, running through several scales. With each note she played, her confidence grew; her touch became surer, scales turning into a melody...into melodies that echoed hauntingly through the silent and empty room.

The hot tears, refusing to be held behind her closed lids, rushed down her cheeks. Grandpapa was gone and would not return. She would never hear him call her lassie again nor would he ever hold her close to soothe away her hurts. Gone forever were the days when he would tell her stories about his beloved Colorado Rockies. Kate had not cried this deeply since she was a small child, since the summer when her mother and father had left her with her grandfather, when she had begged to go to Brazil with them.

Not even when Martin died had she wept like this. Dear God, not even when her husband of eight years had died! Guilt settled heavily upon her and tears ran even more freely down her cheeks. She had loved Martin, and they had been happily married. She simply had not been *in* love with him. In the beginning both of them had thought that would be enough, but while it had seemed to be for him, it had not been sufficient for her.

How innocent his visit to the doctor had been; he had only gone for his annual examination. He had been feeling tired, but both he and Kate had attributed it to his latest project, which had him flying back and forth between the United States and Europe. Kate had begged him to rest, and Martin had agreed to as soon as he completed the contract. He'd promised to take her to Africa for their ninth anniversary.

Kate extracted a tissue from her skirt pocket and wiped her eyes. She and Martin had never gone to Africa. Six months later he'd died of leukemia. As his widow she had inherited his wealth...and an abundance of loneliness. Her parents had not attended the funeral. Somewhere in the Peruvian jungle on a dig, they had not received word of his death until months later. But Kate had learned not to count on them. She had turned to Grandpapa, who had been a tower of strength. Had it not been for him, she did not know how she would have gotten through the funeral.

Now, she did not even have Grandpapa. Without him she was lonely, very lonely, and not at all sure what she wanted to be or to do. Her parents had managed to come home for Grandpapa's funeral, and had begged Kate to take a holiday in Europe with them. She had, hoping she could find her parents; instead she found two dear friends who would always be archaeologists first, and of whom she was extremely fond. Her parent—her grandfather—was dead.

Aware that her grief was turning into self-pity, Kate returned the tissue to her pocket and began to play again. Here she was, thirty-four years old and had never been in love. She had loved; she had been loved, but she had never been *in* love. She wanted to be. Caught up in her music, the tune changed and she played all the harder. The haunting lyrics of "I Want to Know What Love Is" filled the room. How beautifully the lyrics expressed Kate's desire. She desperately wanted to know what love was; she wanted to experience passionate love once in her life. She wanted to go where love was; truly she did, and she wanted someone to show her the way. That someone could have been Brent Carlton, but he had disappeared from her life.

She had never seen or heard from him again after the day when he had taken her to the mountain cabin that he and Caleb were building, and through the years he had become a wonderful memory. Until last night.

Kate's friends thought of her as a staid professor of history at the University of Colorado, cool and unemotional, but that was a facade she had built through the years and behind which she hid to protect herself. Secretly she longed for an intense and passionate romance... one such as Blaze and Caitlin had had, one such as she and Brent Carlton should have shared.

"Kate!" Hayley called.

Kate opened her eyes, lifted her head and saw Hayley at the door. She smiled and nodded, but did not stop playing. A notebook in one hand, Hayley reached up with the other and carelessly raked her fingers through her shoulder-length brown hair. Laughing, she walked into the room and said, "Boy, you're really caught up in your music. I called you twice before you heard me."

"Yes, I am," Kate said, lowering her head so that Hayley would not see the telltale sign of tears.

"Kate," Hayley asked as she drew nearer, "is something wrong?"

"No. I'm fine." Kate's playing intensified. Changing the subject, she said, "I like your dress. It looks springy."

Hayley glanced down at the cotton dress with the unusual, vivid melon-red flowers, and quickly raised her head.

"Bold colors look good on you," Kate continued, talking randomly. "Is it new?"

"Sort of," Hayley answered with an absent air. "I bought it at the end of the season last year and have only worn it a couple of times."

The volume increased. Staccato notes—loud and energetic—bounced through the room, followed by a crescendo. "Your shoes...they're the exact same shade as the flowers."

"Look, Kate," Hayley said quietly but firmly as she moved closer to her friend, "you're not going to sidetrack me. The Caitlin McDonald Musicale is important to the hotel and to me as assistant manager, and I want you to play the role of Caitlin. But nothing means more to me than you do. If this is too soon after—"

"It's not." Kate returned her full attention to the piano, playing louder. Hayley said nothing.

Finally Kate could stop playing; whatever had compelled her withdrew. "I told you that I'd help you celebrate Caitlin McDonald Day, and I shall. After all, I can't let The Stanley down, can I? I can't let Grandpapa down."

"Last year was the first year you didn't attend the Caitlin McDonald Musicale," Hayley mused. "It just didn't seem right without you. Do you realize that for the past ten years you've been the dominant figure in this celebration? You've played the role of Caitlin so long that we at The Stanley seem to think you are our Caitlin."

Kate smiled. "This really hasn't been my day, Hayley. This morning on the way down the mountain I met Nicki, who was out exercising that white Arabian of hers, and she implies that I'm old-fashioned, and now you're implying that I'm old."

Hayley's eyes rounded and she shook her head vigorously. "That's not what I meant, Kate. I'm simply saying you're the only person in the world who seems perfect in the role of Caitlin McDonald. Although Melinda Griffin was good last year, she wasn't you and didn't make a good Caitlin. But I don't want you to be upset like this, either. We can always get someone else."

"No, I'm all right." Kate leaned forward to riffle through her sheet music. "This is the first time that I've played the piano since—since—'' She could not bring herself to say her grandfather's name.

"I know." Hayley lightly ran her fingers over the dark rosewood piano. "Not since your grandfather died."

Kate rose, walked across the room to the north window and stared at the lake. The water was a brilliant blue, rippling gently in the early-summer breeze. Kate leaned her forehead against the cool pane. At one time all she'd wanted had been security, and she had thought wealth would provide it. But wealth had failed her. Through death Martin had abandoned her, and so had Grandpapa.

Now Kate had discovered that nothing mattered but life, and it was passing her by. At thirty-four she was probably more celibate than her dear friend, who was eight years younger. Kate had many friends, the closest of whom were Nicki and Hayley. She was a part of the academic society of the University of Colorado, and until Grandpapa's death had been an active participant in various clubs and organizations, among them the Colorado Storytellers' Association. And she had her book project. She was surrounded by activity and by people, yet she was all alone, adrift with no true purpose in her life.

She turned to look at Hayley. "I'm rather tired. I think I'll go upstairs to my room and rest awhile. What time is rehearsal tonight?"

"Seven." Hayley gazed anxiously at Kate. "Is that all right with you?"

Kate nodded and returned to the piano to gather her music, then walked across the room, but stopped at the French doors. "By the way, who will be playing—" she faltered "—be playing Paddy tonight?"

"Billy Ferguson."

"I don't know him."

"His father is one of our gardeners." Hayley smiled, and her voice softened. "You'll like him, Kate. Your grandfather would have, too."

Kate moved into the foyer, but Hayley's next words stopped her once more. "Aren't you interested in knowing who the dashing Blaze Callaghan is going to be?"

Not really, she thought as she nodded. Many men had played the part of Blaze Callaghan, but Kate would describe none of them as dashing. That adjective she reserved for Brent Carlton and him alone. Waiting for Hayley to reach her, she asked, "Have you and Nicki been at it again? Trying to pair me up with an eligible man?"

"Not trying, Professor. We have succeeded," Hayley announced, sounding rather proud of her endeavor. She moved her head, her golden-brown hair shimmering around her face and brushing against her shoulders. Even as a child, Kate thought, Hayley had been unusually perceptive. No matter what the situation, she was all smiles and positive affirmations. Yet Kate had once been concerned about her, fearing that Hayley would never find the man who could love and appreciate her fragility. But the man had come along. Mason Wilder had recognized and fallen in love with Hayley, treasuring her delicate beauty.

"Ron Townsend," Kate heard Hayley say. "Tall, dark and handsome—all your specifications. Remember?"

Coming out of her ruminations, Kate raised a finely sculptured brow. "How could I forget?" Unintentionally her description of the perfect male had slipped out

at one of those rare moments when she had been thinking about Brent—of late she had been thinking of him
more and more—and Hayley had pounced upon the
tidbit with relish, never to let her forget it.

"Ronald James Townsend, one of Mason's best
friends," Hayley said, holding out her hand and looking down at her engagement ring as she spoke of her fiancé. "They went to college together."

"How much younger than me is Ronnie?" Kate
asked dryly. This matchmaking was really getting out of
hand. While Kate had nothing against women dating
younger men, she preferred older, more mature men.

"He's about your age. He didn't start college until he
was much older," Hayley said, a tinge of impatience in
her voice. "Kate, you're determined to be a spoilsport.
Age differences between men and women don't mean
anything today. If you'll let yourself, you'll like Ron.
He's as passionate about history as you are. Just think!
You and he can spend the entire evening discussing
Henry VIII."

Kate looked suspiciously at Hayley, studying her
young friend's eyes and finding mischief glimmering in
their depths. "Any particular reason why you mentioned Henry VIII?"

Hayley grinned. "Well, he is one of the more passionate figures in English history, is he not?"

Kate smiled. "Thank you for expending so much effort on bringing romance into my life, Miss Austin, but
I suggest you channel it into your own love life. And
speaking of your love life, how much longer are you and
Mason going to be commuters in love?"

Hayley hesitated only a second, then beamed, a trace
of freckles glinting across the bridge of her nose.
"We're going to be married at the end of June."

"How wonderful!" Kate was truly surprised. "Here at The Stanley?"

Hayley's eyes twinkled. "Where else?"

"And where are you going to live?"

"Here." Hayley's laughter, like an artesian well, was refreshing and invigorating; it seemed to bubble up from the very depths of her soul. "Mason is going to open a historical museum in Estes Park, and in his spare time Ron is going to help him."

"How marvelous, Hayley. I'm so pleased for you. Now you don't have to leave The Stanley."

"No, not now."

Smiling, Kate shook her head. "I can remember when you and Nicki were frightened little freshmen, trekking into my American History class at the university. Now both of you are successful business women. You're assistant manager of The Stanley Hotel, and Nicki has her own stables. I'm so proud of each of you."

"And we're proud of you, Kate," Hayley said, "but we're also worried. You've changed so much since Martin died. The only thing you feel passionate about is history, but you can't go through the rest of your life loving a history text or living with legends. The other day Nicki and I were talking and—"

"Hayley, please," Kate began wearily. She loved her friends dearly, but was tired of their efforts to rehabilitate her heart and soul.

The young woman brushed aside Kate's plea. "Kate, you're not going to stop me this time. I've been wanting to say this for quite some time, and I'm going to. Martin's been dead for eighteen months. Dead, Kate, and that means he's not going to return to you. You're alive and have to go on living. You say you want to meet other men, but it's all talk. When given the opportunity, you won't go out with them. It's time you started dating again. You can't spend your life running away from life."

Kate rocked back on her heels. "My, my. Time has really reversed our roles. Are you also a practicing psychologist?"

"I'm not talking as an instructor to a student," Hayley said in a hurt tone. "I'm talking as friend to friend. I care about you, Kate. All of us do."

Kate said, "I know, and I promise, I hear you."

"Are you going to do something about it?"

Kate grinned. Once Hayley pounced on something, she never gave up. "I'm giving the subject some serious thought. That's all I'll promise."

Hayley pushed even further. "Will you go out with the subject if he asks?"

Equally adamant, Kate said, "I'll make that decision if and when he asks. Now I'm going upstairs to rest."

"Okay. I'll see you later."

The women parted, Hayley moving across the lobby toward the dining room and to the antique brass elevator. Kate waited a moment, then turned to scoot under the stairs into the photograph gallery. Standing there, totally absorbed in the Caitlin McDonald exhibit, was a young boy, wearing cutoffs, T-shirt and sneakers. Kate moved to stand behind him.

Aware of Kate, the boy tilted his head and stared up at her. His freckled face suddenly exploded into a smile. "Hey, I know you. I've seen your picture. You've played Caitlin McDonald before, and you're gonna play her this year."

"Yes, I am. You must be Billy Ferguson."

"Paddy O'Grady." He giggled. "I'm going to be your grandpa, Ms. Norris."

"So it seems." Kate's eyes shifted to the collection of photographs in the case.

"He really knew Caitlin McDonald?" Billy's voice was filled with awe.

Kate lowered her head, locking her eyes with the boy's. "That's right. He was about your age and was working at The Stanley."

"Are you named after Caitlin McDonald?"

"I'm named after her, but not Caitlin," Kate explained. "My grandfather loved her so much that he named my mother Caitlin. She in turn named me Kate."

"Where's your mother now?"

"She's in Brazil."

"Wow!" he exclaimed. "What's she doing down there?"

"She and my father are working there," she explained. "They're archaeologists."

"Oh." Apparently losing interest, Billy studied the photographs in the case more closely. Again he looked up and scrutinized Kate. "You look a lot like Caitlin McDonald."

I didn't say you looked like her, Kate heard Brent say as clearly as if it were that day seventeen years ago. *You're reminiscent of her. That's more important than looking like her.*

She smiled. "That's what people tell me."

Billy was quiet for a long while, then asked, "Are you married?"

"I was, but my husband's dead now."

"Was your husband anything like Blaze Callaghan?"

Kate's gaze automatically went to the only known photograph in existence of Blaze Callaghan when he was not wearing his leather helmet and his goggles. "No, not at all." But Brent was. Damn! she muttered, wishing she could get Brent off her mind.

Billy lifted a hand to swat a recalcitrant wave off his forehead. "Blaze raced the Stanley Steamers."

"I know."

"I wish I was old enough to play the part of Blaze," Billy said wistfully. "Then I'd get to drive you to the hotel in one of his cars."

"I think not. The hotel is protective of its car collection, and with reason." Kate could not refrain from passing on interesting tidbits of history. "You know the Stanley Steamers are one of the reasons why The Stanley Hotel is on the register as a historical site."

"Because Blaze raced them?" Billy's face lighted up at the thought.

"No, because F. O. Stanley transported guests from the train depots in Loveland and Lyons to the hotel in an automobile, and opened the western United States to automobile tourism."

"Oh." The monosyllable echoed, signaling the true depth of Billy's interest in history. He finally said, "I guess maybe that's the reason Miss Hayley's having that antique car show."

Kate glanced down at the child in surprise; this was the first she had heard of such a show.

"I just wish we were having a race like the one Blaze was in on the Fourth of July, instead of that silly old parade."

"It's not so silly," Kate said. "A parade really did take place when Caitlin first came to The Stanley."

"I know." He kicked the toe of his shoe against the floor. "I'm gonna ride my palomino, and you get to ride in Mrs. Kelly's fancy white wedding carriage, pulled by Silver Sheik, her white Arabian. Me and her are gonna work on it some more this afternoon. We gotta decorate it with a whole bunch of blue ribbons." He spat out the words as if they were distasteful.

"I know. Nicki had to special-order them, so they would match the color of my dress."

"Kate, is that you I hear?" Hayley called, leaning over the banister.

Kate looked up. "One and the same."

"It's a good thing I heard your voice." Hayley ran lightly down the stairs. "I was headed up to your room to deliver a message. I thought you were resting."

"She better not be!" Nicki Kelly's voice rang through the lobby. "Not while I'm responsible for tying a million little bows over that hansom. I can't understand why anyone would be so cruel and heartless, Kate."

In a fluid motion that had always fascinated Kate, Nicki walked across the room toward Hayley and herself. A white Stetson pulled low over her forehead, Nicki wore jeans and a plaid Western shirt. From the day that Nicki had matured into a woman, Kate had marveled at her innate beauty, a beauty enhanced by Nicki's unawareness of it. Nicki had the ability to be tomboyish and athletic and at the same time to be utterly feminine.

Tall and slender, her long black hair streamed down her back, with soft curls wisping around her face to complement her large brown eyes, which sparkled with life and vitality. Kate had observed throughout her life that many women were transformed by the clothes they wore. Not Nicki. On her, worn jeans, scuffed work boots and faded plaid shirts seemed to be fashionable attire.

"Shall we blame it on Caitlin?" Kate suggested.

"No, we cannot," Nicki teased, then reached into her pocket and pulled out a crumpled sheet of paper. "I've been looking all over for you, Billy. We have to get that buggy ready for the parade. Take this list and go to the drugstore. Mrs. Wilson will get everything you need. Bring it back to the stables and hurry. I'll meet you there."

Billy grinned. "I get to do this instead of tying all those bows on the buggy?"

"That in addition to this," Nicki told him.

"Drat," he mumbled. "We must have a million bows to tie onto it, Mrs. Kelly."

Nicki tilted her head to the side, thought for a minute, then said, "About two million now."

"You'd better hurry, Billy," Hayley said, her eyes glowing. "At the way those bows are multiplying, you're going to have ten million in a second. Sounds like a case of the Tribles to me."

"The Tribles?" Nicki asked.

"Yes." Hayley's melodious laughter floated through the room. "You know, the fuzzy-wuzzies."

"Yeah," Billy said and rushing to the door, flung over his shoulder, "you know, from the old *Star Trek*."

Nicki raised an elegant brow. "I haven't had time lately for TV. I've been working overtime to help my bestest friend with this Caitlin McDonald Musicale. In fact, that's why I stopped by."

"Oh, no," Hayley sighed, "this doesn't sound good."

"Could be worse," Nicki pointed out with her usual bluntness. "I want you to tell those antique car collectors that they cannot park their cars on the bottom acreage. I know they think it's part of the hotel, and if it weren't for—"

"I know," Hayley said hastily, "and I understand. I'm sorry, Nicki, but I'll take care of it."

"If you don't," Nicki returned, a mischievous gleam in her eye, "I'm going to have Jake give them all parking tickets or impound their cars."

Hayley pulled a face and groaned. "All I need is for your husband the cop to be hassling my guests."

"What about this antique car show?" Kate asked. "The first I heard of it was when Billy mentioned it a few minutes ago."

"Well, if you'd stay home and quit running around Europe with your parents, and if you were not so interested in getting that cabin up the mountain rebuilt, you'd know what's happening," Hayley replied lightly, then added, "it was really a last-minute decision. I wanted to add a little bit more fun and color to the celebration this year." She tilted her chin and added proudly, "Drawing from our 1979 agenda, I decided to do another antique car show. Although we will exhibit any antique car that is entered, we will be featuring the Stanley Steamers. From the research I've done, I've found out there are about one hundred of them remaining. Using the roster I was provided by the Horseless Carriage Association of North America, I have invited all the owners to be a part of our annual celebration. The association's magazine offered to do a feature article about us."

At the same time Kate went hot and cold all over. "How many are coming?" she asked, hardly recognizing the strange voice as her own. She wondered if Brent Carlton still owned his Stanley Runabout.

"I have five who have confirmed," Hayley replied. "And one who would like to come, but he wasn't sure if he could fit it into his schedule. He's supposed to let me know."

"Say, Kate," Nicki drawled, "Hayley and I were talking about this the other day. Reckon that man who posed with you for those Caitlin McDonald photographs eons ago will be one of the ones coming? You know the one I'm talking about?"

"Yeah," Hayley said before Kate could answer, "what was his name, Kate? Can you remember?"

Rather than the question being could she remember? it was could she forget?

"His name was—Carlton."

"That's one of them!" Hayley exclaimed, her face glowing with enthusiasm.

Her breath caught in her lungs, Kate's heart felt as if it would never beat again. Hearing about Brent or possibly seeing him did not necessarily startle or surprise her, but his being mentioned after the dream she had had last night did unnerve her.

Eventually, when her breathing had returned to normal and her heart was beating again, Kate inquired, "He's going to be here at The Stanley?"

"That's what I said, Kate," Hayley said, her voice bubbly with laughter. "Caleb Carlton is going to be the driver of one of the featured Stanley Steamer Runabouts in the parade."

Caleb Carlton but not Brent, Kate thought, her heart plummeting to her feet. She barely heard Hayley, who was still speaking.

"Since the show is scheduled for Sunday afternoon, I've asked the owners of the Stanley Steamers to get here early, but Caleb couldn't. He'll be driving in Saturday night."

Caleb was going to be here at The Stanley during the Musicale! The words rolled over and over in Kate's mind. Caleb was not Brent, but he was a living part of that magical day seventeen years ago. After all these years she was going to see him again. While a part of her was eager to see Caleb, another part was anxious, and yet another angry and disappointed because he wasn't Brent. But perhaps it was for the best. Before only eight years had separated them; that gap had now grown to seventeen years. Brent would be forty-two and probably married, with a family.

"Isn't this exciting?" Hayley asked, then before either Nicki or Kate could answer, she added, "I know this sounds rather pompous, but I am proud of myself."

Kate smiled indulgently. "It is exciting, Hayley, and you have every right to be proud. This is going to be one of the best celebrations The Stanley has ever seen."

"Hayley, if only this Caleb Carlton was coming in early," Nicki said, "you could get him to play the part of Blaze, like he did for the photographs."

"It's not the same one," Kate informed them. "This is the photographer, the one you had a crush on, Nicki. He's Brent's younger brother."

"It wouldn't really matter," Hayley said. "He could still play Blaze. What do you think, Kate?"

"I think the two of you belong in the loony bin," she answered lightly. "You said you had a message for me?"

"Chicken," Nicki teased.

"Hayley," a young clerk called from behind the registration desk, "there's a call for you. A Mrs. Simmons from San Antonio, Texas."

"Be right there," Hayley answered, and as she walked away, she said to Kate, "Mrs. Engels called and wanted me to let you know she was coming over with your dress. It's almost finished. All it needs is to be hemmed."

"Good. Send her up when she arrives."

An hour later, wearing a pastel blue-gray lace and linen dress—not at all similar to the one she was wearing in her dream last night, but nonetheless reminiscent of it—Kate stared in awe at her reflection in the antique cheval mirror. Constance Engels knelt on the floor, measuring the hem. Her hair, a mass of tight white curls, framed a full, round face softened by laughing eyes. Between compressed lips she held several straight pins.

Kate touched the delicate lace collar that stood up about her neck. "It's beautiful, Mrs. Engels."

"Yep," the older woman mumbled, "even if I must say so myself. With the description in the old newspaper, that photograph and those reproduced Butterick patterns, I didn't have much trouble. There, now—" She inserted the last pin and pushed herself back, then reached out to smooth the dress around Kate's ankles.

Kate could not get over its overwhelming beauty. Long ago she had thought the ones Linda Barrett had designed for her to wear during the photography sessions were the most beautiful she had ever seen, but this one outshone them. It was simplicity at its most elegant. The skirt was straight, flaring into fullness at the knees. She reached up and touched the mandarin collar; her fingers brushed over the fitted bodice. She turned, the lace rustling through the silence.

The older woman looked up, her gaze fastened on Kate's reflection in the mirror. "I hadn't really noticed before, but the dress is the same color as your eyes."

"Yes, that's why I chose it."

"Now all you need is your hat." Constance grunted as she rose and walked to the love seat at the foot of the ornate four-poster bed. Shaking her head, she muttered, "For the life of me, I can't imagine any woman wanting to wear something like this, especially to a piano concert. Heavens above, but this looks more like a cartwheel than a hat!"

Extracting a dark blue velvet ribbon and a silver brooch from her sewing basket, she returned to stand behind Kate. Draping the ribbon around Kate's neck, she fastened the snaps she had sewn to each end. Then she turned Kate around and pinned the brooch to the center of the ribbon.

"There now," she said with a gentle pat. "You look quite a bit like that photograph of Caitlin McDonald."

Again Kate stared at her reflection in the mirror, her hand going to her chest, the tips of her fingers gently brushing against the cameo. "This is an antique, isn't it?"

"Belonged to my mother," Constance said. "I reckon she and Caitlin McDonald would be about the same age."

"Did she know Caitlin?" Kate spun around to ask.

"Oh, no," the other woman answered with a wave of her hand. "I came to Colorado with my husband about fifteen years ago. I just figured this jewelry would give some authenticity to your costume."

The woman's gesture touched Kate deeply. "Mrs. Engels," she said, "this is priceless, if not in value, in sentiment. I can't wear it."

Constance waved a hand through the air. "Of course you can. What's the point of having something, if you aren't going to get any use out of it?"

Kate threw her arms around the older woman and hugged her tightly. "Thank you, Mrs. Engels."

Constance laughed. "Well, now, you might say I'm being rather selfish about this. I want my name connected with this celebration of the Caitlin McDonald Musicale."

Kate released the woman and blinked back the tears. She was getting a little irritated with herself. Normally she was not a person who indulged in tears, yet today she had never been far from them. "Everyone will know you created my dress, whether I wear the brooch or not."

Constance returned to her basket. Her back to Kate, she said, "I have something else I want to loan you."

She turned and held out her hand, a ring resting on her palm. Kate stared at the golden topaz. Set in white gold, the stone was surrounded by small diamonds. As if the ring...no, the topaz...were a magnet, it drew her closer and riveted her gaze.

"I found it a long time ago, when I was at the Caitlin McDonald and Blaze Callaghan grave site. I took it to the jeweler's and had it cleaned and polished. He said it went back to the turn of the century. I advertised it in the newspaper, but nobody ever claimed it. I guess it was selfish of me, but that appeased my conscience and I never told anybody about it, for fear they would try to take it away from me. But today I felt real strong that I should bring the ring and let you wear it."

Kate trembled with excitement; she closed her fingers over the ring. A warmth emanated from the stone and pulsed up her arm and throughout her body. She was both frightened and exhilarated. Dumbfounded, she opened her hand and stared at the ring in fascination. She had argued with the seamstress about wearing the brooch, but no such argument came to mind about the ring. Kate knew she must wear it. A force, a knowledge she did not understand affirmed this to her. No longer did she feel as if she was in control of her life. It was as if she were being controlled by forces far beyond her realm of comprehension. She felt very much as she had done that day seventeen years ago, when she had been posing as Caitlin McDonald for the thesis project.

Constance smiled, obviously embarrassed by her own sentimentality. "I thought maybe you'd like to wear it for the concert. Maybe it'll give you a feel for the era."

Kate slid the ring onto the fourth finger of her right hand and moved to stand in the sunlight that streamed into the room through the opened French doors. She stared at the mysterious, seductive topaz; it seemed to have a life and vitality all its own, seemed to be drawing her into itself, and she had no desire to fight its allure.

"Yes," she said, "I'll wear it for the performance."

Chapter Three

After Constance had left, Kate walked to the French doors and stood on the small balcony, holding out her hand to look again at the topaz that twinkled so seductively, the sunlight splintering into a rainbow of color as it touched the diamonds. Eventually Kate returned to the room, and deciding not to wear the ring until the night of the performance, slipped it off and placed it in her jewelry box. She undressed and lay down, but was unable to rest.

Clad in her underwear, she got up again and walked to the antique desk. There she seated herself and took into her hand a very old photograph to stare at the image of a man. The sepia tones had faded, so that she could hardly discern the man's features. Blaze Callaghan, the man whom Caitlin McDonald had loved and married, the man to whom many claimed she had been unfaithful.

Kate felt as if she were standing next to him. His dark hair was combed back in thick waves from his face, a lone lock looping across his forehead. Wearing a white, long-sleeved dress shirt with dark, peg-legged trousers and striped suspenders, he leaned against the trunk of a large tree. His face, ruggedly handsome, wore a pensive expression, his eyes narrowed as he stared into the distance. An air of melancholia seemed to surround him, reaching out to touch Kate.

Unable to escape the eerie feeling, she pushed herself away from the desk and moved to the dresser to pick up the ring and to gaze at it once more. She squeezed it tightly in her fist, liking its warm emanation; it gave her a sense of peace and well-being. Quickly forgetting her decision not to wear it until the performance, she slid it over her fourth finger. It felt right, as if it really belonged on her hand. Although the ring did not fit as tightly as Kate would have liked, it was not so loose as to fall off. She held out her hand and stared at the deep golden color of the gleaming topaz.

Returning to the desk, Kate glanced at the photograph again, and suddenly felt the urge to go to the tree that marked the Caitlin McDonald and Blaze Callaghan grave site. Without taking the ring off, she leaped to her feet and donned her skirt and blouse. Purse in hand, she rushed out of the room in such a hurry that she did not wait for the elevator. Instead she raced down the stairs, across the lobby and into the parking lot.

It seemed as if only seconds had passed rather than half an hour; she parked the silver Mercedes-Benz in front of the huge tree—the tree where Blaze's car had crashed, where he had died and been buried next to his beloved Caitlin. Kate walked closer and stood there staring at the graves, which were now surrounded by a waist-high picket fence, so that no one could desecrate them. This was a historical memorial to a man and a woman, who for the most part still remained an enigma to historians.

Taking the photograph out of her purse and studying it again, Kate walked around the tree until she
thought she had discovered the direction in which Blaze
had been looking. She leaned her left shoulder against
the trunk and gazed into the distance to see the majes-
tic mountains. At what had he been staring? she wondered. About whom was he thinking? Caitlin. Yes, he
was thinking about Caitlin; this Kate knew. Had the
photograph been taken after Caitlin died? The faded
inscription, written in a man's scrawl on the back of the
original, had dated it July 3, 1910, two days after Caitlin's death and the day before the fateful automobile
race.

Still holding the photograph in her hand, Kate looked
at it once more. So much remained a mystery. If only
she could unearth some new piece of evidence, either to
prove or disprove Caitlin's infidelity to Blaze. Naturally if there was proof of Caitlin's infidelity, Kate
would be hurt and saddened. At the same time she
would be happy because the puzzle, at least, had been
solved. Disappointed and frustrated at her lack of success, Kate dropped the photograph into her purse and
snapped it shut. After years of research, she had found
nothing more than bits and pieces of information...
and probably would never find more than that. All she
had really accomplished was having this old sepia photograph of Blaze duplicated and colorized, based upon
a newspaper description of him.

Sighing and moving away from the tree, she gazed
wistfully down the modern, black-topped highway that
snaked through the mountains—then a haze, rising
from the asphalt almost like steam in the summer heat,
began to dance before her eyes.

THE HIGHWAY DISAPPEARED and was replaced by a dirt road. A large crowd was assembled there. Three racing cars—old-fashioned models, like those of the early 1900s—were parked in a line across the road. In the distance she saw a small boy, who looked about nine years old. He was so familiar that she knew she should recognize him. He moved closer, and then she saw him clearly. It was Grandpapa! The boy looked like Grandpapa must have done when he was a child. A huge banner, bearing the legend July 4, 1910, waved in the air. Smaller ones, each inscribed with a name, fluttered beneath the larger one. Kate read them quickly: Josh Reilley; Arnold Hansmueller; Reuben Gladstone; Blaze Callaghan.

This was the Fourth of July Tournament, and these people had gathered to watch the race. Kate felt the excitement that rippled through the crowd as they turned and moved down the road toward an approaching car. Jumping up and down and shouting, the boy ran ahead. Kate craned her head to see the arrival of the Stanley Steamer. It drew nearer until she could discern the name of the entry on the placard that hung from the rear: The Legend.

Her hand on her forehead to shade her eyes from the sun, Kate slumped against the tree trunk and gazed in awe at the scene before her. The driver wore a beige linen duster, and his head and face were covered with a dark brown leather helmet and goggles. She saw no identifying features, yet knew he was Blaze.

He stopped the car, slung his legs over the side and stood still, staring directly at her. He reached up to take off his goggles, then unfastened the helmet and stripped it from his head. Now Kate was staring directly into the face of Blaze Callaghan. Holding the helmet and goggles in one hand, he raked the other through his hair. He lifted his lips in a crooked smile and began to walk toward her. As if he were motioning to her to join him, he waved.

Compelled by an unknown force to obey him, Kate's palm slid down the trunk, the bark pulling the ring over her knuckle. As she pushed herself away from the tree, the ring fell to her feet, but she did not take the time to pick it up. At the moment it was unimportant. She wanted to reach Blaze; she wanted to be with him. As if he could read her thoughts, his smile widened, and he nodded his head encouragingly. Her eyes never leaving his, Kate took a step, then another.

Her heart beat wildly and her breath was short. Each step was carrying her on a journey into the unknown. While she was curious and excited, she was also frightened. She stopped, and again Blaze waved and encouraged her with a nod and a smile.

She could no longer distinguish reality from imagination. She stopped once more, closed her eyes and breathed deeply. She knew that she was totally obsessed with Caitlin's legend. Perhaps she was sufficiently infatuated with Blaze to hallucinate, but she would not allow the story of two dead people to control her like this.

She opened her eyes. Now the scene was a blur and fading, but Blaze was still discernible and moving toward her, still beckoning to her. He seemed to be calling to her, but she could not hear his voice; she could only see him mouthing her name. Then he dropped his hands to his sides and simply looked, his eyes dark with pain. The boy raced forward, frantically motioning to her with both hands. She felt as if her feet were nailed to the ground; she could not make them move. The boy faded, then Blaze. He smiled sadly and waved good-bye; she saw the tears in his eyes.

"Blaze!" Kate screamed and raced forward, but he was gone. She stopped, her hand going to her mouth. Desperately she looked around; she sought the crowd, the boy... Blaze. None of them were to be found. She rushed back to the tree. Still nothing changed.

HER LEGS FELT as if they were made of Jell-O. Unable to stand, she leaned against the tree and reached up with trembling hands to massage her forehead. During the past three months, both Hayley and Nicki had had paranormal experiences. The strange little man Harry Peabody had appeared one day at The Stanley and had given Hayley a magical golden apple, reputed to have belonged to Atalanta. With it had come three wishes, and all three that Hayley made had come true. After the third one was fulfilled, Harry had then appeared and taken back his apple. A little later, Nicki had uncovered the murder and murderer of her first husband, Hayley's brother, through psychic dreams.

Although Kate had heard about all these experiences and had been indirectly affected by them, this was her first direct involvement with anything paranormal. While one part of her had been frightened and had pulled back, another part had wanted to join the boy. She'd wanted to be transported to the past. And it was the past that she had seen! The people were real, particularly the little boy and Blaze. She would swear that both had beckoned her to join them... in their world.

What was their world, and where did it really exist? The questions, for which she had no answers, spun around in Kate's mind. She was confused and wondered how she could have experienced this. All her life she had studied the legend, had made annual pilgrimages to their memorial, yet nothing like this had ever happened. Why now? she wondered. More significantly, she wondered how it had happened. If only she knew, perhaps she could make it happen again.

When her trembling eventually subsided and strength returned to her legs, Kate walked to the car. She slid in, closed the door, but did not immediately turn the key in the ignition. Abruptly she realized that she no longer wore the ring. She opened her purse. She knew she had been wearing the ring when she put away the photograph. Desperately she raked through the contents, but found no ring.

Frantic with fear, she threw open the door and raced back to the tree. Slowly she circled the trunk; there it lay, nestled between two exposed roots. Breathing deeply, she stooped, picked it up and held it tightly in her fist. Weak with relief, she leaned once again against the tree, promising herself that she would not put the ring on again until the night of the performance, and even then she would wrap some tape around it to make the fit tighter.

She thought about returning to the hotel, but quickly dismissed the idea. She wanted to talk with someone about her experience. She turned the key, and the engine softly purred into life. It was not just a simple matter of wanting to talk about what had happened to her; she had to tell someone.

She eased the Mercedes off the shoulder and headed back to Estes Park. If anyone could help her sort through these bizarre feelings and experiences, it would be Nicki. Hayley was too busy with the celebration.

"I WAS AFRAID you wouldn't be here," Kate said.

"I shouldn't be," Nicki replied as she set two cans of

diet colas on the table, then returned to the counter to stack sandwiches on a platter. "But you're in luck today. I decided to come in for lunch. I also needed to run into town to get more ribbon for the carriage. You know, to match the color of the dress you're wearing, I had to special-order them," she teased.

Kate managed a smile, but at the moment the parade and the celebration faded in significance when compared to what she had just experienced. She picked up her soda and poured it into the glass, watching the carbonated drink fizzle over the ice.

"Nicki, I want to talk to you about psychic visions."

"Why?" Nicki grabbed the bag of potato chips, ripped it open and popped one into her mouth, munching loudly, then poured the rest into the bowl.

Kate knew that Nicki had always been uncomfortable with her own psychic dreams, even though they had proven her innocence to everyone, including Hayley, who had known all along that Nicki couldn't have killed her brother. Even so, the experience had been a cruel, almost brutal test of their friendship. No wonder Nicki had been glad when the dreams finally ended! Not wanting her friend to get the impression that she wanted to discuss Nicki's dreams, Kate said quickly, "Psychic visions in general, not anyone's in particular."

Setting the last of the food on the table, Nicki drew out her chair and sat down. She pulled the tab from her cola, poured it into her glass and looked across the table.

"Why the sudden interest in the paranormal, Kate?" she asked. "Are you finally getting interested in something besides Caitlin?"

Kate grinned. "No, it concerns the research for my book."

"Interesting," Nicki drawled, her brown eyes sparkling with curiosity. "Tell me more."

Kate needed no more urging, telling Nicki everything that had happened to her from the time Constance Engels had given her the ring until she had driven to the stables. "I saw them, Nicki," Kate said. "Just a little, and I would have been a part of—well, of the—"

"Of the past," Nicki said.

"Yes, of the past," Kate agreed, finally admitting it. "At the same time it was both frightening and exciting."

Nicki nodded. "That's the way I felt about the dreams. There was something exciting and wonderful about them, but they were also one of the most frightening experiences I've ever been through."

"It happened," Kate said slowly. "I know that, but I don't know how. That's what's confusing me. I must find more information on this—this—" Not knowing what to call it, she grasped for a word to describe her experience. "This time travel phenomenon. I thought perhaps you could help me."

"I can't help you understand what or how it happened," Nicki said, "but I can recommend someone who can. She's a renowned psychic in Denver, has her own radio and television show. While I get her address and phone number, you get the ring Mrs. Engels loaned you. I'm more than curious about it." Rising from the table, she popped another potato chip into her mouth and headed for her bedroom.

SEVERAL HOURS LATER, Kate found herself seated in an opulent office, its mauve and gray decor softened by the muted light from the table lamp. Wearing a pastel pink skirt and matching silk blouse, Lucille Knight sat behind the desk. Her curly blond hair was pulled from her face and clipped at her nape with a gold barrette; bangs hung softly over her forehead. As Kate talked, relating the entire incident at the grave site, Lucille took notes. When Kate finished, the psychic laid her tablet on the desk, then leaned back in the chair, her face barely within the arc of lamplight.

She brushed the tips of her fingers against her temples and said in a deep, husky voice, "Nothing like this has ever happened to you before?" When Kate shook her head, she asked, "No experiences with déjà vu?"

"No," came Kate's quiet answer.

"What you've experienced is not at all unusual. To people who recognize their psychic abilities, traveling the paths of time is a common occurrence."

Gripping the arms of the chair tightly, Kate listened to Lucille. She had made an appointment to consult this woman, but was not sure she was prepared for what she was hearing. How true the old adage was: thinking something was far different from knowing it. "You're telling me I actually went back in time."

Lucille smiled and nodded. "We use the phrases 'went back in time' or 'time travel' in order to have common symbols of communication, but in reality, time has no barriers such as past or future. Again these are merely symbols used by us as points of communication. Time simply is. It's always the present."

Understanding what Lucille was telling her, but not sure that she concurred with its underlying philosophy, Kate said, "I really don't care if time has barriers or not, I simply want to know *how* I saw the past as if it were actually happening right now." Kate's palms were sweaty, and she felt herself shaking. "And why did I see this today and not any other time that I've visited that grave site? I've been to that memorial hundreds of times during my life, and nothing like this has ever happened.''

"You've asked me a question that I can't fully answer," Lucille said as she leaned forward, her blond hair gleaming in the lamplight. "No one really comprehends all the facets of the time continuum. We are only beginning to unravel its complexities. I can only guess that you're being pulled back by some strong force in the past, and today you were more receptive to it."

Again Kate was not sure that she and the psychic saw eye to eye, but now was not the time for debate. If she were going to understand how she happened to see the start of the 1910 Fourth of July Tournament, she had to know more about time travel.

"But why?" Kate insisted, edging forward in the chair. "Why did I see into the past this time? As you put it, why was I more receptive now and not at all before?"

Closing her eyes, Lucille was quiet for a moment. "The answer to your question must come from within. To help you find the answer to that question, I'll need to know what was different about your visit today."

"Nothing! There was nothing different about today." But even as she uttered the words, the truth dawned upon Kate. In itself the visit to the grave site had not been different, but all the precipitating events that led up to her going had been. Beginning with her dream last night, everything that had happened today had been different, and all of these acting together or one of them in particular had made the difference.

"Something had to be different," Lucille insisted. "Tell me all that has happened to you today."

"All?" Kate answered.

"Every detail," Lucille instructed, "whether it seems important to you or not."

Nodding, Kate began to talk. She began with her dream of Brent Carlton, then recalled playing the piano and the vivid memories of her grandfather and Martin that had flashed through her mind. She spoke of her feeling of abandonment by her parents, Brent, her husband and her grandfather—and lastly of the ring that Constance Engels had found at the grave site and given her.

"Do you have the ring?" Lucille asked as soon as Kate stopped talking. When Kate nodded, she said, "Let me see it."

Opening her purse, Kate extracted the ring and handed it to Lucille, who laid it in her palm.

"It's possible this could be the link. You said Mrs. Engels found it at the grave site?"

"Yes."

"Have you ever heard of psychometry?" Lucille asked.

"Yes, but I'm not sure that I clearly understand what it's all about."

"A person can glimpse the past or the future through an emotional bonding with an object that belonged to a particular time, place or person."

Kate stared at the topaz, glittering brilliantly on Lucille's palm. "You're saying that because I was wearing this ring, I bonded with—with someone from the past. I brought him to me."

"Yes, that's what I'm saying, but you're not necessarily being called back by a person. It may be an event that happened incorrectly or out of sequence," Lucille replied.

Kate was silent for a long time, then said, "I've felt unusually close to my grandfather today. Perhaps he's the one. He motioned for me to join him, and he did love Caitlin."

"It's a man calling you, but I cannot see or sense him. His face and eyes are covered by something," Lucille said. "I do sense that it is not your grandfather and that you are going to be out of phase. You'll be existing in two places at one time, or where time has bent on itself. The time continuum is one straight line. Sometimes it bends back or loops on itself, and we have an intersection of two different times."

"How is this going to affect me?" Kate asked, not really comprehending most of what Lucille had said.

"You've become the pivotal force to break this loop and put time back on its path." Lucille paused, then said, "You see, Kate, what you experienced today was a psychic vision. You could have stepped back in time either as spirit or as a manifestation. If you were manifested, you would have to assume the identity of a person in existence at that time, and since you cannot inhabit anyone's body but your own, you would have to return to one of your earlier incarnations."

"You're saying that time travel and reincarnation are one and the same?"

"Some say they are the same. Others say not. I tend to think they are. As I said before, your going back to the past is for a purpose. You must either learn a lesson or teach someone. Something in the past was left unfinished, and you must go back and finish it. This is all I can tell you. You must discover the answers within yourself."

Lucille returned the ring to Kate, who dropped it into her purse. Although the day had been different and in a way bizarre, Kate was not certain she could accept all that the psychic was telling her. While she had read about reincarnation, she had never accepted it as a possibility for herself. Rising, she said, "Thank you for your time, Miss Knight, but I really must be going. I have to practice tonight for the Musicale at The Stanley."

"You don't believe me, do you?" Lucille got to her feet and walked around the desk to stand next to Kate.

"I don't disbelieve you," Kate answered honestly, "but mostly I'm too confused to believe anything right now."

"The ring is your key to finding the truth."

"Perhaps," Kate replied.

"There is no perhaps about it. I know the ring is your medium. Don't run away from this, Kate," Lucille admonished her. "I know you didn't come here for a reading, and I haven't given you one. But I know that you've let life pass you by and have taken the easy way out. You wanted security at any cost, and that's what you received. Now is your opportunity to find what you've secretly desired out of life. Someone is giving you the opportunity you consciously or subconsciously asked for."

The words were cutting too close to the bone. "For what?" Kate challenged.

Lucille studied Kate closely. "The opportunity to find the love you're seeking."

WHEN KATE RETURNED to The Stanley, she walked to the registration desk. "Is Hayley here?" she asked.

The young clerk tossed her head, a thick mane of blond hair swirling through the air. "No, ma'am. She's gone to town to make some last-minute arrangements for the antique car show.''

Kate sighed. The last thing she wanted was to be alone with her troubled thoughts, and the idea that she could have—that she had—traversed time both unnerved and troubled her. If she were quite honest with herself, it frightened her. ''Have you any idea when she'll be back?''

The girl shook her head again. ''Sorry. She said for us to expect her when we saw her.''

''Thanks.'' Kate smiled and moved toward the elevator, but stopped short of entering. She was not ready for the solitude of her room and her thoughts. What she wanted and needed at the moment was a cool drink. Turning, she headed for the Dunraven Grille. Hesitating on the threshold, her gaze brushed hastily over the elderly couple who sat close to the door and the two men at a table in the corner.

''Hello, Mrs. Norris, may I get you something?'' the young waitress asked as she passed Kate.

''A margarita, Nancy,'' Kate replied and moved toward one of the smaller and more secluded tables. Before she reached it, one of the men stood and lean, muscular legs encased in snug fitting jeans moved out of the shadows toward her. Before she could clearly discern his facial features, she knew who he was.

''Hello, Kate.'' His lips curled into that old, familiar smile.

Kate went weak all over and was glad that she had the chair for support. ''Brent,'' she murmured, her eyes devouring his face, and automatically extended her hands for his warm, firm grasp. ''What a surprise.'' Even to her own ears, her voice sounded husky. ''I was expecting Caleb.''

As if time had slipped back seventeen years, Brent chuckled, laugh lines creasing the corners of his eyes—eyes that were still warm and friendly, that still twinkled with mischief. His grasp tightened. "I told you before, I don't let anyone drive my Stanley Steamer, not even my brother. Trust a woman to forget such an important fact."

Trust me not to have forgotten one thing about you, Kate thought. Then she saw the other man rise, a lock of blond hair falling over his forehead as he moved. A familiar grin creased his face. Brent released her hands and stepped back.

"Hello, Kate," Caleb said, also taking her hands in his, but Kate missed Brent's clasp; it seemed warmer and more protective. "Long time, no see."

"Too long," Brent murmured.

Certainly not by my choice, Kate thought, but only replied, "Too long, indeed. Would the two of you join me for a drink?"

"I'll let Brent have the honor," Caleb said quickly.

Kate felt her heart flutter erratically at the thought of being alone with Brent. The years had clearly done nothing to diminish her attraction to the man.

"I'm on my way to take care of the cars," Caleb continued, "and to make sure they're registered and parked in the right place. That woman who owns the stables gets right testy when it comes to where we park."

Kate laughed. "I think testy is a mild word for Nicki's feelings, when it comes to parking those antique automobiles on her property. Do you know where to go?"

"Sure do. She told me so in no uncertain terms." Brushing his hair from his face with one hand and balancing his Stetson in the other, Caleb laughed and winked at Brent. "See you later, Big Bro."

"Later," Brent said and pulled out a chair for Kate as Caleb departed.

Not sitting down immediately, she stared into his face; the room and the people faded away.

"I hope you were serious about that drink," Brent said softly.

"I was," she answered, wanting to reach up to feel his face, to assure herself that Brent Carlton was real, that he was no figment of her imagination or extension of her dream. She was beginning to doubt her own sanity, she realized.

Brent's smile widened, his eyes softened, and he leaned forward. One hand brushed her cheek as he pushed an errant curl behind her ear, his knuckles grazing her temple. The gesture was innocent, yet provocative. "You haven't cut your hair?"

"No." Kate shook her head, willing her heartbeat to slow down; thankfully she slid into the chair.

"I'm glad," he said and moved to sit down on the opposite side of the table. "Somehow I can't imagine you with short hair. You haven't changed, Kate. I would have recognized you anywhere."

"You haven't, either," she answered, her gaze riveted on the left hand that rested on the table before her—a left hand naked of a wedding band. She looked up in time to see his eyes fastened on her own left hand, on the wide gold band with the solitary four-carat diamond twinkling in the setting—her wedding ring from Martin.

The waitress appeared. Setting the margarita on the table and turning to Brent, she grinned broadly. "What'll you have?"

"Another beer." As soon as Nancy was gone, he said to Kate, "So you're performing as Caitlin Mc-Donald?" Taking a sip of her drink, Kate nodded and he continued. "Will your grandfather be here?"

She set down her glass. "No, he...died...six months ago."

Brent reached out and laid his hand over hers. "I'm sorry," he whispered. "I didn't know."

"Of course not," Kate returned.

"How?"

"A heart attack," she replied, blinking back the tears that suddenly misted her eyes. "The—the storyteller is gone."

Brent's hand tightened over hers. "I don't think so. I remember a young girl who had a gift for storytelling. She had me so convinced that she could have been Caitlin McDonald herself that I wanted to be Blaze Callaghan."

"I'm a good storyteller, but I'm a better story writer," Kate admitted without conceit and freed her hand from the gentle pressure of his.

"I haven't seen anything you've written, so I can't judge."

"You wouldn't have," she answered, then explained, "For the most part I've written scholarly articles. I'm a professor of history at the University of Colorado."

"I heard," he said, "and I'm quite proud of you."

"Thanks," she murmured, warming under his praise. "Right now I'm concluding my research, so that I can write a book on Caitlin and Blaze."

Leaning back in his chair, Brent's eyes narrowed and he scrutinized her. "You're still obsessed with them, aren't you?"

Kate felt herself bristle slightly at his comment. He was not the first to accuse her of this. Most of her close friends thought the same thing. "The love Caitlin and Blaze shared has always fascinated me," she admitted. "It seems...to be...eternal. It's as if Caitlin and Blaze will always be alive and in love. Grandpapa immortalized them with his storytelling. I'll immortalize them with my story-writing."

"Your husband must be proud of you and your accomplishments."

Kate blinked at him in surprise. For some reason she had expected him to know. "Martin's dead," she answered. "He died from leukemia about eighteen months ago."

Brent leaned forward again and reached out to take both her hands in his. He squeezed them gently and comfortingly and listened as she quietly talked about Martin. He had not planned to enter his car in the antique car show, but something—a force he could not explain—had drawn him back. And now that he was here, staring at and listening to the woman who had been a wonderful, haunting memory for the past seventeen years, he found himself mesmerized by her, caught up in the magic that she seemed to weave around him and herself. He was saddened to learn that she had not had the children she desired and that she had lost her husband, but at the same time was glad that she was a single woman again.

"Now it's your turn," Kate said.

Leaning back in the chair, Brent shrugged and took a swallow of the beer. He set the bottle on the table and said, "After that summer I returned to university, finished my degree, then on assignment from Elk Ridge I went abroad to study European mountain resorts."

"How wonderful," Kate breathed.

"It wasn't bad," Brent admitted. "I was getting the best of both worlds, earning a salary and living in luxury resorts all over Europe. But I missed home. The Colorado Rocky Mountains have a magic that no other place has. And by this time I had enough money to buy a partnership in Elk Ridge." Brent sighed and shifted his weight in the chair. He found it difficult to talk about himself, and this was the hardest part. "I married while I was over there, but Alyce wouldn't return to the States with me. We ended up getting a divorce."

"How long ago?" Kate asked.

"Two years."

"Any children?"

Brent shook his head. "No."

"I'm glad you came," she said and smiled at him, the smile that he had remembered all through the years, the special one that completely transformed her from a pretty woman into a beautiful one, that made her indescribably precious to him.

"I am, too," he answered, then asked, "Kate, will you have dinner with me tonight?"

"I WISH we could have gone out tonight," Brent said as they walked out of the restaurant into the lobby of The Stanley.

"Me, too," Kate murmured, "but I couldn't. I promised Hayley that I'd be there for rehearsal, and The Stanley is sparing no expense this year with the celebration. They're going all out with costumes and the works."

Resting his arms lightly around her shoulders, Brent grinned. "I don't suppose you need someone to play the part of Blaze Callaghan."

Kate sighed, remembering that she had almost promised to go out with Ron Townsend. "No, I'm afraid that Hayley Austin—"

"The assistant manager of the hotel?" he asked. "One of the little girls who watched Caleb take those photographs of us?"

"One of those little girls all grown-up," Kate answered. "She's already arranged for someone to play the part."

"Such a shame," Brent said. "I make such a good Blaze Callaghan. Oh, well, another time and place."

Feeling at peace with the world, Kate laughed. "Just thinking about Hayley being grown and on the brink of marriage makes me feel old. How about you?"

Brent stopped and turned toward her. "I feel like a man who has a new lease on life, Kate." He stared into her eyes. "I don't understand what's happening or why, but for some reason I know we've been given another chance. And I don't intend to let this one pass me by. I know it's only been eighteen months since Martin died, that you said that you haven't dated since and that we haven't seen each other in years, but you have always been with me, Kate, and now is the time for us to be together forever."

Kate smiled. "Are you asking me or telling me?"

Brent caught her hands in his own, and when she lifted her face to his and stared into those compelling eyes, she saw the fear and uncertainty. "I'm telling, but I'm really asking. Please don't say no. Let's give it a try."

"I'd like to see you, Brent," Kate said and really meant it. She pushed to the back of her mind her worries about the ring and her glimpse of the past and concentrated on the present, on having a second chance with Brent. She would be the first to admit that Blaze was a marvelous hero, but Brent was here, he was real, and so was the pull she felt toward him.

"After the rehearsal," he suggested and Kate nodded. "I know this isn't going to sound too exciting, but would you like to ride up to the Blaze Callaghan cabin?" In the same breath he added, "It's still there, isn't it?"

"Oh, yes, it is, and yes, I would," Kate said. "Are you going to stay for rehearsal?"

"Now that I've found you," he answered, "nothing is going to keep me from you."

"Brent!" Caleb's shout echoed across the lobby. "I've been looking all over for you. You have to come look at the Runabout. I think something is wrong with one of the cylinders, and if we're going to be driving her in the parade, she needs to be in tip-top condition."

Kate looked up at Brent and grinned. "Nothing?"

Brent chuckled. "Well, almost nothing."

Hayley walked out of the office, her arms piled high with papers and portfolios. "Kate," she said, her tone harried, "I'm glad to see you."

"What's wrong?" Kate asked.

"Everything and nothing," Hayley answered. "It's just the last-minute details. Nothing has gone right today, so I don't expect it to tonight. I finally had to turn the parade arrangements over to Nicki and Jake, so I could get back here and get the rehearsal going."

"Hayley," Kate said, "have you met Brent and Caleb Carlton?"

"Caleb I've already been introduced to," Hayley said, a smile brightening her face. She cast a suspicious glance from Brent to Kate and back to Brent. "Brent,

I'm so glad to see you again. It's been a long time. Are you going to join us for the rehearsal?''

"I think not. Caleb just told me that I need to check out the Runabout."

Hayley sighed, and Kate could almost have sworn it was with relief. "Well, I have to rush. I'll see you later. You, Kate, I want to see sooner, so head for the Music Room."

Kate laughed. "Yes, ma'am."

"I'll be waiting on the front porch," Caleb said and sauntered to the door.

"What time is rehearsal over?" Brent asked.

"I'm not sure," Kate answered. "Give us a couple of hours."

Brent smiled and reached up to brush away a curling tendril from her cheek. "I'll see you about nine."

ALTHOUGH Kate loved playing the role of Caitlin McDonald and truly enjoyed Billy Ferguson's impersonation of her grandfather, she found Ron Townsend a bore and could hardly wait for nine o'clock to arrive. She wished that Hayley's immediate goal in life might have been something other than matching her up with Mason's best friend. Finally rehearsal ended, and the crowd of actors began to disperse. Kate remained on the stage while she put away her music.

"Kate," Hayley called, "do you want to go out with us for something to eat?"

"No, thanks, I ate earlier."

Hayley walked closer to the stage and said in a lower voice, "You don't have to eat, Kate. You can just order something to drink."

"Not tonight," Kate answered. "Brent and I are going out."

Clamping her hands on her hips, Hayley playfully glowered at her, then said, "Well, Kate Norris, I'm not altogether pleased, because I did hope you would consider going out with Ron, but I'm not altogether displeased either, because you are at least going out with a man."

"Thank you," Brent said behind them; both women turned. He smiled and nodded to Hayley, then asked Kate, "Are you ready?"

Closing the portfolio, Kate handed it to Hayley. "Put this away for me, will you? I'll see you later."

"Anytime," Hayley said.

Kate grinned as she picked up her sweater and ran down the steps, holding Brent's hand. "How's the Runabout?"

"She's okay," Brent answered, "but in need of some new parts that I bought before we left home. That's one of the reasons why we towed her. I didn't have time to change them. Once we do that, she'll be ready for a road test and for the parade."

"We're not going to take her up to the cabin?"

"Nope. I'm afraid we'll have to make do with the Bronco, if that's okay with you?"

"That's fine," Kate answered, glad when they exited the building into the coolness of the night.

Taking the sweater from her, Brent helped her into it, then led her across the porch and down the stairs to the parking lot. Half an hour later and after a great deal of reminiscing, Brent parked the truck in front of the cabin and turned off the headlights.

"It's odd that these past seventeen years have made such a change in some ways, but haven't seemed to affect the cabin," he said.

"It was built to endure," Kate murmured and snuggled closer to Brent, glad for the warmth of his body next to hers and his arm around her shoulder. "I guess it's symbolic of Caitlin and Blaze's love."

Brent laughed softly. "You don't think it's symbolic of good workmanship and exceptional lumber?"

"These past seventeen years haven't seemed to affect you either, Brent Carlton," Kate pouted teasingly. "You're as much a cynic now as you were then."

"Not really a cynic," he corrected. "Just a realist." Moving closer to her, he reached out and began to pull the pins from her hair, and Kate did not stop him. One by one the pins fell into her lap, then the coil of her chignon slid down her back and her hair hung about her shoulders. "Your hair is beautiful," he said and ran his fingers through it.

She lifted her face and he lowered his. "I've thought of you, dreamed of you and loved you for years, Kate Norris, but now I think I'm falling *in* love with you. What do you think of that?"

"I'm not sure," Kate whispered, wanting him to kiss her and at the same time fearful of it. Her fear won out, and she averted her head, to lay her cheek against his chest. "Maybe we're in love with a memory, an idea."

Brent's arms closed around her and held her close. "Not me, sweetheart. I'm in love with Kate Norris, my Lady Luck."

"Is your car still named *la dama de suerte*?"

"Forever," he said. "Some things are eternal, Kate Norris, and that's one of them."

"Because of me?" Kate asked; it seemed that the years were quickly slipping from her shoulders. Could she really have found the love she had so desperately missed?

"Yes." They lapsed into silence, and he continued to hold her in his arms. After a long while he said, "Shall we get out and walk by the brook?"

"I'd love that," Kate said and reluctantly freed herself from his embrace. She gathered her hairpins in her hand and was about to recoil her hair, when Brent reached out and stopped her.

"Let it hang loose tonight," he said, "for me."

Kate stared at his face in the moonlight, then nodded her head. She opened her purse, dropped the pins into it and snapped it shut. "Let's go," she said.

Holding hands, they walked in the silvery light along the brook until they reached the narrow log bridge. "Did you and Caleb ever complete your cabin?" Kate asked.

"Finally," Brent answered. "I'd like for you to come see it. It's odd, but Blaze's cabin makes me think of mine."

Kate laughed. "One cabin looks very much like another."

"It's something more than appearances," Brent replied. "It's the way it's located on the side of the mountain, the way the trees form a canopy over it." He shrugged. "I don't know how to explain the similarity."

"You don't have to," Kate answered. "I understand what you're saying."

On the bridge now, they stood and stared into the moon-glazed water that rushed beneath them. An evening breeze stirred and Kate shivered. Brent pulled her into his arms and held her close. His hand touched her chin and he gently lifted her face.

"Kate," he murmured, "I'm not going to rush you. I've been waiting for seventeen years. I can afford to wait a few more, but I am going to kiss you, the way I wanted to all those years ago.''

This time Kate did not avert her head. Her palms slid up his chest and her hands locked around his neck. His arms tightened around her as she pressed herself against the hardness of his body.

When he finally lifted his mouth from hers, he laid his cheek against the crown of her head and softly began to speak.

I have been here before,
But when or how I cannot tell:

. . . .

You have been mine before,—
How long ago I may not know:

"You didn't forget," Kate said and pulled back to look at him wonderingly.

He shook his head. "Those words have haunted me through the years. When I saw you today in the Dunraven Grille, I felt as if I had found a part of myself, as if I had really come home."

"Brent," Kate said, "I'm not sure. At the moment I'm confused. I'm glad you're here and I enjoy being with you. But I don't want to rush anything."

Kate turned and walked to the other side of the bridge and looked at the star-studded sky. Brent walked up behind her and placed his hands on her shoulders.

"I didn't mean to rush you."

"You didn't," she replied. "I wanted to be with you and I wanted you to kiss me. But I also want time to think." Now she turned to look at him. "Although Martin was good to me and we had a wonderful marriage, I was wrong to have married him without loving him. You also made a mistake in your first marriage. I don't want either of us to make another one.''

''We won't, love,'' Brent said. ''I promise you that.''

Chapter Four

The Music Room of The Stanley Hotel was brilliantly lighted; the crowd was absolutely enthralled with Kate's playing. When she finished her last number, "I'll Take You Home Again, Kathleen," which she sang to Brent and to him alone, the audience rose to its feet, applause thundering through the room. As she rose and bowed, Ron Townsend, attired in a white suit in the style of the early 1900s, strode down the aisle with three dozen red roses in his arms.

Smiling broadly, he handed her the bouquet. "Miss McDonald, these are from your many admirers."

Looking over Ron's shoulder at Brent, who was sitting there in his blue suit, she said, "Thank you, Mr. Callaghan."

"And this—" glowering, Ron pulled a yellow dandelion from behind him "—is from me. The roses are lovely, but this reminds me of you. Wild, untamed and beautiful. A part of God's natural beauty."

Her eyes closed, Kate imagined Blaze saying these words to Caitlin. She heard a husky masculine voice, much like she imagined his to be, much as Brent's sounded. She felt tears behind her eyelids and hated herself for being so easily overcome by nostalgia. She would be glad when this celebration was over. It was really getting to her. Hayley and Nicki had a right to be worried: she was losing herself in someone else's identity. This nonsense had to stop. Opening her eyes, she reached out and took the wildflower, her fingers brushing against Ron's.

"Again I thank you," she said.

"It is I who thank you." His voice lowered to a suggested whisper, yet was not so low that the audience could not hear. "May I take you riding tomorrow?"

Smiling, Kate's gaze skimmed over the crowd; again her eyes locked with Brent's. She smiled for him. "You are audacious, sir, to ask me in front of so many people. What if I were to turn you down?"

Ron threw back his head and laughed. "But you won't."

Kate leaned forward and tucked the wildflower into his lapel. "But I have, sir. Tomorrow I am going riding with Mr. Patrick O'Grady." Holding her roses in the crook of her arm, she swept the room with her other hand. "Tonight I belong to my admirers."

Applause deafened Kate; she and Ron caught hands and bowed time and again. When the performance ended, the people thronged around, congratulating them. Finally they made their way through the crowd into the lobby.

Running a finger around his collar, Ron said, "I'm glad we don't have to wear these stiffly starched collars anymore today. I feel like I'm suffocating. Don't you?" The minute he said the words, he looked at Kate and smiled. "Of course you don't. You're beautiful. You don't look a bit perturbed."

"No," she murmured, searching the crowd for Brent, "I'm not."

"Ron! Kate! Over here!" Kate looked across the lobby to see a tall, lanky man standing outside the restaurant, grinning and waving to them. It was Mason Wilder, Hayley's fiancé. "Join Hayley and me for something to drink."

"Shall we?" Ron asked, an expectant look on his face.

"Not right now. I'd like to get a breath of fresh air and rest awhile." Kate hid her face in the roses and inhaled deeply. "You go ahead, and I'll join you later."

"All right." Although he looked disappointed, he said, "Hayley told me about your renovating the Blaze Callaghan cabin. I'm quite interested in it and would like to discuss it in more detail."

"We will," Kate said.

"Promise?" he asked.

"Promise." She tried not to let her irritation show, but all she wanted to do was to get away from him, to see Brent.

Finally Ron turned and walked to the other side of the lobby to join Mason.

"I believe Mr. Townsend has settled into his role," Brent said in a low voice behind her.

Kate turned and smiled at him. "He gets on my nerves. I thought he would never leave."

"Do you talk that way behind my back?" Brent teased.

Kate nodded. "To be honest, Mr. Carlton, you do get on my nerves...but in the best sort of way. Now are you ready for dinner?"

"That is what I wanted to talk to you about," he said. "I thought I had the right parts for the Lady Luck, but I don't. Caleb and I are going to have to haul the

Runabout into Boulder. A friend of mine special-ordered them and is going to help me install them."

"Now?" Kate demanded.

"Now, if I intend to drive the Runabout in the parade tomorrow."

Kate looked up to see Caleb smiling and waving from the door. When Brent turned, he motioned to him.

"I'll be back before dawn."

Kate smiled. "I'll be waiting." Leaning toward him, she planted a kiss upon his cheek. "Be sure to come by the room and get me for a sunrise breakfast."

Brent grinned. "I wouldn't miss an invitation like that for anything, love."

"Not even the Runabout?"

"Well..." he drawled over his shoulder as he walked across the lobby. When he reached the door, he turned, smiled and blew her a kiss. Then he disappeared into the darkness.

Smiling and greeting people as she walked, Kate headed for the privacy of her room. With Brent gone, she had no desire to remain below; besides, she was exhausted. Before she reached the stairs, however, Hayley ran up to her.

Her face flushed with excitement, she said, "Kate, this has been a star-studded night for the hotel. We completely sold out, and because of you, the Musicale was one of the greatest successes we've ever had. Needless to say, you were marvelous."

"Thank you for the kind thoughts," Kate said, "but you're the one who deserves the credit, Hayley. You were the driving force behind this success."

"Oh, Kate—" Hayley glowed with happiness "—ever since Harry appeared in my life with that golden apple, things have changed for the better. I was happy before, but now I'm happier. I was successful, but now I'm more successful. Everything is so much better."

"I believe someone over there is trying to get your attention," Kate said and pointed to Mason, who stood across the lobby.

Hayley turned her head, to see her fiancé waving at her. "And I've found the man of my dreams," she murmured, then quickly looked back at Kate. "You *are* going to join Mason, Ron and me for a drink, aren't you?"

Kate looked from Hayley's expectant face to Ron, who stood beside Mason. She knew that Hayley wanted her to be with them, but she really did not want to spend an evening with Ron. He was probably nice, but definitely not her choice of a date. What was more, she wanted to be by herself for a little while. "Give me a few minutes."

"You're not going to your room, are you?" Hayley frowned in dismay.

"I'll be down in time to do some dancing," Kate said.

"No, before that. If you're not going to join us for a drink, I want you to promise to join us for dinner."

"I'm not hungry, and besides, in real life Caitlin didn't eat dinner. She went to her room and rested. So I'm still in character."

"Caitlin may have gone to her room, but Kate Norris cannot. Two of Kate's best friends and their respective fiancé and husband are here, and we would like to have the pleasure of her company for dinner. Besides, what will I tell Ron?"

Seeing the desperate look in Hayley's eyes, Kate reassured her again, "I'll be down."

"For dinner?"

"For dinner."

"Well," Hayley said, "to make sure, I'll send Ron upstairs to get you. Okay?"

"How about sending Billy?"

Hayley shook her head. "He'd be too easy to turn down. You'll think twice with Ron."

Laughing, the two women parted. Hayley returned to the party, and Kate climbed the steps to the second story. When she arrived at the suite, she stood for a moment and stared at the brass door plaque that bore Caitlin McDonald's name.

When she entered, she moved through the moonlit room to her desk, where she laid down her sheet music. She turned on the desk lamp, the light softly glowing over the two photographs, one sepia-toned and the other colorized, which lay where she had left them earlier in the day. Soon, Kate thought, this phase of her life would be over. Once she had her book published, her obsession would end. Caitlin and Blaze would cease to be a part of her life and thoughts.

But as this phase closed, another one opened. Brent Carlton was again a real, not imagined part of her life, and this time he wanted a relationship. Instinctively Kate knew that he wanted to marry her and that she wanted the same thing. But she wondered why, fearing that her loneliness and Brent's resemblance to Blaze were unduly influencing her.

She walked to the French doors. Opening them, she stepped onto the small balcony. A light summer breeze danced through the curling tendrils that had escaped her chignon. Couples milled on the grounds, and soft orchestra music wafted up to remind her that the celebration was still in full swing. But she was in no hurry to join the festivities.

The other day she had wanted neither the solitude of the room nor of her thoughts but tonight she did. This had been a strange weekend, and she still did not understand all that had happened to her. She held out her hand and looked at the topaz ring. After her bizarre experience yesterday, she had not wanted to put it on again. But neither had she wanted to disappoint Constance Engels. Directly before her performance began, she had slipped it onto the fourth finger of her left hand, having removed her wedding band. She had not "traveled" back in time since then and probably never would. Probably Lucille was wrong, or perhaps she herself was too much the skeptic.

Either way, it did not matter. She turned and reentered the room, looking again at the strange, fascinating ring. As the golden yellow turned into a deep whiskey color, a warmth spread through Kate. She moved across the room to touch the furniture—the desk, the rocker, the dresser—all reputed to be the original pieces that had been there when Caitlin and Blaze lived in the three-room suite. Something—she was not sure what—compelled her to return to the desk. She picked up the colorized photograph of Blaze and stared at it.

His hair was dark brown, almost black. The pristine white of the shirt contrasted with a sun-browned complexion. His eyes were green, reminding her of the forest in springtime. A five o'clock stubble shadowed his face. Wide, blue and red suspenders lined each side of his shirt, accenting the breadth of his chest beneath the starched cotton. A secret smile lurked in his eyes and touched the corners of his mouth.

Yes, she thought, the description of him in the old newspapers had been perfectly duplicated in this color shot. He was handsome, handsome in a rugged way like Brent. Dark and intense with an all-or-nothing temperament! He was the kind of man who appealed to her. The mystery surrounding him and his brief, tragic marriage fascinated her. And the fact that he was a race car driver with a fiery Irish temperament both frightened and attracted her.

With a fingertip she traced the outline of his face. Oddly she did not wonder about the texture of the skin beneath her finger; she knew. She knew the man. She brushed the lips, the powerful neck, the suspender line down to his waist, moved to the other suspender and up again. For some reason she felt close to him, this man who was both Blaze and Brent, and it frightened her. Once again she was having a difficult time discerning fantasy from reality.

A BRONCO, pulling a flatbed trailer that was covered with a tarpaulin, sped through the dark, its headlights beaming across the mountain highway. "Pour me another cup of coffee, Brent," Caleb said.

"You've drunk too many now. I know you want to get me back to The Stanley in time to have breakfast with Kate, and I appreciate the thought. But I would rather get there later and be in one piece. Why don't we stop for the rest of the night, Caleb?"

"I promised I'd have you back and I will," Caleb told him. "Now, if you're not going to pour the coffee, Brent, hand me the thermos and I'll do it myself." Caleb slid one hand along the seat, while the other negotiated a sharp curve. The Bronco swerved off the road, the tires throwing pebbles into the air.

"I'll pour you the coffee, but for God's sake, watch what you're doing!" Brent exclaimed as Caleb twisted the wheel and jerked the car onto the pavement. "If you have no concern for me, at least think about the Runabout."

"Okay," Caleb said, his voice subdued.

"We're going to stop at the first motel we find," Brent insisted. "We'll get up early in the morning and be there in time for the parade." Pouring the coffee into the plastic cup, he handed it to his brother.

"Thanks," Caleb murmured.

"Did you hear what I said?" Brent said. "We're going to stop—"

"I heard you, but don't be silly, and stop the father act. We're too close to stop now."

"So close, yet so far," Brent said and thought about the barrier Kate was erecting between them. When they'd first met, it had been the difference in their ages; now she seemed to doubt her own emotions. "Maybe the old saying is true, Caleb, that you can't return home."

"Sure you can," Caleb assured him. "You just have to remember that both of you have changed. You can't pick up the past where it was, but you can take the present and create a future from it."

"I'm not so sure." Brent sighed.

"Well," Caleb said, looking at his watch, "it won't be long now. We're almost at the Caitlin McDonald and Blaze Callaghan grave site."

He switched on the radio and country and western music softly filled the automobile. Brent leaned his head against the back of the seat and closed his eyes, visions of the auburn-haired woman flashing through his mind. He had almost drifted into sleep when he felt the Bronco swerve to one side.

Startled, he opened his eyes and shouted, "Caleb, what's wrong?"

The Bronco was rolling down the side of the mountain, and as he looked out his window, Brent saw a huge tree straight ahead. He lifted his hands to his face, heard the splintering of glass and tearing of metal. Caleb's scream pierced the night.

The quietness surrounding Brent was louder than any noise he had ever heard. He was in no pain, but when he touched his face, it was wet, very wet and sticky. Blood, he thought hazily. He wanted to find Caleb to see if he was all right. But he was unable to turn his head; he tried to speak, but failed.

He had to get up; he had to! Pushing his right hand through the broken window, he pressed his palm against the dirt and pushed with all his strength, but still could not move. Angry at his helplessness, he dug his fingers into the soft soil.

LOOKING at the porcelain clock on the mantel, Kate decided it was time for her to return to the festivities below. She straightened her desk, methodically returning each piece of her research to its proper file. The soft strains of "I'll Take You Home Again, Kathleen" drifted through the window as she picked up the color photograph once again. Kate began to hum the tune that the newspapers claimed had been Blaze's favorite and rested her finger on his picture. This time, however, she did not become immersed in the image of the man; rather the ring seemed to beckon to her. She became absorbed with the play of the light upon the topaz.

In the depths of the gemstone she saw a grave marker zooming toward her, getting larger, the closer it came.

Before it consumed her, she saw Blaze Callaghan's name. She became a part of death. Whirling through an abyss, a huge black void, she saw a wrecked Bronco and the body of a man, his arm outstretched through a broken window. She saw the bloody face and recognized Brent.

"Brent!" she screamed.

Then the whirling stopped and Kate ceased her screaming. She was in the bedroom at The Stanley. She moved her hand, refusing to look at the topaz, but could not shut out Brent's voice. So sure that he was calling to her and that she must answer, she rose and moved toward the door, where she was enveloped by a brilliant white light.

She seemed to melt into it, becoming a part of its energy, wisdom and power. Every fiber of her body was permeated with peace, her fears abated, and she became one with time. She knew only that she was going to Brent. Then she was floating somewhere above the wrecked Bronco.

"Hello, my darling," she murmured, kneeling and taking him into her arms, not caring that his blood was saturating her beautiful costume.

"Kate," he whispered.

"Don't worry, darling," she assured him. "Lady Luck is with you, and this time she's going to set things right. She's going to take you home." She pushed the topaz ring onto his little finger, which it fitted snugly. "Take this, and don't lose it."

The gravestone swallowed both of them.

BEFORE the whirling finally stopped, Kate heard a man screaming her name. Then she felt his hands as they gently examined her. Whispered words she could not hear well enough to understand touched her ears and soothed her frayed nerves. She was lifted from the ground and pressed tightly against a firm, masculine body. She felt the warmth of his chest and the strength of his arms. She could tell by the way he was straining that they were climbing up the side of the mountain, away from the car accident. She knew she was safe.

"Don't worry, love," he whispered, his lips brushing through her hair, "I have you now. I'm not going to let anything happen to you."

Her palm slid up his shirt and she smiled to herself. It was Brent; she had saved him and now he was here with her. Believing him, she closed her eyes and went to sleep.

When she awakened, she lay on a soft bed, a pleasant herbal scent touching her nostrils. It was a familiar yet elusive scent. A cool, damp rag covered her forehead.

"Has she come to yet?" A woman's voice penetrated the cloud that enveloped Kate.

"Not yet, but she will," a man replied in a soothing and quiet tone that was tinged with concern. "*She must.* She's my *dama de suerte*."

"Your what?"

"She's my Lady Luck," the man said. "Up to now the women in my life have been shadows. Kate is the first one of substance. My *dama de suerte* forever."

Not fully conscious, her lids still too heavy for her to open, Kate lay there, listening to the voices and wondering whose they were and whom they were discussing. Then she remembered. Objects and names flashed through her mind: the dream or vision or whatever it was; Brent; Blaze Callaghan's grave marker.

La dama de suerte. Lady Luck. The phrase should mean something to her. It did, but she simply could not place it at the moment. Her thoughts were hazy and elusive. Every time she reached for one it eluded her.

"She won't make it," the woman sniffed. "Not after the fall she took down the side of the mountain."

The voice was strange, the conversation even stranger.

"I said she will and she will," the man promised.

The mattress gave as someone moved, the someone who smelled like herbal cologne...or after-shave. A hand—a masculine hand—gently brushed the hair from her face, lifted the cloth and replaced it with another one, fresher, cooler. She struggled to open her eyes, but her lids were too heavy, the effort too much. Breathing deeply, she relaxed.

"Poor dear girl," the woman said. "She deserves better than this. I hope the doctor gets here in time."

"He will."

Kate wanted to speak, to find out who they were and what they were doing in her suite, but her clouded mind made it difficult for her to pull her thoughts together. She lifted her hand, pain shooting down her side and arm. Moaning, she twisted her head into the pillow.

"Don't try to move, love," the man said and caught her hands in his, squeezing them before he laid them on the bed. Then Kate felt his warm breath against her cheeks, his soft voice close to her ear. "You fell down the side of the mountain, love, but you're going to be all right. You have a few minor cuts and bruises, but no real damage has been done."

No, I didn't fall down the side of a mountain, Kate wanted to say but could not speak. I simply fainted. I was trying to get to Brent. No, that was a dream. I was resting after my performance at The Stanley.

"Is she conscious?" the woman asked.

"I believe so," the man said.

"Thank God," the woman sobbed.

The man wiped Kate's face with the cloth. She took a deep breath, gasping as spasms of pain shot through her chest.

"It's all right," a man soothed, concern evident in his deep voice. "Everything's going to be all right. You're here with me, and I'm going to take care of you."

Kate desperately wanted to open her eyes and to know why she was lying here, when she should be downstairs, having dinner with Hayley, Mason and Ron. She wanted to know who this kind man was who kept reassuring her, whose voice was the most beautiful she had ever heard, whose touch was like that of a ministering angel. Again she raised a hand to her forehead and she tried to sit up, but cried out when excruciating pain racked her body.

Gentle hands against her shoulders urged her back into the softness of the bed. "Lie still, darling. The doctor's on the way."

Kate's head began to spin, and she seemed to be sinking in a thick mire that threatened to suffocate her. The man and woman were talking, but she could no longer make out what they were saying; their voices blended to create nothing but a blur of noise. She was losing consciousness. Suddenly she was alone, all alone. There was no one to help her, no one to save her. Grandpapa and Martin were dead. Brent was dead!

The impact of that thought hit her with full force. This man was not Brent. He was gone forever. She fought the panic that rose in her. Before she had been comforted by the thought that he was alive, but now she was denied even that. The blackness began to engulf her, and she fought the hands that firmly grasped her shoulders. She struggled to bring more air into her lungs; they hurt so badly that she thought they would surely explode.

"Stop fighting, love." The man gathered Kate into his arms, and although the movement hurt her physically, Kate did not care. He held her against himself, and she felt the steady beat of his heart. She was not alone; he was saving her, bringing her back from the bottomless pit into which she'd been sinking. Despite the pain, she threw her arms around his shoulders and clung to him.

He cradled her as if she were a child to be comforted, rubbing her head with his hand. "You're all right, sweetheart. I have you now and won't let anybody hurt you."

"Yes," Kate muttered, her face buried against the man's chest, her eyes still tightly shut.

"Thank the good Lord!" the woman exclaimed. "The child has spoken. She's going to be all right!"

"Yes," he murmured, his voice thick, "she's going to be all right."

"Where—?" Kate's mouth felt as if it were stuffed full of cotton. "Where am I?"

"At The Stanley," he answered. "Don't you remember?"

"Yes," she breathed. *This is Ron,* she thought, her head swimming as she vacillated between reality and dreamland, as she wrestled to separate fact from fantasy. This had to be Ron. Hayley had sent him to get her. She had gone to sleep and was having a nightmare when he arrived. First Brent and now this.

"What about—"

"What about the Arabian?" the man said. "He's fine. You suffered far worse than he did."

"What . . . about . . . dinner?" she murmured, wondering why on earth he was talking about Silver Sheik. Everybody knew that Nicki never allowed anyone to ride her horse.

Soft laughter filled with relief echoed through the room. "We'll have dinner brought up, love. Don't you worry. Let's just wait until Doc Stover looks you over, okay? You've given us quite a fright."

Love. The man had called her love several times and darling and sweetheart. Yet the words were neither condescending nor flirtatious. They sounded warm and sincere. Now she knew this wasn't Ron. Licking her lips, Kate whispered, "Who is Doc Stover?"

"Local doctor," the man answered and slowly withdrew his arms, placing her gently on the bed. "I don't reckon you've been here long enough to know."

"Of course I have." What was wrong with these people? Kate wondered. Either they were crazy or she was. By sheer willpower she forced her eyes open and tried to sit up a second time, but the dizziness returned. Her stomach churned with nausea and intense pain shafted through her body. Although her lids felt as if they weighed tons, she forced them to stay open; she wanted to see the man, but could not. He was nothing but a blur. Hurt, frustrated and confused, she fell back against the pillows with a low groan.

"Please lie still, darling," he said. "You're badly bruised from the fall and are hurting yourself by moving."

"If you don't mind, sir, you can leave the room, and I'll be happy to help the missus undress and put on her nightclothes."

"Thank you, but I'll undress her. Will you get her nightclothes out of the armoire, please?"

Footsteps faded away as the woman left the room. The conversation was getting stranger by the minute, Kate thought, and this man had a great deal of audacity to think he was going to undress her.

"You—you won't—undress me," she said, irritated because her voice was so feeble.

"I won't hurt you," he promised and again changed the wet cloth on her forehead. "And you'll feel much better if you're in your nightgown."

"Here they are, sir," the woman said, returning to the room. "I'll lay them on the love seat."

"Thank you, Mrs. Adams."

"Is there anything else you'd like for me to do?"

Mrs. Adams. The words ricocheted through Kate's mind. Caitlin McDonald's personal maid had eloped with her lover soon after she and her mistress had arrived at The Stanley. Flora Stanley had hired Sally Adams to be Caitlin's maid during her stay at The Stanley. *No,* Kate thought, *this cannot be!* This was even more bizarre than her dreaming about Brent and the accident. Hayley and Nicki were right; she was absolutely too obsessed with the past.

"No, I don't think so," the man said.

"I reckon I'll go down to the kitchen and fix a pot of tea. Reckon she might want a cup when she comes around."

"She may," the man said absently.

Kate tried to laugh, but the effort proved to be too painful. She thought she was insane, her head hurt so badly that she thought she was dying, and the woman was going downstairs to brew her a pot of tea.

"Let F. O. and Flora know that she's coming around, Mrs. Adams."

"I'll do that," Sally answered and closed the door.

The man's hands moved over Kate's body, and soon she found herself naked with no time to be embarrassed. Just as quickly he lifted her body into his arms, crooning softly to her all the while, and slipped soft, white material over her head, cool material that caressed her bruised and aching body. When she was lying down again, tucked beneath the covers, the man wet the cloth again and wiped her face. Breathing easier now, she slowly opened her eyes. Still the man was nothing but a blur of color; then she blinked several times, and he began to take shape.

She found herself staring into the face of Blaze Callaghan. "No," she whispered and pushed back into the mattress as if to get away from him, "it can't be you."

Yet it was. She would recognize him anywhere, anytime. She was dreaming; worse, she was hallucinating. Forgetting her head, forgetting her pain, she bolted up again. She had allowed this man to undress her, to see her naked!

"Please, lie down, darling—" his hands on each shoulder, Blaze gently pressed her into the pillows "—you're only going to make your head hurt worse."

At that moment she did not care about her head or the pain. Wildly she looked around the room. The furniture was basically the same; the four-poster bed; the white wicker rocker; the mahogany writing desk and matching chair; the slipper chair; the two armoires; a marble-topped nightstand and round reading table; the cheval mirror; a corner washstand, the bowl and pitcher matching the yellow and red wallpaper. An antique light fixture hung from the center of the ceiling, casting a soft glow over the room.

Nonetheless nothing was the same; everything was changed!

Her gaze returned to him. "Who—who are you?"

"You've really dented my ego," he said, a half smile curving his lips. "I'm your husband."

"No." Her eyes rounded in fear; she was not married to Blaze Callaghan. "You can't be."

"But I am...unless you know something I don't." He cocked an eyebrow and stared at her. When she shook her head, he continued. "I'm sorry about the accident, darling."

"The accident?" she repeated inanely.

Blaze stared at her for a few minutes. "I guess the fall has disoriented you."

Love. Darling. Sweetheart. And he claimed that they were married. Despite the pain, Kate twisted away from him, the washcloth falling onto the pillow. There must be an explanation for this. She had not assumed Caitlin McDonald's personality. She had not!

"You were riding the white Arabian—"

"Silver Sheik," Kate interrupted.

"Whatever his name," Blaze said dismissively. "You were out riding when your horse was spooked. He bolted, and you fell down the side of the mountain. Thank God, I happened to be driving by, darling, and saw what happened. If I hadn't been there—" He broke off with a shudder.

Her head pounding furiously, Kate lay down again. Blaze picked up the washcloth and dipped it into the basin on the night table next to the bed. He twirled it through the cool water, wrung it out and flapped it through the air a time or two, then replaced it on her forehead, his fingers remaining on her temples.

His hand trembled against her skin. "You're lucky to be alive."

"I'm—I'm *la dama de suerte*. Surely you knew that Lady Luck can't die." She spoke the words, but was hardly aware of their significance. It was as if someone else inside her were saying them.

"Yes, my darling, I knew that." His voice sounded teary.

"I'm your *dama de suerte*."

"Yes, darling, my *dama de suerte* forever."

Kate closed her eyes and breathed deeply. She felt life ebbing from her body.

"Dear God," the man cried in anguish, "please don't let her die!"

Chapter Five

Later when Kate came to, she seemed to be drifting between two worlds, one of which was getting dimmer and
dimmer, but she did not have the energy to keep her eyes
open. She had no energy to wonder where she was or
whom she was with. "You were driving the Stanley
Steamer," she said. "The one in the lobby?"

Blaze laughed. "Hardly."

Several sharp raps on the door was followed by a
young boy's voice. "Mr. Callaghan, Doc Stover is here.
Is Miss McDonald all right?"

Miss McDonald. The child had called her Miss
McDonald, so she was not married to Blaze.

"She's all right. You and the doc can come on in."

Kate was too confused and too tired to open her eyes.
The door opened and closed, and two sets of footsteps,
one heavy, the other light, echoed through the room.

"Well, now," a gruff but friendly voice said, "what
have you done for your little missus, Blaze?"

I am married to him, Kate thought. She felt the mattress give as Blaze stood. "Didn't know what to do,
Doc, so I've just been putting a cool, wet cloth over her
forehead. No bones are broken that I can tell, but she's
badly bruised and suffered a blow to her head."

"Miss McDonald, I'm Dr. Stover. Phillip Stover. I'm going to examine your head." The legs of a chair grated over the floor and his hand caught her head, turning it gently. Kate moaned. "I'm sorry, ma'am. I don't mean to hurt you, but I have to see the wound."

"Is she going to live?" a child asked.

"She sure is," the doctor answered.

The small, frightened voice compelled Kate to open her eyes. At the end of the bed, a hand wrapped around one of the bedposts, a boy peered at her. He couldn't have been more than nine or ten years old. A lock of auburn hair fell across his forehead, and his big, blue eyes were shadowed with anxiety.

Standing at the foot of the bed was Patrick O'Grady, Kate's grandfather, the child she had seen in her psychic vision, but he no longer beckoned her to join him in his world. She intuited that yesterday afternoon he had recognized her as Kate Norris. Now he recognized her as Caitlin McDonald. From the way the child talked and acted, Kate knew that she was part of his world, and she felt at home here, very much at home.

Doc Stover rummaged through his medicine bag. "We'll give her some aspirin, Paddy, and that should soothe her headache."

"And a cup of good, hot tea." Sally Adams walked into the room, the china clattering against the tray as she moved.

"Don't know that it'll do her any good, but it sure won't harm her," Doc muttered, lifting his hand to push up his spectacles on his nose. He rose and moved to the window, measuring the white powder into a glass and adding water.

"Reckon you think something stronger would be better for her?" Sally set the tray on the dresser.

"I reckon I do, Sally Adams," Doc declared.

"Humph!" Sally flounced around. "Will you have a cup of tea, Blaze?"

"I don't think so, Mrs. Adams. Will you stay with her while I go take care of the Steamers? I'll be back directly." He walked to the door. "Paddy, do you want to come with me?"

"Paddy?" Kate murmured and held her hand out. "Paddy O'Grady?"

"Yes, ma'am." The boy removed his cap and slowly moved around the bed to take her hand. "I didn't think you'd remember me, Miss McDonald."

She fixed her blue-gray eyes on the boy's face. "I'll never forget you, Paddy."

His face flushed with pleasure, and he mumbled, "I got your horse, Miss McDonald. He's in the stables."

"Thank you." She squeezed his hand. "You're a fine lad."

"Well, now, Paddy—" Twirling the glass in his hand, Doc Stover returned to the bed "—how about your moving out of the way? Let me give her this medicine."

"Is she going to be all right, Doc?" the boy asked as he backed away, still clutching his hat in front of him.

"Of course she will. She'll be up and about in no time at all. Now, I suggest all of us leave except Mrs. Adams and let Miss McDonald rest. You gonna want me to have someone sit with her tonight, Blaze?"

"No," Blaze answered, "I'll be here with her."

Kate pushed herself up on an elbow and swallowed the medicine. Lying down again, she smiled to herself. Blaze would be here with her. She would never be alone again. Somehow she had lost Brent but had found Blaze. Drifting off to sleep, she smiled to herself again and snuggled beneath the sheet. Somehow the two seemed alike, as if they were the same person.

When the door closed, Sally Adams walked to the bedside. "I'll be here until Blaze returns, dearie. Just let me know if you need anything."

"Thank you, Mrs. Adams," Kate murmured, then added, "I'm glad Mrs. Stanley recommended you for my maid. You're very good."

"Why, thank you, ma'am." Sally beamed at Kate. "Seeing as I'm getting up in age, I don't like to work all the time, but in the summer when the hotel is open and Mrs. Flora needs help, I'm always glad to lend a hand. And seeing how your maid up and left you in the lurch—not that I rightly blame any young lady for getting married, when she finds the man she wants to spend the rest of her life with—I'm right glad that I was able to be of benefit to you."

Sitting down in the platform rocker in front of the window, she picked up her needles and yarn and began to knit. Kate dozed, then awakened. As she reached up to push a tendril of hair from her face, she saw the shimmer of the golden topaz and lifted her hand to stare at the ring—the ring Constance Engels had found at the Caitlin McDonald and Blaze Callaghan grave site—the ring that she had pressed into Brent's hand during the...the dream in which he had been dying at the grave site.

All her life Kate had heard that truth was stranger than fiction, and while one part of her wanted to deny that she was in the past, another part quickly, surely affirmed that she was.

"Mrs. Adams, what day is this?"

Sally gave her a quizzical look. "Why, it's June 25, child."

Kate looked at the lace and linen dress that swayed gently in the afternoon breeze. She was startled. That was the dress that Constance Engels had made for her...not for Caitlin McDonald. Baffled by all that had happened to her, Kate closed her eyes again and laid one arm over her forehead. That was her dress; therefore she was Kate Norris, not Caitlin.

"The year, Mrs. Adams?" she whispered. "What year is this?"

The knitting needles fell into Sally's lap as she stopped rocking and stared curiously at Kate. "It's 1910."

"And I'm here for the first anniversary of The Stanley?"

"That's right. Right wonderful Musicale it was. One of the best The Stanley's ever had." Sally laid aside her knitting and walked to the bed, where she laid her palm against Kate's forehead. "Do you reckon I ought to get the doctor up here again, Miss McDonald? You feel like you might have a fever."

"No, I'm all right now," Kate answered. "I was . . . disoriented."

"You took a mighty heavy blow. Good thing Mr. Callaghan was there to save you." She shook her head vigorously. "You're fortunate to be alive, ma'am, and mighty fortunate to have a man like Blaze Callaghan love you."

"Yes, I am." Her headache abating somewhat, Kate closed her eyes and breathed deeply. For some unknown reason, she was in the past. The psychic had told her that when one traveled in time, there had to be a reason: either she was here to learn herself, to teach someone or she was here to right a wrong that had been done. She closed her left hand over her right, the topaz digging into her tender flesh. She knew how she had traveled back in time, but did not know why. "I think I'll rest awhile now."

Later in the evening someone entered the room. She quickly recognized Blaze's deep voice, such a contrast to others and so reminiscent of Brent's. She roused to hear him and Mrs. Adams whispering. Then she drifted back to sleep, only to be awakened when someone slipped into bed with her. Groggily she thought about Martin and smiled.

"How are you feeling?" the man asked.

"Better," she mumbled, again recognizing Blaze, "now that you're here."

"Sorry, I was late," he said. "But one of the wagons needed some repair work, and there was no one else who could do it but me."

He spooned his body against hers, and Kate sighed. It had been a long time since she had been snuggled.

"Good night, love," he whispered, dropping a kiss onto her neck below her ear.

"Good night . . . love," she murmured.

"I'LL BE drawing your bath," Sally called from the bedroom.

"All right," Kate answered.

Wearing a white cambric dressing robe that buttoned up the front and had a lace yoke and stand-up collar, she moved from the opened window to the kettle table beside the love seat. After pouring herself a second cup of tea, she glanced at the four-poster bed and her face grew warm at the memories of Blaze Callaghan lying next to her during the past night, his arm over her.

"When do you expect Mr. Callaghan to return?" Sally called from the other room.

Sipping her tea, Kate walked into the center of the second room of her suite; there she was surrounded by five huge armoires and innumerable trunks and valises. "He said he would get back late this evening. He wanted to experiment with the automobile."

"I'll tell you, Miss Kate," the maid said, "one of these days Blaze Callaghan is gonna regret racing them cars."

A shiver of apprehension ran down Kate's spine. "He's the best racer in the country," she said rather defensively. "I'm sure he knows what he's doing."

"Humph! I'm not worried about what Mr. Blaze is gonna do, I'm worried about them tomfool automobiles. I ain't one for them things, anyway."

Kate smiled. "They're really the thing of the future, Mrs. Adams. Why, I'll bet in about fifty or sixty years every family will own two or three, possibly more."

"Lord have mercy on us if that's the truth, Miss Kate." Mrs. Adams clucked her tongue.

Setting down her empty cup, Kate began to investigate her wardrobe. Moving from armoire to armoire, she could understand why Blaze had been irritated with Caitlin the day he had picked her up at the train. All of the wardrobes were filled to overflowing with her gowns, shoes and accessories, and still there were more. Trunks, valises and dresser drawers contained her underclothes and the transparent stockings she had brought to match all of her dresses.

Opening the door of one armoire after the other, Kate examined her—Caitlin's—wardrobe. All of the dresses were beautiful, expensive and of the latest in fashion, all designed either in Paris or England. Many were of striped material and needed no applied decoration; others had peplumed bodices with tassels at the points.

The straight and narrow skirt of one dress had a small train, and the jacket was three-quarter length, cut away in front below the waist, the buttons very large. Another, in a soft gray and pink, was cut in the Empire style with an overskirt of chiffon embroidered with diamanté. A royal-blue dress, bold in color and design, had a tiny, pointed train coming from the side—a degenerate wisp with little in common with the sweeping dignity of the other trains. The dress had no collar, so the neck was bare.

On the higher shelf were four beautiful muffs, one of sable, another of moleskin, still another of luxurious, gray chinchilla, and the last one of skunk. Kate reached out and caressed the fur.

In another armoire Kate discovered large-crowned hats in a multitude of colors, all laden with ostrich feathers, aigrettes, birds of paradise and big flowers. Kate smiled as she thought of the fashionable proportion in 1910, according to the latest designers. It was three to two: circumference of hat six feet, of dress hem four feet.

All of this belonged to her; yet none of it was hers. Everything rightfully belonged to Caitlin. Kate moved to another armoire, which contained nothing but shoes: black and white, laced ankle boots; brown kid high-top boots; leather high-heeled shoes in bold, bright colors; thin, high-heeled shoes and satin slippers.

Kate slid her foot into one of the house slippers, much surprised when the shoe fitted as if it had been made for her. She put on the other and stepped back. Moving to the full-length cheval mirror, she stared at her reflection. She was Kate Norris; she still looked like

Kate Norris; yet everyone here thought she was Caitlin.

She kicked off the shoes and began to unbutton the dressing gown. Lucille Wright had told her that time travel was really nothing more than a person's returning or moving forward to another incarnation. If that were true, Kate and Caitlin were one and the same.

Kate could accept the theory of reincarnation but not the reality of it. If this were true, she was Caitlin. She may have been reminiscent of her, but she did not even look like Caitlin. She had played the role of Caitlin through the years, but never had she thought of herself as the other woman.

Yet, a small voice said, why have you been so preoccupied with this woman all these years, diligently searching for every bit of information you could find on her? Remember how people have always noticed the similarity between the two of you.

"Are you ready for your bath, ma'am?" Sally asked, breaking into Kate's thoughts.

"Mrs. Adams," Kate said and turned to look earnestly at her maid, "have you noticed a difference in me since the accident? Do I look different?"

Sally Adams sank her hands into the pockets of the white apron that covered the entire front of her dress. "Well, ma'am," she said, "you're a little more peaked, what with your color not having come back yet, and you're still a little disoriented. Other than that, I don't see no difference in you. Now, ma'am, if you'll take off your jewelry, I'll put it up for you while you bathe."

Kate looked at the ring on her left hand. "I'll keep it on," she answered, not about to take off the ring. It was her only real link with the world from which she'd come, and she did not wish to part with it. "I—feel rather naked without it."

"Yes, ma'am," the older woman said. "I guess most of us womenfolk feel that way about our wedding rings."

"My wedding ring," Kate murmured.

If indeed Lucille Wright was correct, this was the object with which she had traveled through time. This ring was her mode—her only mode—of transportation. If she were ever to return to her own time, she must have it. She could not—would not—take the chance of misplacing or losing the ring. As long as the decision remained hers, the ring would not leave her possession.

As she clasped her ring hand with the other, she thought about her last dream of Brent and remembered pressing the ring into his hand as he lay on the mountainside. When she had come to, Sally and Blaze had been talking about her falling down the side of a mountain. In her vision that was where she had been with Brent. She must keep the ring; it was the key to unlocking the mystery of her being here in the past; it was the key to getting back to her own time...but what if she could not return? Kate quickly discarded that thought.

"Which dress do you wish to wear this morning, Miss McDonald?" Sally asked, breaking into Kate's ruminations.

"The—uh—the blue and ecru one," Kate said.

"Oh, yes, ma'am," Sally said. "That's my favorite. I love the gathered yoke and insets on the skirt. I'm so glad you're going to wear it today."

Kate walked to the desk and riffled through the small writing table, the third time she had done so since she'd awakened this morning. She had hoped to find a diary or some personal letter that would better explain Caitlin. Instead she'd found a small leather-bound book of verse, but it was not hers. She knew before she turned to the frontispiece she would find Blaze Callaghan's name written on the flyleaf. She closed the book and held it against her breast, feeling extremely near to him at that moment.

Kate's dress draped over an arm, Sally walked to the door. "I'll be downstairs, ironing this for you, ma'am. I'll be back shortly."

"No hurry. If you're not back by the time I'm through, I'll put on my dressing gown and write some letters." Kate paused, then asked, "Do you have any idea where my diary is, Mrs. Adams? I can't seem to remember where I put it."

Her hand on the knob, Mrs. Adams turned. "The last time I saw you with it was yesterday morning. You were sitting in the chair beside the bed, writing in it. Reckon you put it in the drawer of the night table?"

"No, I've looked there," Kate said.

A grin suddenly appeared on Mrs. Adams's face and she strode briskly into the other room. Doors opened and closed with a loud bang, then the maid returned with the book.

"Where did you find it?" Kate exclaimed, her heart beating so fast and furiously that she did not know if she could contain it. Her hand closed around the precious book.

"I remembered you were wearing your combing sacque and the pockets are quite large. Thought maybe you dropped it into one of them."

"Oh, Mrs. Adams, you're such a jewel."

"Don't know about that, ma'am," she said, "but I reckon for a woman of my age, I got a pretty good memory. Well, I better get going, if I intend to get back with your dress fitting to wear.''

As soon as Kate locked the door behind Mrs. Adams, she opened the diary to the last entry on June 24:

I have never known such love as that which I share with my husband. He can be the most passionate human being that I have ever known, and at the same time the most tender. I live for the moment, not knowing what lies ahead for us...what with his dangerous career of racing automobiles. Daily I fear those machines will take his life but cannot, in all good conscience, ask him to give them up because they are his life. Like a child, he is anticipating the Fourth of July Racing Tournament here in Estes Park, and in a way so am I, for we shall be making a trip together to Boulder.

The last time he raced, Blaze lost to one of the contenders, and this year he hopes to best him. When I think about his racing, I cannot help but be afraid. It's as if I see a dark cloud hanging over his head and know that death is his constant shadow. But Blaze laughs it aside and says that death is everyone's constant shadow and is only a breath away from each of us. He is right, I know. Therefore I live each day fully, knowing full well that it could be my last.

Sitting at the desk, Kate picked up the pen with trembling hands and dipped it into the inkwell. Today's entry would be hers, and she wondered, if she managed to put the diary where it could be found and handed down, if anyone would notice the difference in their handwriting. In bold cursive, she described her accident as best she could remember it, highlighting Blaze's heroic rescue of her as it had been repeated to her by both him and Mrs. Adams. She ended with a declaration of love for Blaze. After she blotted the page, she thumbed through the diary, noticing that Caitlin had already been lavish in her praise and admiration for her husband. But still Kate felt the need to add her own feelings. As Caitlin she had loved Blaze; as Kate she continued to love him.

Inexplicably her thoughts turned to Brent and she leaned back in the chair. It was difficult for her to separate the two of them, and she wondered why she had dreamed about him the night she'd returned to Blaze. She vividly recalled the golden-white light that had encompassed her and again felt its peace. As if it were an entity, it dispelled her doubts and fears and assured her that no matter what happened to Brent, he was fine. He had the key to life and would know what to do. So at the moment her most pressing concern was the diary.

Closing the book, Kate stood and looked around the room for a hiding place. Not the furniture, she decided. That could be moved and the diary lost forever. Wondering if perhaps there were a bishop's nook or an equally good hiding place secreted within the room, her lips eased into a smile. How fanciful she was getting! Nicki and Hayley—strange how her past, that is, her future—life was becoming hazier and hazier. Nicki and Hayley in their wildest dreams would never imagine her as she was now.

But even if she did manage to hide it in a place where it could possibly be found, Kate thought, how would she know where to look? During her future life she had not known that she was Caitlin; she had searched every conceivable place for material on Caitlin and Blaze and had returned empty-handed.

Would she ever return to that other life? Kate wondered, unafraid now to face that question, then laid the book on her desk. For the time being, she knew of no other place to put it. Slowly undressing, letting her clothing lie where it fell, she moved to the bathtub.

She had luxuriated in the water for a long time and was stepping out of the tub, when a key was inserted in the door and the lock clicked. "What marvelous timing, Mrs. Adams," she called, dabbing her body with the soft, terry cloth towel.

The door closed and she heard the soft click that announced it had been locked once again.

"Indeed it is good timing."

Kate spun around to see Blaze Callaghan lounging against the door. Gasping in surprise and embarrassed that he had caught her naked, she wrapped the towel around her, holding it together in front with her fist. A smile on his face, Blaze moved toward her. Kate's gaze quickly raked over the buff-colored suit he wore, the fitted jacket unbuttoned to reveal a dark brown waistcoat. He tossed his straw hat onto a vacant chair.

"You're—you're early!"

"What a way for a bride to greet her new groom!" He chuckled softly.

"Oh, no!" Kate licked her lips. "I didn't mean it like that. I'm glad that you're back. You've—you've surprised me. It seems like you've been gone forever."

"Only part of a day," he replied.

"When they're all you have," Kate murmured, "days can be a lifetime." And they would have to be for her. She was locked in this body, in this particular time; she was in love with her husband and had been all her life ... her lives. Still, he was a virtual stranger to her, and mature though she was, she was still shy.

"Kate McDonald Callaghan, you're truly the most beautiful woman I've ever known, and intelligent, too." For every step forward Blaze took, Kate took one back. "It's no wonder I fell in love with you and couldn't wait to get back to you. You're one of the most enigmatic persons I've ever known. One minute you're all fire and passion, the next you're a starry-eyed innocent."

Kate had backed into the wall and had no place to go. He came closer, and she saw how really tall and broad-shouldered he was. Exactly as she remembered seeing him in the doorway before. She closed her eyes, confused by her thoughts. She was Kate Norris and had never been married to Blaze Callaghan. Yet she knew him.

His hand closed gently over hers, and he bent to plant a soft kiss on her forehead, so sweet, yet so sensuous that she felt pleasure spread hotly through her entire body. His warm breath fanned her cheeks.

She lifted her face, and he captured her lips with his, thoroughly kissing her. His hand slid over her breast and down her midriff to settle on her hip, which was covered with nothing but the soft terry cloth. Through the thin material she could feel the hard imprint of his entire body. She was flooded with a delicious warmth. He lifted his mouth and whispered against her lips, "I brought you a gift."

"What?" she murmured, pressing one hand against his chest. When he was close to her like this, loving her, she had need for nothing else. He was her world, her entire world, and she was content with only him.

He stepped back and held up a brown package. "This."

"Oh, Blaze," she exclaimed, momentarily in that gulf between two worlds, and reached for it, "how sweet of you."

Smiling impishly, Blaze said, "I'll hold the towel for you while you open the gift."

Suddenly shy, Kate lowered her eyes. She had been married before and had no idea why this man affected her emotions so deeply. Yet he did. Blaze tucked a crooked finger beneath her chin and raised her face, his eyes catching hers.

"I mean it, Caitlin Callaghan, you're an enigma," he said softly. "You're a woman in every sense of the word, yet you're so innocent and ethereal. At times I wonder if you really belong on earth at all."

"Oh, yes," Kate whispered. "I belong here and to you."

And with certainty Kate knew why she had been allowed to traverse time. She was Caitlin McDonald, and Blaze Callaghan was her soul mate. They had journeyed through the universe together. In a faraway life, in another world she vaguely remembered a friend who had been given a golden apple, with which came three wishes. Kate had been given something even greater than a magical apple: her ring—yes, her ring—had taken her through the ages back to her lover and had given her a second chance to find the passionate love for which she had longed so desperately. She might only have a few days at the most, but they had been given to her.

The gift slid out of her hand, falling to the floor; she melted into Blaze's arms and lifted her face for his kisses, hot and demanding. Eventually her hands slid up his chest to lock about his neck; his hands, searching out the sweet curves of her body, worked the towel loose so that it, too, slipped to the floor around her feet.

Then when she was so weak with desire that she thought she could no longer stand it, he swept her into his arms and carried her to the bed. Gently he deposited her there, and she lay on her back waiting for him, as she had done so many times before, yet had never done before. *But you're not his wife* came the nagging thought from somewhere in her brain.

"No," Kate mumbled and rolled over, her hand going to the base of her neck.

"Oh, sweetheart," Blaze murmured and immediately sat on the edge of the bed. Brushing her hair aside, he began to press soft kisses against the knot on her neck. "I'm sorry. I didn't mean to hurt you."

"You didn't," Kate assured him, her eyes burning with tears of joy. Never had she basked in such total love. The man whom she knew to be so chauvinistic and fiery was also one of the most tender she had ever encountered. From such fragile care bloomed eternal love, and it was for her and her alone.

"Mrs. Adams is going to be returning shortly with my dress," she said.

"And we mustn't shock Mrs. Adams, must we?" He stood and walked to the end of the bed and picked up her underclothes, returning with them. "So I suggest we get you dressed, so that you're presentable, Mrs. Callaghan."

Laughing with him, Kate allowed him to put the garments on her. Then she slipped into her dressing gown. Arm in arm the two of them walked onto the balcony and gazed at the crystal-blue lake in the verdant valley below.

"Beautiful, isn't it?" he murmured quietly.

"It's my favorite spot in the whole world. No matter where I may go, I'll always return here."

"I feel the same way."

Kate did not hear him move, but she was so attuned to him that she knew that he had gone. She turned her head and saw him bending to pick up the package. Then he saw the bouquet of flowers in the center of the reading table.

"Where did these come from?" The sharp tone broke the magical moment the two of them had created and caused Kate to lift her head. A hint of a smile still lingered on his lips, but his expression was guarded. His hair was combed back from his face, a tiny speck of silver dotting his left temple. Odd; she had not noticed that before. Laugh lines lightly etched their way from the bridge of his nose to the corner of his mouth. At last her gaze rested on his full, sensuous lips. "An admirer?" he asked.

"Yes," she agreed without hesitation. "One of my greatest."

"With so many I should think it would be hard to gauge which one is the greatest. Tell me, wife, exactly how do you measure an admirer's devotion?"

Kate stared into the intense green eyes, her love forgiving him for his jealousy, yet her humanness prodded her to tease. "I'm not sure I have a fixed answer for that, Mr. Callaghan. Measuring devotion is not quite like arithmetic. When one adds two and two, the answer is always four. Not so with emotion and caring."

Blaze did not move, yet Kate felt as if he were closer to her. His cologne filled her nostrils, the fragrance coming from another time and place. She could see the texture of the skin that softened the chiseled planes and angles of his face.

"But something has found the giver of the posy a special place in your affections?"

"Yes." Kate continued to tease as her delicate laughter filled the room. "Paddy O'Grady is in love with me. He robbed his mother's flower garden to bring me this bouquet."

Blaze smiled, looked rather sheepish, and tension ebbed visibly from his large frame. "Although I don't have a flower garden from which to pluck fresh posies for you, my love, I will give you the flowers of my soul." Ripping the wrapping paper from the package, he returned to the balcony.

"Opening my gift?" Kate said lightly and gazed into his brilliant green eyes. The flush of pleasure that warmed her cheeks by merely looking at him surprised her.

Holding a small, leather-bound book in one hand, he waved it through the air. "This is not necessarily the gift. The beauty lies therein." Moving to her side, he opened the book and began to read in a rich, mellow voice.

"I have been here before,
"But when or how I cannot tell:
. . . .
You have been mine before,—
How long ago I may not know:"

Kate was silent for a long time after Blaze had stopped reading. Inside she was trembling so greatly that she did not think she could stand. This was the poem that had come to her mind that long-ago afternoon, when she and Brent had been posing for Caitlin's death scene. Brent had held her in his arms, and she had remembered it from another lifetime.

"Oh, Blaze," she finally cried, her eyes sparkling with tears, "how beautiful! I didn't know you liked poetry, especially Rossetti."

"You, Kate Callaghan, have brought many new things into my life and heart, among them music and poetry."

Blaze caught her in his arms, and they stood for a long time in the sunshine, but it was in the warmth of their love that they basked.

Chapter Six

The day had been one of the most beautiful that Kate had ever spent, one full of discovery about Blaze, Brent and herself. Earlier Blaze had brought her to a quiet spot on the other side of the mountain, the spot where he and Caitlin would someday be buried. Ironically, Kate had not felt depressed or grieved as she stood beneath the tree's spreading branches and listened to the melody of the wind rustling through the leaves.

Sitting on a boulder, she had turned to see him leaning against the trunk and staring across the valley below. "I want a photograph of you just like that," she had said, and he smiled.

"I don't like photographs unless I'm wearing my goggles, helmet and racing jacket," he said, his smile turning into a crooked grin. "That way, no one knows exactly what I look like."

"But I want to know what you look like. I want at least one photograph of you without your racing gear. Please," she begged.

"I will," he promised.

Now she stood on the porch of his mountain cabin, her arms wrapped around one of the columns, and gazed into the distance. She marveled at how closely this cabin resembled the one that Brent and his brother had begun building so many years ago, even to the cellar. With a small chuckle she had to stop to correct herself. They had not built their cabin years ago; it would be years into the future before they even began.

When she had first entered the cabin with Blaze, she had gasped when she saw the gun rack above the fireplace. It was almost identical to Brent's; yet Brent had never seen this one. Hanging on it was the full-stocked military version of the legendary Winchester '73. Blaze had explained to her that he, like Brent, was a collector and trapshooter, not a hunter—Kate reflected—and she had confessed to him that she knew how to handle a weapon herself.

Now she awaited his return from target practice, having declined to go herself. She absolutely loved it up here, especially when the sun began its descent in the western sky, leaving a multicolored ribbon in its wake and a splintering of golden rays through the foliage. Now she understood why as a child she had been drawn to this place; it was here that she and Blaze had spent some of the happiest moments of their life. Their love was what had bound her to the land.

The door opened and closed. "Here you are," Blaze said, his booted feet clipping against the hardwood floor as he moved to stand behind her, his hands lightly clasping each shoulder. "I wondered where you were."

In the distance their horses, tethered to a low-hanging limb, whinnied, and birds chirruped as they fluttered through the leaves of the aspens.

"I wanted to watch the sun set," she murmured. "Although I've seen it hundreds of times, I never tire of it."

"Nor do I," Blaze said. "That's why I shall always have a mountain home."

"Look over there," Kate said and pointed to a cluster of tiny, dark clouds on the far horizon. "Do you think it's going to rain?"

"Perhaps," he answered, "and again they might dissipate before they ever reach us. Are you worried about them?"

"No," she murmured, tilting her head and brushing her cheek against his hand, "I love storms."

"More than you love me?" he teased.

She laughed softly. "Never more than you, my darling. I never dreamed that I could love someone as much as I love you." She turned and was in his arms in a warm embrace; then her arms tightened about him and she drew him even closer. Not sure where she really belonged in the time spectrum, if or when she might be departing this present phase, and quite sure that if she remained here, she had not much longer to live, she feared losing Blaze.

"What's wrong?" he asked, rubbing his hands up and down her back in a soothing motion.

"I worry about your racing that automobile," she said, her voice muffled against his waistcoat. If history repeated itself, Kate knew that he would outlive her, but she had to warn him about the dangers of the race. She knew that he would think she was nagging him, but with her knowledge she could do no less. Even if she died, there was no need for Blaze to do so. He was a brilliant designer and had much to give the world of automobile design. "It's so dangerous, Blaze."

"Nothing can go wrong, darling," he said. "Remember, you're my Lady Luck."

"Don't, Blaze," Kate whispered. "Luck is fickle."

Something about the words jarred her, and she remembered her dream from the other lifetime, the dream in which Brent was lying in the mangled ruins of a wrecked Bronco. But she could not remember what she had told him.

"Lady Luck may be fickle, darling, but you're not," Blaze said, "and that's what matters."

"Blaze, I don't want you to race anymore...ever."

"But it's my life and my career. You knew that when you married me. I thought we had come to an agreement." His hand moved to cradle her head and press it against his chest. She listened to the steady rhythm of his heart; she felt the rise and fall of his chest as she breathed.

"Perhaps at that time we came to a verbal agreement," Kate conceded, "but that was before I fell so deeply in love with you, my darling." She drew back her head and gazed into his face, hoping he could read the love and adoration in her eyes. "I understood the word love and what it was supposed to mean before we married," she said, "but it wasn't until after we were intimate that I began to grasp it totally. I don't want to lose you."

"You won't," he promised. "It's just that every time I race, I learn something new that can be changed and perfected in the Steamers. Right now, Kate, we're making a major breakthrough in our steam generators. Automobiles are here to stay, Kate, whether they are steam- or gasoline-powered, and they're going to change our entire life-style. I want to be a part of that change. I want to forge the road for generations of Americans. I want to be an automobile pioneer."

"I want you to be an American pioneer. I want you to design Steamers—or gasoline automobiles, for that matter," Kate returned, "but I don't like the idea of your racing, Blaze. Think what you'll be denying the world if you let racing cut your life short!"

"I think you reckon me much greater than the world does, love—" Blaze smiled at her "—but lately I've been doing some serious thinking. I'm getting a little too old for this racing business. The Fourth of July Tournament will be my last race. I promise."

If he only knew that the Fourth of July race *would* be his last one, Kate thought. "No!" she exclaimed. "I want you to give it up now, Blaze. No more races, period."

"What if I said I didn't want you to perform again?" he countered.

"That's different," Kate retorted, "and you know it. My career does not endanger my life. Please promise me that you won't race on the Fourth?"

"Don't be silly," he said, speaking now as if he were admonishing a child. "I've compromised with you. I'll give up racing, but I want the Fourth of July. I want the chance to outdo Josh Reilley. Winning over him would be enough victory to last a lifetime. Okay?"

Although Kate remembered all that Lucille Wright had told her about time travel, she no longer thought about her reason for being here; all she knew was that she loved Blaze and wanted to be with him for as long as she could. Perhaps the wrong she could right would be in getting them out of Estes Park before Sam Donovan arrived, before his quest for revenge would destroy their world. If she and Blaze were to escape, they would have a chance for a life of their own; they could see the fruition of their hopes and dreams. She had no idea what the present…what the future held, even if she could return to the 1990s. She had a surer guarantee of love and happiness if she and Blaze could find a way to live out their lives here in this present world.

"Don't be so pensive, love," he murmured and lifted her chin with the curve of his finger. She loved the feel of his callused hand against her flesh. He lowered his head to touch her mouth gently with his own, his breath brushing her cheeks, his lips moving evocatively over hers. For a man who was so passionate and powerful, Blaze was also tender and sensuous. Contrary to all that she had learned about him in her life as Kate Norris, Blaze was a caring individual who gave as well as took in his relationship with Caitlin.

Yielding to the sweetness of his kiss, Kate wrapped her arms around him. After long, pleasurable moments he finally lifted his mouth from hers, swung her into his arms and walked inside the cabin, kicking the door shut with his foot. His boots clicked over the smooth, wooden floor as he walked into the bedroom, where he laid her on the bed.

The scene was so reminiscent of another that Kate was again lost in the mist-filled gulf between the two time phases. She seemed to be everywhere at once, both Kate and Caitlin, in love with Blaze and with Brent. Gazing into Blaze's face, she knew that as surely as he and Caitlin were in love, so were she and Brent. Which of the two, she wondered, were the star-crossed lovers? Kate and Brent? Possibly... but she would probably never know.

Blaze knelt on the side of the bed and gently began to unbutton her blouse and to pull the material off her shoulders. Her skin was a creamy white and smooth as satin to his touch. He trembled to think that this fragile beauty was his wife, that she loved him, that she had canceled her concerts for several months so that they could enjoy their honeymoon here. Bending, he pressed his lips to her shoulder and using his teeth, pulled down the strap of her chemise. Lowering his face still further, he kissed the upper swell of her breasts and felt beneath his cheek her intake of breath and the erratic tempo of her heart. He marveled that his touch could affect her so greatly.

"Is it too soon?" he asked softly, his fingers gently kneading the small knot on her nape before they spread into the loosened tresses of her auburn hair.

"No," she murmured, thinking of the years that separated them, "it has been far too long, my husband. Please make love to me."

"Not only shall I make love to you, my beloved," he whispered, "I am deeply in love with you."

The refrain of a song that she had played so desperately only a few days ago ran through Kate's mind. She had wanted to go where love was, to know what love was and to have someone show her. Now her deepest wish was coming true.

When he had undressed her and she lay naked on the bed, Blaze stood and divested himself of his clothes. Their eyes were riveted on each other. The evening light, flowing through the window, cast a golden haze around her, making her look even more ethereal than before. Her hair was a fiery halo, her eyes were wide and luminous, her gaze almost virginal.

She radiated innocence, yet Blaze knew that behind the air of eternal youth lay a wealth of maturity and experience. Still, he was puzzled. The only certainties about her were the elusive beauty of her eyes and his growing desire to love her, to know her physically, intellectually, spiritually. Nothing else seemed to matter; nothing else was important. He had to unravel the mystery that was Caitlin McDonald. His confusion lay in the fact that the more he learned about her, the more mysterious she became.

"You're beautiful," he murmured.

"So are you," she whispered softly, and Blaze chuckled. Every time he was with her was a new and wonderful experience. When he had first met her, she seemed to be a most daring and shocking woman, but beneath that facade was a shy creature who never ceased to amaze him, who seduced his senses all over again, who rendered him helplessly and wondrously in love.

He knelt beside her, slowly leaning over her, his lips capturing hers in a kiss that was deep and long and searching, a kiss that both of them wanted. Stretching out beside her, he pushed her hair out of her face, tucking it behind her ears; he planted small kisses from her ears down the side of her neck and across her collarbone. He felt her pulse throb against his lips.

Kate's fingers tangled in Blaze's thick black hair, and she pulled his face away from her body and up to her lips. She wanted his kisses, letting them become more prolonged and intoxicating, yet she knew that they made her aware of her deep emptiness and loneliness. Although she and Martin had shared a wonderful marriage and he had often made love to her, he had never reached her heart. Never had her emotions been touched by his lovemaking. Even as a teenager of seventeen, she had known that only Brent could reach that special place. Already Blaze had taken her to emotional heights that she had known existed, but had thought beyond her reach.

Blaze's hands cupped her breasts, and Kate drew in a deep breath as his thumb circled the sensitive flesh. All inhibitions were burned away. Kate wanted to know him fully because she loved him. There would be no holding back. There would be no denial. She was his love, he her beloved. As surely as Caitlin had been married to him, so was Kate. She and Blaze were soul mates through all time.

Gently, reverently his hands moved over her body as he prepared her for total union. He breathed soft endearments into her ears. Her hands caressed his body as his caressed hers, giving him the same pleasure as he gave to her. Both were learning, discovering and delighting in the feel of each other. When they were breathing quickly and heavily, when both were trembling at the point of not being able to wait any longer, he lovingly moved over her and lowered himself into her welcoming softness.

"I love you, my darling husband, and will love you throughout all eternity," she whispered and gave herself up to the perfect, sweet communion. She had never shared this with Martin. She had never dreamed that it was possible to feel this way, alive all over.

Emotionally and physically Blaze carried her to such heights that she did not think she could endure the pleasure. She caught her breath as her body seemed to explode into a million splinters of elation. No sooner had she reached this pinnacle of fulfillment than Blaze joined her. Then their shudders ceased, their trembling quieted, and they lay in the security of each other's arms, lingering in the afterglow, her face hidden in the dark hair that covered his chest. She breathed deeply, filling her lungs with the smell of him, her heartbeat slowly returning to normal.

"You're the most wonderful thing that has ever come into my life," he said. "Every time I make love to you, it's as if it were for the first time. Each day that I'm with you, I love you more and more.''

"I love you the same way, my darling," she whispered and using her fingernail, drew designs on his chest. She watched the play of the waning light on the topaz ring, the ring that had brought her to him—the ring about which she knew virtually nothing.

As if he sensed her thoughts, he caught her hand and brought it to his lips, kissing the tip of each finger. Then he turned over the hand and stared at the ring. "Remind me to take this to Boulder and have it cut down for you," he said. "I don't want you to lose it."

"Nor do I wish to," Kate said. "To me it's a priceless heirloom."

Blaze laughed softly. "That's sweet of you to say so, love, but I don't know that it's as priceless as sentimental. My great-grandfather gave it to my great-grandmother when they were married, and it's been handed down through the remaining generations."

Kate laughed with him. "When you met me at the depot in Loveland, did you have any idea that you would fall in love with me?"

"All I could see was luggage," he said. "Trunk after trunk and when those ran out, there were the valises. I'll have to be honest, love, and confess that my thoughts about you that day were less than charitable."

"You were quite the bore," Kate said on a stifled giggle, "quite pompous and self-righteous, you know."

"How well I know. You told me and the entire world when we arrived at The Stanley."

Curiously Kate asked, "Exactly when did you fall in love with me?"

"The moment I walked around the Steamer and opened the door for you to step out," Blaze said without hesitation. "That's when I first really saw you. Your eyes were the most beautiful I believe I have ever seen, then you smiled and it transformed you. From that moment on, sweetheart, I was snared for life. I knew I had to have you for my wife, and that you were the one to whom I would give my great-grandmother's ring."

"Your great-grandmother was a Scorpio also," Kate said rather than asked.

"Yes, like you, she was born in November. She was all passion and fire, a worthy match for a Leo."

"My lion," Kate murmured, extracting her hand from his and rubbing his chest. They laughed together, basking in the pleasure of their love. Then she said, "Darling, please don't race on the Fourth."

He grinned and reached up to tweak the end of her nose. "Don't be a nag."

"I'm not. I just have this feeling," she began, then stopped when she felt him tense.

"Kate, don't use what we just shared as—"

Propping herself on one elbow, her hair fanning across his chest, she laid a hand over his mouth. "I would never do that, my darling. I'm trying to make a confession, trying to make you understand why it's important that you do not race, that we do not remain in Estes Park at The Stanley."

"What kind of confession?" he asked in the sharp tone she had come to identify with jealousy.

"Earlier today you spoke about my being ethereal and not of this world."

She paused. Impatiently he said, "Yes?"

"I'm of this world, Blaze, but I'm also of another world. I don't quite understand how, but I've been transported back through time. I live...I lived eighty years in the future. Having lived there, Blaze, I studied the past, your life and Caitlin's in particular, and I know in general what's going to happen.''

"You're not making much sense, love," he said gently as if talking with a child, a faint smile accompanying his words. "That tumble has affected your thinking much worse than we thought."

Kate shook her head. "The fall had nothing to do with what I'm talking about, Blaze." She rose and slipped into her chemise and petticoat. Walking to the window, she leaned against the frame and gazed down the mountain at the rushing stream—the same stream where she and Brent had stood on a day long ago, when she had told him the story of Caitlin and Blaze. "No matter how bizarre it sounds, Blaze, I'm Kate Norris, a woman from the future."

Blaze chuckled. "And I'm a prehistoric man from the past."

"You may well be." She turned to look at him. "I'm not joking, Blaze, and I want you to stop taking this so lightly and listen to me. What I'm saying is very important to both of us."

As if he sensed how much what she was trying to say meant to her, Blaze quietly listened as she talked. By the time she had finished the story of Caitlin and Blaze in both of the versions that had been handed down through the generations, Blaze was completely dressed, sitting in the rocker on the far side of the room. She could tell that while he had listened respectfully, he did not believe her. But she could not blame him; if someone had come to her with such a weird story, she would have laughed at it, too.

"Can you imagine how this makes me feel?" he asked, and without giving her an opportunity to answer went on, a tinge of desperation in his voice. "Like a character out of fiction. Why are you doing this to me, Kate? Do you think I'm such an idiot I would believe this?''

Knowing how difficult it was for him to believe her, Kate went to kneel in front of him. "You must believe me, Blaze. It's the truth."

His hands gripped her shoulders and he stared into her face. "I may be a steam jockey, love, but I'm not daffy, and I won't have you playing such tricks on me."

"Believe me, it's no trick, darling. So help me God, it's the truth."

He reached out and caught her face between his hands. "I've never loved another person in my life like I love you, Caitlin McDonald," he said in a low voice. "But don't take me for a fool. I don't believe a word of what you've told me. People don't jump back and forth between the past and the future. We live now. Right now and no more."

"You're right, Blaze," she contradicted softly, her mind reliving a similar scene with Brent, "we do live right now, and right now I'm Caitlin McDonald Callaghan, your wife, but also right now I'm Kate Norris." She pushed herself closer so that she could wrap her arms around his waist and press her cheek against his chest. "You must believe me. Only by believing me do we have a chance of living."

"All of this that you're talking about," he said quietly but firmly, "is a horrible nightmare. That's why you're not really sure of anything. It's a dream, Kate." Blaze caught her arms and pulled them away from his waist so that he could stare into her face.

"No," she whispered, "it's not a dream, Blaze. It's the truth."

"I'm taking you to the doctor in Boulder first thing in the morning," he announced and stood, tugging her up with him. "No matter what you think, that fall has affected you far worse than we thought."

"No matter what *you* think," Kate said, "the fall has not affected my thinking, but I'm willing to go to Boulder right now and under any circumstances. At least it'll get us away from Estes Park and Donovan."

Dumbfounded, Blaze stared at her and eventually said, "You're really worried about this, aren't you?"

Kate nodded, and he reached out to cup her head in his hands. "Honey, nothing is going to happen to me. I don't know anyone named Sam Donovan, and my automobile is one of the finest in the nation. This race really isn't for speed. It's for endurance."

"Blaze, believe me," Kate said, despairing of convincing him of the seriousness of the situation, "if we stay here, both of us are going to be killed. As I told you, a man named Donovan is coming to The Stanley in search of you."

"Claiming that I ran off with his wife, whom I ditched after I got her pregnant!" He almost spat out the words. "That's preposterous. I never went out with a married woman in my life."

"Not that you knew about," Kate argued. "Perhaps she didn't let you know."

"I'll have to have some time to think about this," Blaze said, a frown creasing his brow.

"Time is the one commodity we don't have much of," Kate said.

Blaze nodded. "We'd better get going if we expect to be back at The Stanley for dinner."

"Blaze," Kate said, picking up her blouse, "you're not dismissing what I told you, are you?"

"No, I'm just thinking about it and trying to figure out what I—what we should do."

Kate was disappointed at Blaze's reaction to her confession, although she knew she should not be. The whole idea of time travel still sounded preposterous to her, and she was the one who had actually been transported from one time period to another. She could imagine how much more difficult it was for Blaze to believe in the phenomenon. If only she could persuade him to leave Estes Park. The farther away from there she could get him, the safer they would be.

The ride back to the hotel was a quiet one. Kate had done all she could and had nothing else to say that would convince Blaze of the truth. Now it was up to him to believe or disbelieve what she had told him. When she had first arrived in the past, she had thought about what Lucille Wright had told her about the purpose of time travel, but now she was concerned only with saving Blaze's life. If that meant leaving The Stanley, they would leave. But deep in her heart Kate was plagued with questions. She wondered if she had the willpower to defy acts carried out in the past. Could she go against what she had done in an earlier lifetime? Even if she did have that power, did she have the right to do it?

At that moment she was not concerned with the morality of her decision. She only knew that Blaze was the most important person in her life. She had waited for several lifetimes—quite literally—for his love, having been thwarted in the last one. Now she was getting a second chance, and she was not going to make the same mistake.

When they arrived at the hotel, night had begun its gentle descent. They dismounted, the groom taking the horses and leading them to the stables. His hand cupping her elbow, Blaze guided her up the flight of stairs, across the wide veranda and cool lobby to the front desk.

"Any mail for us?" Blaze asked the smiling clerk.

"Nothing today," she answered. Then dangling a key between her thumb and index finger, she called out, "Mr. Donovan, here's your key."

Kate felt as if her bones had turned to butter, and Blaze's fingers gripped her elbow. Slowly, like a sleep-walker, she turned to look at the man who sprinted briskly down the stairs and moved toward them. Deb-onair, he wore a Palm Beach suit—the fashionable outfit favored by men who lived on either the Eastern or Western seaboard—light in color with a shaped jacket and waistcoat. Around the wing collar of his shirt he wore a dark bow tie, and peeking from beneath the pegged trousers with the deep cuff were shiny, black patent leather shoes. He wore leather gloves and carried a cane, which tapped in cadence with his steps. As he neared the counter, he looked at Kate and smiled.

"Good evening, madam," he said in a pleasant voice, curling his lips into a bigger smile to expose even white teeth. "Please forgive me for being so presumptuous, but aren't you Caitlin McDonald?"

"Yes," Kate answered, her voice strange to her own ears, "I am." She felt Blaze's grasp tighten even more on her elbow and knew that he was just as affected by the man's appearance. Out of the corner of her eye she saw his ashen face. Donovan took a step closer, his co-logne assailing her nostrils. It was a highly distinctive odor, heavy and sweet, which nauseated Kate.

"I'm Samuel Donovan, and while you won't recog-nize me or my name, I most assuredly recognize you. I was at your performance in—"

Kate felt as if she were going to faint, not only from the odor of his cologne, but from the mere presence of the man she had judged to be Blaze Callaghan's arch-enemy all these years. Here she was face-to-face with a man whom she had come to hate through her years of research into Caitlin and Blaze's lives. She could not rid her mind of the maniacal laughter she had heard in her dream. She shivered and pressed herself closer to Blaze. She looked into the stranger's face and watched his mouth move, saw that pasty smile, but did not hear a word he spoke. She heard only his laughter and it mocked her; it told her that she would never succeed in running away from him.

"I'm Blaze Callaghan," Kate heard her husband say and marveled at his aplomb. "I'm Caitlin's husband. We're pleased to make your acquaintance, Mr. Donovan."

"Likewise," Donovan said, but his gaze never left Kate's face. "May I invite you to be my guests for dinner? I would love the pleasure of your company."

"Thank you, Mr. Donovan, but my wife and I have plans for this evening. Another time, perhaps." His face set in a frown, Blaze guided Caitlin toward the stairs.

"Another time, indeed." Donovan's words followed them more like a threat than a promise.

"I don't like him," Kate murmured as they ascended the stairs to their second-story suite. "He's evil, Blaze. And it's just as I told you."

"You're overreacting," Blaze said, but Kate heard the doubt underlying his words. "And the man clearly said he had gone to one of your concerts, so that's where you could have learned about his coming here to The Stanley."

Kate jerked her arm from his hand and spun around on the landing between the floors to glare at him. "You're determined not to believe me, aren't you? Are you just going to wait for him to shoot you? Are you going ahead to race in that darned tournament, no matter what I tell you?"

Blaze's hand shot out to cover her mouth. "Be quiet," he ordered. "Everyone in this hotel can hear you and will think you're insane."

Her cheeks coloring with embarrassment, Kate's gaze swung around the ground floor, and she did see several curious glances directed their way. Quietly she allowed him to lead her up the remaining stairs to their suite. Knowing that Caitlin and Blaze had indeed argued on the stairs, she should have known better, but her thoughts were no longer very clear-cut. It was becoming more and more difficult for her to know if she was thinking as Caitlin or as Kate; the two seemed to be merging, her identity becoming a composite.

She could not allow that to happen, or she would not be able to save Blaze. She, Kate Norris, had to keep her wits under control. She had to plan an escape for them.

Blaze slid the key into the lock and turned it, the click echoing down the hallway. They walked into the room, soft with evening shadows. He touched the switch and muted light spread throughout the huge parlor. He walked to a long, marble-topped table that stood against the wall and lifted the crystal decanter to pour himself a glass of whiskey. Because he was not ordinarily a drinking man, Kate knew he was upset by the turn of events. Leaving him to his own thoughts, she moved into the bedroom and began to undress.

Blaze paced back and forth in the parlor. "There has to be an explanation, Kate," he finally muttered.

Wearing only her chemise and petticoat and holding her brush, Kate moved to the door. "I've told you what this is, darling. I've also told you what will happen if we remain here. At the hands of that man I shall be murdered. Three days later your car will crash in the race and you will be killed."

His hand tightened around the empty glass. "If what you've told me is true," he said, "perhaps you did not die because of Donovan. Perhaps I'm the one who killed you."

Kate dropped the brush and rushed to Blaze, throwing her arms about him. "Don't torture yourself like this," she begged; yet she was tormented by the same thought. "You're not capable of killing anyone, much less me. You're in love with me."

"I'm not sure of anything anymore, love," he murmured, burying his face in her hair, still clutching the empty glass. "I'm confused and don't know what to do. Running away isn't my style, but I can't stay if my staying is going to result in your death."

Kate felt the shiver that ran through his large frame at such a thought. Never had she felt more loved.

Then he pulled back to gaze somberly into her face. "Can one run from one's destiny?"

"I have knowledge of future events," Kate told him. "Providence would not have allowed me to return, if there was nothing I could do with the truth I have."

Blaze sighed. "That might be so if you had the truth, but you're not sure what the truth is. You have two stories that have been handed down, either of which may be right—or both may be wrong."

Kate felt the blood drain from her face. "I had never thought of it like that," she whispered. "What can we do?"

"We'll take one day at a time. First of all we'll go on to Boulder to hire a private detective to investigate Sam Donovan," he said and walked to the table to set down his glass. "You said he was from Daytona Beach, Florida, so that should be a relatively simple chore. If what you know about Donovan turns out to be fact, we'll find exactly whom his wife did run away with and present him with the truth. When we return to The Stanley, if he still happens to be here, we'll tell him what we learned, he'll have no reason for revenge and will leave us alone."

"Yes," Kate murmured. His solution seemed so logical and simple. "That's marvelous, Blaze. When are we leaving?"

"Tomorrow." He smiled. "I'll run downstairs and make the travel arrangements, while you're getting prettied up. Then I'll take you to dinner and we'll dance the evening away."

After Blaze left, Kate walked to her desk and sat down. Opening her diary, she began to write. She was quickly learning that perhaps she had no control over destiny and could not change that which had already happened. But surely Providence would ordain that she could leave a record of what really had transpired. All the same, she knew of no place where she could put her diary for safekeeping, somewhere it could be located by Kate Norris at a future date.

Reaching up, she pulled the chain on the lamp, and soft light fluttered over the desk to gleam richly on the dark mahogany. She stared at her topaz ring, her wedding ring.

But no matter how long she stared at the gemstone, she saw no visions, had no dreams and found no answers. Sighing, she rose, locked the diary in the drawer and dropped the desk key into a pocket of her purse. She promised herself that she would find a place—one so obvious that it would be overlooked for years, but which would be found by a true searcher.

Chapter Seven

Blaze, wearing a black evening suit, gazed at his wife, who stood in front of the cheval mirror. Her hair was piled high on her head, a mass of curls and braids with feathers, pearls and crystal combs twined among the glowing red tresses. Her gown, an elegant creation in pink silk, was heavily beaded with imported crystal that matched the combs. The neckline featured an Art Nouveau butterfly and trim of palest pink satin, silver ribbon and lace. White chiffon panels were draped from the scooped neck to the gloves and fluttered to the hemline.

"Tonight, love, you will be fire and ice rolled into one. You and the Pacquin creation are the fire." A small jeweler's box in his hand, he walked toward her. Opening the box, he pulled out lead crystal earrings and a matching pendant on a long platinum chain. "This is the ice."

"Oh, Blaze," Kate breathed, turning to look into the mirror as he draped the chain around her neck. She reached up and touched the pear-shaped pendant. "This is so expensive."

"Nothing is too expensive for you, my love." He leaned over and pressed light kisses down the gentle curve of her shoulder and neck. Then he watched as she put on her earrings, the crystals shimmering in the overhead light. "You've been stunning before, Mrs. Callaghan," he said, "but tonight you'll dazzle them. Never will a more beautiful woman grace The Stanley Hotel."

"The old saying is so true, love, that beauty is in the eye of the beholder."

Blaze tucked her hand into the crook of his arm and they walked out of the suite, pausing for him to lock the door. When they stepped from the ornate brass elevator, they moved through the brilliantly lighted lobby to the dining room where they ate dinner by candlelight, more engrossed in each other than the food. When they were through, Blaze led her into the Music Room, which, like the lobby, was ablaze with light. Soft music came from the string orchestra in the alcove. Chairs and tables, ordinarily scattered through the room, now lined the wall, and couples danced the Viennese waltz.

"May I have this dance, Mrs. Callaghan?" Blaze asked.

"I would give it to no other," she murmured, delighted when he caught her in his arms and swept her across the floor. For such a tall man, Blaze was graceful and light on his feet, an excellent dancer as Kate had known he would be. They fitted perfectly together and moved in complete harmony. Looking into each other's eyes, lost in a world of their own making, they spun around the room, the delicate chiffon panels of her gown furling through the air.

"You look like a fairy princess," Blaze said.

"I feel like a woman who is very much in love," she told him and gazed into his adoring eyes.

Then over Blaze's shoulder she saw Sam Donovan enter the room and stand against the wall, his eyes coming to rest on them. Unable to stop the shiver of apprehension that ran down her spine, she stiffened. The man frightened her. As Blaze twirled her around the room, she watched Donovan out of the corner of her eye. He followed them with his gaze, and it seemed to Kate that they were the only ones he was watching. So evident was his scrutiny that Kate lost her concentration and tripped, causing Blaze to look at her in surprise.

"I'm sorry," she murmured. "It's Donovan. He's been staring at us ever since he entered the room."

Blaze whirled her around so that he could see the man. "Don't worry," he consoled her, "I'm not going to let him hurt us. Hopefully we'll be on our way to Boulder long before he awakens in the morning."

An older man appeared in the door, his gaunt face sporting a snowy-white beard. Looking toward Kate, he smiled.

"There's Mr. Stanley," she said and waved. "He's looking at us, darling. Have you told him about our plans for tomorrow?"

"I have."

"I thought so. The way he's smiling, I have a feeling that he's up to something."

"I wonder what?" Blaze asked, not bothering to look toward the door.

"I'll bet he's looking for a good game of billiards," Kate answered as they continued to spin about the room. "Especially if he knows that we won't be back from Boulder for several days. He's waving to us, Blaze."

When the music stopped, Kate moved out of his embrace, putting her hand on his arm. They moved to the door where F. O. Stanley stood, holding the lapels of his coat in either hand.

He smiled and said, "I don't suppose I could interest you in a game of billiards tonight, could I?"

"Of course you could," Kate replied and smiled at the older man. "Although Blaze promised me a full night of dancing, I know that he'd much prefer to be in the billiard room with you, talking about Steamers and racing and ideas for new designs."

The older man looked at Blaze and laughed softly. "Looks like you have a woman who not only loves but understands you, Blaze, my boy. She's a rare creature. Take care of her."

"I will, sir," Blaze answered quietly.

"Perhaps an old man like me should not interfere with you newlyweds."

"You're not interfering with us," Kate said and began to walk toward the billiard room. "I'm quite tired and shall enjoy sitting down and watching a good game of skill."

"Few men can really challenge me," F. O. said. "Among them is Blaze."

In contrast to the lightness of the other hotel rooms, the billiard room was heavily paneled in dark wood and had massive raised benches cushioned in leather, where ladies might sit to watch the games. Chandeliers hung low, casting their light over the individual tables. Taking off his coat and laying it on the bench beside Kate, Blaze leaned over her and said, "I'm sorry, darling. I truly meant for this to be an evening for you."

"I don't mind. In fact, I was telling the truth a moment ago. I'm quite glad to sit out a few dances."

His eyes searched her face. "Are you feeling all right?"

Although she was in fact slightly nauseated, Kate shook her head. "I'm a little warm. I'll be all right as soon as I cool off."

"We'll go to the room," Blaze said, solicitous about her health.

"No, I'm not ready to leave," she told him. "I enjoy watching you play billiards, but I do get tired of your letting Mr. Stanley win."

"What makes you think I let him beat me?"

Her smile turned into a grin. "Because you're the best. Now beat him several games tonight. By the time we return from Boulder, he'll be over his irritation."

"Just remember, sweetheart, he's my employer. I have to be a little cautious. The old man is rather prickly where his billiard skills are concerned."

"Let me see you win at least one."

"One," Blaze said.

Kate settled back on the bench, watching the men concentrate on their game and listening to the music that wafted into the room. Once in a while she would look out the window, to see threads of lightning streak the sky. Also in the distance was a faint roll of thunder. The later it grew, the larger the threads became, the louder the claps of thunder, and the closer the storm. Kate was humming one of the tunes the orchestra was playing next door when she felt someone approach her. Then she smelled a familiar, heavy, sweet fragrance and knew it was Sam Donovan.

"May I?" he asked and bowed low, his manners as impeccable as his evening attire.

"Of course." Kate framed the words with a smile and wished more air were circulating in the room. "With so

many other billiard tables vacant and begging for oc-
cupancy, Mr. Donovan, I wonder that you sit with me
on the sidelines and watch."

"Please call me Sam." He looked at her and smiled,
and while he was not handsome, she had to admit that
he was attractive in a wholesome way with a trusting,
persuasive smile. Although he was talking to her, Kate
sensed that his attention was really centered on Blaze.
He continued. "I don't really play the game that well
myself, but I do enjoy a good game, if you don't mind
my saying so, Miss McDonald. Or shall I call you Mrs.
Callaghan?"

"Mrs. Callaghan," Kate murmured, knowing that he
wished to call her neither. He would have liked them to
be on a first-name basis, but she would not tolerate that.

"Ah, Mrs. Callaghan, I wanted to talk with you. You
have no idea how popular a man I shall become, when
people learn that I've actually met and talked with you.
Being able to recount your performance, which I saw
personally, brought me a certain amount of fame and
prestige, but this shall surely outdo that."

Deciding that this would be as good a time as any to
learn something about him, Kate nodded her head in
gracious acknowledgment. "What a compliment you
pay me, sir. But who, pray tell, will be interested in
knowing that you have met Caitlin McDonald Callaghan?"

"All of my acquaintances," he replied vaguely.

"And what about me shall be of the most interest to
them?" she asked curiously, having always been glad
that she enjoyed popularity, but never quite sure what
had pushed her to such heights.

"I suppose the one item they will find most interesting is your recent marriage to—" his eyes shifted to the billiard table "—Mr. Callaghan."

Kate laughed softly, glancing at her husband. "Then I am in agreement with my public, Mr. Donovan. My recent marriage is certainly the most interesting fact in my life."

"May I get you a glass of punch or lemonade?" Sam asked as a waiter unobtrusively moved through the huge room, a tray balanced on one uplifted hand.

"Yes, a lemonade, please," Kate said. "I'm quite thirsty."

Kate returned her attention to the game, watching Blaze as he moved around the table, visually measuring his shots, then posing. The sharp click of a billiard ball hitting another ball or being hit by the cue echoed through the decidedly masculine room. Blaze was poised for a shot when he looked up, his eyes locking with Kate's. At that moment Donovan returned with the lemonade.

Standing so that he was between her and Blaze, he said, "Here you are. It is quite cool and appears to be most refreshing." He moved past her and sat down.

Holding the glass in her hand, Kate's gaze again caught her husband's. His eyes were narrowed, his face set in unyielding lines. After a second—one that seemed much longer to Kate—he lowered his head, looked at the billiard table and shot.

F. O. Stanley's laughter rang through the room. "Another shot or two like that, Blaze, and I'll be better off playing by myself. It's as if you're giving the game to me."

Blaze laughed, but the sound was hollow and devoid of humor. "Believe me," he answered, "I would never willingly give you this game. Winning is much too important to me.''

When Blaze looked at her again, Kate smiled tentatively. Naturally she was concerned about him. His mind still had to be reeling from her confession earlier in the day, and now he was clearly thinking about Sam Donovan—and her—at this moment. Blaze smiled back at her. The gesture was comforting and reassuring, yet she saw the undercurrent of anxiety.

Other men entered, their drinks and cigars in hand, and circled different tables.

"How long will you be staying at The Stanley?" Sam eventually asked, his tone and question seemingly casual.

"As soon as my husband concludes his business," Kate replied, instantly on guard.

Donovan nodded, his eyes again moving to Blaze. "I hear tell that he's really working hard to come up with some really innovative changes in the steam boiler."

"I really don't know about that," Kate answered, again gracing him with a smile. "You would have to discuss that with Blaze, and I'm sure he'd be happy to talk automobiles with you. It's one of his favorite subjects. But what about you, Mr. Donovan?" she asked. "Is your trip to Colorado for pleasure or business?"

"It's a combination," he replied. "At the present, my business and pleasure are working hand in hand."

A gust of wind blew through the opened windows and Kate shivered, but not from the cold. She feared the implication of Donovan's words, one of which only she could be aware. Yet her lack of knowledge about this man was her greatest weakness in this life. She knew that Donovan had played a role in Caitlin's death, but had no concrete evidence as to the nature of that role.

Deep down she knew that Caitlin had never been infatuated with Sam Donovan and had certainly not had an affair with him.

"If I'm not being too presumptuous, sir," she said, "may I ask what your business is?"

"I am a real estate developer, a financier of sorts and a dreamer," he replied. "I figure that soon tourism will be one of the major businesses on the Eastern coast, and naturally cities and towns that are building their economy on tourism must furnish the tourists with accommodations. I like what Stanley has done here," he said, "and I want to copy and expand it across the United States so more people can enjoy it."

Kate leaned back in surprise. She had never expected such depth from Sam Donovan. In all her research he had always appeared so one-dimensional that she had experienced difficulty in accepting him as a real, living human being. Now his intelligence and sound ideas really caught her off guard. She was prepared to dislike him; she wanted to think evil of him; yet she was finding that while she distrusted the role he'd played in Caitlin's life, he was not quite the blackguard she had presumed he was, nor was he necessarily the epitome of a villain.

"Your wife, Mr. Donovan," Kate said, grasping for a delicate way to broach a subject that directly tied Donovan to Blaze. "What does she think about your ideas on tourism?"

He clenched his teeth, a muscle ticking in his jaw. Eventually he spoke and turned tear-filled eyes toward her. "My wife is dead, Mrs. Callaghan. She died... recently in childbirth."

"I'm so sorry," Kate murmured, her heart going out to him.

"Yes, I am, too," he said, again turning his head. After a long, poignant pause, he added, "Part of me died with her. But that part that is left must go on living, if one can call it living."

Not knowing what to say, Kate remained silent, sipping at her lemonade, which was suddenly tasteless. Donovan did not move, nor did he make an attempt to revive the conversation. He appeared to be concentrating on the game. Kate was glad when the game ended and Blaze walked to the bench.

"That was an excellent exhibition of skill, Mr. Callaghan," Donovan said, and Kate wondered if she imagined the cutting edge to his tone. "At one point I didn't think that you could pull it out."

Blaze reached down between Donovan and Kate and picked up his coat. "My whole life is predicated on racing and on winning, Mr. Donovan. I can always pull into the lead," he answered in a deathly quiet voice.

Sam Donovan rose, and Kate realized that he was almost the same height as Blaze, though not as broad and muscular. Yet Blaze seemed to dwarf the man. "But life is fickle, isn't it, Mr. Callaghan? It doesn't guarantee that a winner will always be a winner. Always there comes along another who is much faster and more determined to win."

Kate rose and slipped a trembling hand around Blaze's arm as he replied, "Life gives us exactly what we demand," he said. "To avoid being a loser, one must step aside while he's still a winner."

Donovan nodded his head and smiled. "That's a good philosophy to live by. I've heard that the Fourth of July Tournament is going to be your last race, so evidently you have decided that your winning streak is over."

Blaze smiled and laid his other hand over the one Kate had curled around his arm. He looked down at her. "The Fourth of July race will be my last, but you're wrong about my concept of my winning streak. I think I'm on the biggest roll of my life. It's just a different one than racing. Kate and I are ready to settle down and start a family."

Donovan's sharp intake of breath caused Kate to look at him. His eyes were dark, his face set.

Quietly she said, "Mr. Donovan's wife recently died in childbirth, darling."

"I'm sorry," Blaze said. "I didn't mean to—"

Donovan held up both hands in a silencing gesture. "Not to worry," he said. "I didn't mean to get sentimental. Now, if you'll excuse me, I think I shall retire for the night. I've had a rather exhausting day, and tomorrow doesn't promise to be much different."

"Good night," Kate and Blaze murmured and watched him walk out of the room.

Dropping an arm around Kate's shoulders, Blaze gently steered her to the exit. "Shall we dance the night through, love?"

"No," she said softly and looked up into her husband's face, "I think not. I have much more pleasant things I would prefer to be doing tonight."

"Ah," he drawled, "an invitation I cannot resist."

Laughing and talking quietly, they walked to the elevator, but were stopped by a call from the other side of the lobby. They turned to see Donovan descending the stairs and moving in their direction.

"Could I meet with you for either lunch or dinner tomorrow?" he asked Blaze. "I've been talking with your wife about a possible real estate venture, and I would like to get your advice on the practicality of having an automobile taxi service like The Stanley employs. I spoke with Mr. Stanley a moment ago about such a meeting, but he suggested that as supervisor of his Steamers and of the fleet, you would be the one to speak to.''

"I would love to talk automobiles with you," Blaze answered, "but I can't meet with you tomorrow. My wife and I are leaving for Boulder early in the morning." Glancing at Kate, Blaze smiled indulgently. "A shopping trip. She's suddenly discovered that she doesn't have nearly enough clothes to wear."

"Perhaps when you return," Donovan suggested.

Blaze nodded. "Certainly."

Donovan walked back to the staircase, stopped, then turned back. "Mr. Callaghan," he called, "I understand that you're quite an outdoorsman?"

"Yes, I suppose so," Blaze answered.

"I'm an avid hunter myself."

Kate's heart pounded with such fury her chest hurt. Every word Sam Donovan spoke seemed loaded with innuendo.

"I'm a trapshooter, Mr. Donovan, not a hunter," Blaze replied.

Donovan shrugged as if there were no difference between the two. "Although I sound rather arrogant, I must admit I'm quite a good marksman myself. I should love to pit my skills against yours before I conclude my stay at The Stanley."

"If time permits," Blaze said quietly.

"Of course. I've brought my gun with me, but it needs a minor adjustment. Could you recommend a good gunsmith to me?"

Blaze hesitated for a half second before he nodded his head. "I use Tom Hannibal. He's—"

"Please," Donovan interrupted, pulling a piece of paper and pencil from his pocket, "I'm so new here. I don't know one person from the next or one place from the other. Would you write his name and directions to his house?"

"Surely." Blaze took the sheet of paper and pencil and walked to a long desk in front of the arched window. Donovan followed, but Kate waited at the elevator. Blaze quickly wrote down the information, then returned the writing apparatus.

"Thank you so much," Donovan said, folding the paper and slipping it and the pencil into his inner coat pocket. He followed Blaze across the lobby, moving up the stairs as Blaze joined Kate. "Now I'll say goodnight." He inclined his head, turned and disappeared from view.

"I can hardly wait for us to be away from here," Kate said in an undertone as she and Blaze stepped into the elevator. "Donovan frightens me. He's baiting you."

"Everything will be all right, darling." He patted the hand that was curled around his arm. "I promise."

Somewhat reassured, Kate said no more but was glad when they were in their room. As Blaze locked the door, she moved into the bedroom, turning on the desk lamp, then stripping off her clothing. A cool wind blew through the room, billowing the lace curtains.

"Why, Blaze?" she asked. "Why did Donovan have to come and spoil our paradise?"

"I've been wondering the same thing, love." He entered the room, moving to the dresser where he shed his coat, tie and cummerbund. Draping them over the valet, he began to unbutton his shirt. "When I saw Donovan sitting with you, Kate, I was angry. But more than that, I was afraid. For a minute I was jealous, jealous of the attention he was paying to you. Jealous of your laughing and talking with him. Kate, what if—?''

Kate rushed to where he stood, threw her arms around him and pressed herself against him. ''Don't think that, Blaze. Put thoughts like that out of your mind. We're going to Boulder tomorrow. How long do you think it will take to find out something about him?'' she asked, knowing they were running out of time. They did not have the luxury of weeks to search for an answer, and the few days left were quickly turning into hours. And they were beginning to distrust both themselves and their motives.

His embrace tightened. ''It won't take long,'' he reassured her. ''Perhaps a day. A reputable private investigator will have connections in the major cities, whom he can call by telephone, and if necessary, he can travel by train.''

Kate lifted her face and he lowered his, their lips touching in a tentative kiss that quickly deepened into desire. When Blaze finally lifted his mouth from hers, he murmured, ''We'll find a way out of this, love.''

''Yes, we will,'' Kate murmured, but she wondered if it would be the same way they had gotten out of it before. Or would the strength of their love give them the will to change their destiny?

Blaze smiled. ''In the meantime, don't you think we ought to retire, Mrs. Callaghan?''

''Yes,'' she replied, and arm in arm the two walked into the bedroom, Kate's eyes going to the desk, to the drawer in which her diary was locked.

Chapter Eight

The French doors and windows were open. The evening breeze, growing stronger as the hours passed and the summer storm approached, wafted through the room, billowing the lace curtains. The room, dimly illuminated by the desk lamp, was quiet, the only sound that of Kate's pen as it moved across the pages of her diary. Naked with a sheet stretched across his lower body, Blaze slept.

Kate wrote with no concept of time until the clock chimed the early-morning hour. She paused to look at the porcelain clock, but even then she would not have stopped had her entry for the day not been completed. She laid down the pen, blotted the page and quickly re-read it. Satisfied, she closed the book, held it against her breast for a brief second, then returned it to the drawer. After locking it, she dropped the key into the pocket of her white cotton dressing robe and leaned back in the chair to look at her ring; the topaz glimmered in the pale light.

Kate did not know much about psychometry, but she knew that if she were to return to her former life, she would not be able to take the diary with her. It had not physically manifested itself in her former life; therefore there was no way of taking it back with her. She also remembered that as Kate Norris she had not been able to unearth Caitlin's diary. She knew it existed now, but where could she hide it, she wondered, so that it would be found and Caitlin's true story revealed?

Now more than before, now that she really knew and loved Blaze, Kate wanted the world to know the true story behind the Caitlin McDonald legend. She wanted them to know about the true love these two people shared. She rose and walked to the bed to look at her husband. So precious had their hours together become that she was tempted to wake him, but did not.

Instead she stood and enjoyed looking at him. His lashes, dark and long, rested against sun-browned skin; sleep softened his expression and gave his rugged face vulnerability. She pushed the strand of dark hair from his forehead and ran her fingertips lightly over his beard-stubbled cheeks. Blaze roused, breathed deeply and turned onto his back, the dark hair that swirled on his chest in direct contrast with the white sheet that still covered him.

Love for him swelled in Kate's heart to such proportions that she could not voice it. Words could not begin to explain her feelings, a blend of joy and sorrow. She had never felt complete because she had never loved passionately, but Providence had given her another chance, and now she had experienced a love that was deeply consuming. But in giving her this opportunity, Providence, the double-edged sword, was also taking from her the very joy that it had given.

At most she had little time left with Blaze, and although she was Kate Norris and had all her knowledge of the past, she was impotent to change it, powerless to save her beloved or herself. No matter what she had done up to this point, the basic outcome would remain the same. She had an explanation of sorts about the reason why and the manner in which she had traveled back in time, but she had no idea how, when or if she would ever move forward again. As Caitlin she had only a few days to live, but the thought of dying was not frightening. Somehow the fact that she had traveled in time lessened the fear of the unknown and assured her that there was life after death. Her fear was of leaving Blaze.

Buttoning her dressing gown, she walked to the door, unlocked it and slipped into the hallway. Her slippered feet silently descended the steps and walked across the lobby, which was dark except for the quicksilver flashes of lightning. Quietly, so as not to disturb the night clerk who snoozed behind the registration counter, she slipped into the Music Room, then closed the door and walked to the alcove. Sitting down on the round stool, she lifted the lid of the Steinway, and her fingers touched the keys as she played her favorite classical music, Tchaikovsky's piano concerto No. 1 in B-flat minor, op.23.

Strong and vibrant, the notes resounded through the room, her imagination adding full orchestration. She closed her eyes and gave herself to the music, her hands nimble and strong, delicate and firm, caressing and loving the most beautiful tones from the ivory keys. Time ceased to exist; the echo of thunder was far beyond the plane on which she lived; lightning was the hand of fate, playing with the heavens as if it were a harp. Her fingers, playing the ageless classic, created a new world for her as they moved from one end of the keyboard to the other. The sharp, staccato notes seemed to flow into softer, delicate tones, swelling once again to vibrant, full tones as Rossetti's poem floated through her mind, the words that her beloved had spoken to her.

> I have been here before,
> But when or how I cannot tell:
> . . . .
> You have been mine before,—
> How long ago I may not know:

Finally Kate dropped her hands into her lap and sat for a long time staring at the piano. Her sorrow and anxiety purged, she lowered the Steinway's lid and walked out of the room as quietly as she had entered, closing the door behind her. When she turned, she saw the night clerk moving toward her.

A tall, lean man, gaunt and bent with age, he smiled. "That was lovely, Miss Caitlin. I never dreamed that I would be privileged to hear such a concert. I hate to see you and Mr. Blaze leave. The Stanley will never be the same. Your music has brought us a beauty that can never be surpassed."

Kate caught the old man's hands in her own and squeezed gently. "Thank you, Mr. Strickland." She looked over her shoulder as a streak of lightning illuminated the entire lobby. The lightning was especially bright this time, she thought. "Caitlin McDonald shall always be a part of the history of The Stanley. At a time when you least expect it, she'll return to play the Steinway. Her music will always be here for posterity to enjoy."

"I hope so, ma'am," he said. "I surely do."

"Good night," Kate said. "It's past time for me to be in bed."

Catching the gold chain with a gnarled hand, he withdrew his watch and stared at the large, round face. "That's for a fact," he agreed, then returned it to his waistcoat pocket. Walking closer to one of the large, arched windows that graced the lobby, he said, "Big storm brewing tonight. Travel's going to be mighty dangerous tomorrow."

"Yes, it is," Kate said and laid her hand against her breast, a gnawing fear returning to plague her.

Slowly she turned and walked up the stairs, down the hall to their suite. She eased the key into the lock, opened it and entered. Quietly she closed and locked it again, dropping the key onto her desk as she switched off the lamp. The room fell dark for a moment, then was filled with a flash of silver light. She was still not ready for bed; she wanted to waste none of her precious time on sleep. There was much left undone, much more she wanted to do.

She walked outside to stand on the balcony and to enjoy the exhilaration of the approaching storm. The evening breeze, having gained momentum, was now a gusty wind, and the night sky was covered in clouds. Not a star was in sight. Kate watched the spindly fingers of lightning as they crawled up and down the sky. Booming peals of thunder, growing louder, followed in its wake.

Having been fascinated rather than frightened by storms, especially electrical storms, since she was a small child, Kate remained where she was. The wind whipped her hair from its pins and molded her robe to her body. The nearer the lightning came and the louder the thunder cracked, the more exhilarated Kate became. Even when the rain began to fall in huge droplets, she did not move. She lifted her head and let it splatter against her face. She welcomed the cool, refreshing touch of the elements.

As if the clouds were a trapdoor beneath the heavens, they opened and the rain fell in torrential force. In minutes Kate was soaked to the bone, her face still uplifted, her hair plastered to her back, rain running in rivulets down the long strands. Without her realizing it, her tears were mingled with the rain expressing the joy of having tasted love and the sorrow of having to part with it so quickly.

"Kate!"

She slowly opened her eyes and rolled her head against the wall to see Blaze standing in the shadows beyond the door. In a flash of lightning that brightened the room, Kate saw that he was wearing only his slacks. Her eyes moved over his chest, down the swirl of hair to his waistline.

"Honey! What are you doing out here in this storm? It's dangerous," he said, his voice heavy with concern.

"I love storms," she said. "Lightning is beautiful."

"It's deadly."

"But exciting," Kate said, wondering why she was suddenly walking on the edge. She had always been a circumspect person, looking for security at all costs. Now she was throwing all caution to the wind.

Their gazes caught and locked, the two of them alone, their purpose one. Each turned toward the other, moved by the beat of thunderclaps that heralded the arrival of the storm. They were caught up in the current of electricity as bolts of lightning danced across the sky, again and again. Long strides carried him through the door and onto the balcony.

"Blaze," she whispered.

His large hands curled over her shoulders and he drew her closer. She lifted her face to his, his lips closed over hers, water streaming down his cheeks and onto hers, their kiss a reflection of their fear of losing one another.

A grotesque flash of lightning with a multitude of gnarled fingers clawed through the air, illuminating the balcony, and their soaked bodies. Blaze swung Kate into his arms and carried her into their room, setting her down beside the bed. Quickly he stripped the sodden garments from her body.

Looking at her, he murmured, "You're beautiful, Kate." He flicked the damp hair from her forehead.

She reached out and unbuttoned his slacks, pushing her hands beneath the wet material and sliding them down his legs. Stepping out of them when they pooled at his feet, he picked Kate up again and laid her in the middle of the huge bed and knelt over her. As streak after streak of lightning split the night, Kate lifted her hand, dragging her fingernails down Blaze's chest. Blaze lowered his head, his lips touching Kate's breasts. His breath was warm on her skin, his lips stirring new desires within her.

He slid his body alongside hers and ran his hand down the smooth line of her waist and hips as her fingers tangled in his hair. Her stomach quivered beneath his touch, and she gave herself with abandon to the fiery taste of his kisses and the demand of his hands on her body.

His fingers stroked her, and she rolled her head from side to side as little whimpers of delight escaped her slightly parted lips. He captured her mouth, pressing his lips into hers, and moved his other hand to her breast, slowly and expertly building her passion. His lovemaking reached the same intensity as the raging storm, carrying both of them to the heights of pleasure.

Later, Kate lay in the cradle of Blaze's arms, staring at the rivulets of rain on the window. She stirred and pressed her body against Blaze's hard warmth.

"Daylight will be here soon," she said.

"Mmm," he droned and rubbed his cheek against the top of her head.

"I don't suppose we'll be going to Boulder."

Breathing deeply, Blaze rolled over and slid out of bed, picking up his trousers and slipping into them. He walked to the French doors, and bracing his hand against one side, leaned on the other. "You're really worried about this Donovan fellow, aren't you?"

Kate pushed herself up, reaching to lift her damp hair off her shoulders. "Yes."

"Then I'm going on to Boulder and see what I can find out."

Careless of her nudity, Kate bolted up in the bed. "You're taking me with you, aren't you?"

"No." Blaze shook his head and slowly returned to her. "Not after the rain. The roads are too dangerous. Besides, I'll make better time by myself."

"Don't do this to me," Kate pleaded, fear wrapping its tentacles around her heart and squeezing.

Sitting on the edge of the bed, he drew her into his arms and held her close. "If what you know of the future is true," he said softly, "you have more to fear from me than from this man. I'm the one he wants."

"Blaze, we have so few hours left. I can't bear to be separated from you. No matter how dangerous it is, I would rather be with you than here."

He caught her by the shoulders and pushed her back so that he was looking into her face. "Providence let you return to me," he said, "and for a reason. You have a chance of doing something this time that you didn't do the first. Let me go on to Boulder and see what I can learn. I promise that I'll be back as quickly as I can."

Kate wanted to argue with him, but even as she opened her mouth, she knew that it would be useless. Her will was strong enough to go against the events as they had been enacted, but not her conscience. At times when she was thinking more like Kate Norris than Caitlin, she believed she had the right to recreate the past, to insist that they defy destiny, but at that moment she felt that if she did so, she would be a blasphemer. Tears sparkling in her eyes, she lifted her hands and cupped his face.

"Trust me, darling," he murmured. "I'll take care of you. I promise."

"All right," she whispered and leaned forward to kiss him softly on the lips.

THE DAYS passed slowly, and still Blaze did not return. Every time Kate ventured downstairs, Sam Donovan seemed to materialize out of nowhere and to glue himself to her. Warm and friendly, he pressed his company upon her until she felt as if she were suffocating and made some excuse to return to her room. The longer she was around him and the longer Blaze was gone, the more fearful she grew.

On the third morning after Blaze's departure, Kate received a letter in which Blaze told her that he had hired a private investigator by the name of Amos Tubman, who had put in several calls to Daytona Beach. So far they had learned nothing about Sam Donovan; but Blaze was going to wait a little longer to see if they received more information. In the meantime he was buying some needed equipment for his racing car. He admonished Kate to be careful and sent his love, ending with a promise to be home no later than the first of July. He planned to be home by early afternoon.

Happy that Blaze had sent her the name of the investigator, but disappointed, both because they had uncovered nothing about Donovan and that Blaze was still going to race his Steamer on the Fourth, Kate refolded her letter. Unlocking the desk, she tucked it into her diary; then she changed from her day dress into a divided skirt and blouse. As she sat in the slipper chair, putting on her boots, Sally Adams walked into the room.

"Going out?" she asked.

Kate nodded. "For a walk. I'm tired of being cooped up."

"I don't think that's such a good idea," Sally said. "The trails are dangerous, and you're such a newcomer."

Kate smiled. "Thank you for the kind thoughts, Mrs. Adams, but I'll manage. I'm not going that far, really. Just up to the cabin."

Going to the wardrobe, Kate searched through her purses until she found a large one. Returning to the desk, she tucked her diary into it along with her writing paper, pen and ink. Last she added several other books, among them Blaze's two volumes of poetry.

Observing from the doorway, Sally asked dryly, "Going to be gone awhile?"

Kate smiled. "I may stay overnight."

"Do you think that's wise, Miss Caitlin?"

"I don't know," Kate answered, "and I don't know if you can understand this, Mrs. Adams, but I feel closer to Blaze when I'm at the cabin."

Her arms folded over her chest, Sally nodded and said softly, "I understand. I'm just worried about you. I sure don't want something to happen to you."

"It won't," Kate answered with certainty. *Not until July 1,* not until tomorrow.

The handle of the bag looped over her shoulder, Kate walked out of The Stanley and made her way to the path that she had traveled with Blaze the day they had gone to the cabin. She had not gone very far when she saw Paddy O'Grady, a fishing pole in one hand, a pail of bait in the other.

When he saw her, he grinned and transferred his pail into his other hand, so that he could snatch off his cap. A shock of dark auburn hair fell over his forehead. "Morning, Miss Caitlin."

"Good morning to you," Kate said. "Going fishing?"

"Yes, ma'am. I know a spot up here where the fish bite real good. Mr. Blaze helped me find it, and we're the only two who know about it."

"You come up here often," she said.

"As much as I can," he answered. "But with Papa being dead, I have to help Mama around the house, so I don't get the chance too often."

For the first time Kate thought about Paddy's mother—her great-grandmother. "I suppose your mother will appreciate your catching a lot of fish, won't she?"

Paddy grinned. "She likes fish real well, but what we don't need, we generally sell to the hotel."

"Do you usually have quite a few to sell?" Kate asked, remembering how hard times had been on Paddy and his mother after her great-grandpapa had died.

Paddy nodded. "I'm a good fisherman, and Mr. Stanley promised me that he'd always buy fish from me first." He smiled. "I'm taking real good care of my mother."

"Yes," Kate said, a small lump in her throat, "I know you are. I'd like to meet your mother one of these days, Paddy."

"Yes, ma'am. I think she'd like that, too." He bobbed his head energetically, then said, "Did you know, Miss Caitlin, that one time I was up in the mountains, fishing, when Old Harry—?"

Kate laughed softly as she remembered the tales her grandfather had often told her about his fishing excursions. The two of them fell into step and continued to walk the narrow path up the side of the mountain. As they traveled, Paddy entertained her with fish stories, and Kate listened in fascination. Even at this young age, he was already a storyteller. When the path split, she took the right fork, Paddy the left.

"Would you like to come fishing with me?" the boy asked. When Kate hesitated, he said, "I'll show you my favorite fishing spot, a place that nobody knows but me."

"Yes," Kate said and smiled, because she had a feeling that she did know where Paddy was taking her. "I think I will go with you, Paddy. While you're fishing, I'll read."

Again they chatted as they trudged up the mountain path, finally cutting away from the broken trail to push through the brush. When they arrived at a clearing by the side of the rushing brook, Paddy threw out his hand.

"What do you think?" he asked proudly.

"It's beautiful," Kate whispered and marveled that it was so little changed; Patrick had often brought his little granddaughter to this same spot, and the two of them had sat on the narrow bridge, fishing and talking. As Paddy, the lad of nine, scurried down to the bank of the stream, Kate slipped the leather strap from her shoulder and let the purse gently thud to the ground. Seating herself on the huge boulder to one side of the narrow path, she gazed at the valley below.

"There isn't a place on earth equal to this," she sighed, viewing the scene before her as if for the first time.

The valley was surrounded by snow-capped mountains that peaked into the sky; arcing through the fine mist that hovered over the valley was a delicate rainbow. Nestled in a south-facing slope overlooking the alpine mountain bowl was The Stanley Hotel with its bright yellow and red exterior. Stretching before it were green meadows, where wildflowers grew in profusion. Rising behind it was a great rock outcropping.

Paddy, having laid his fishing paraphernalia on the bank, moved to where she stood and looked across the valley with her.

"The Stanley is elegant and regal," Kate said, amazed at how easily the words flowed from her lips, words that she would hear repeated to her in the future, when as a child she stood at her grandfather's knee. "You might call her the Queen of the Rockies. Her entire domain consists of the valley, the village and Longs Peak."

"Do you believe in magic, Miss Caitlin?" Paddy pressed even closer to her, his blue eyes open and searching.

Kate only hesitated a second before she said, "Yes, I do. All you have to do is pretend that the mist, touched by the sunbeams, is a delicate golden veil, behind which hides a magical land. If you believe hard enough, you can cross over anytime you wish, Paddy. Through books and stories, you can go anywhere in the world you wish."

He squinted and peered into the distance. "I believe, Miss Caitlin. I really do." He returned those solemn blue eyes to her face. "My mother believes in magic, too. She says there's magic in telling stories."

"There is," Kate answered, "and I have the feeling that one of these days, Paddy O'Grady, you'll be spreading magic all over Colorado as one of the state's foremost storytellers."

He grinned. "Mama tells me that I can already spin a good yarn about my fish stories."

Kate chuckled softly. "That you do, laddie. Now you'd better get to fishing or the afternoon will be gone."

Sitting beneath a tree and leaning against the trunk, Kate took out her diary and pen and dutifully recorded in detail everything that had transpired since her last entry. When she had finished, she returned the diary to her purse. Seeing that Paddy was still fishing, she extracted the books of poetry, which she read for the remainder of the time. Several hours and three fish later, the sun was well into the western sky and Paddy announced that he needed to get home to do the chores.

"Are you going back to the hotel?" he asked.

"No," she answered, "I'm going to stop at the cabin."

"Do you want these fish?" he asked.

"I can't take your fish," Kate said.

"You're not taking them," he said reasonably. "I'm giving them to you."

"I'll... buy them," Kate said.

He shook his head. "No, I'd like to give them to you."

Not wanting to offend him by not accepting his gift, Kate said, "I'll tell you what. You take them home to your mother first. If she doesn't want them, I'll take them. No." She stopped in midsentence, then said, "I'll go with you, Paddy. I'd like to invite you and your mother to have dinner with me."

His gift forgotten, Paddy's eyes rounded like saucers, and he stared at her for a full minute, then bobbed his head energetically. "Come on, Miss Caitlin, let's go."

Grinning, Kate repacked her boots and watched as Paddy scampered away to gather his fishing gear. Together they headed down the path, turning right where they had turned left earlier and going beyond The Stanley to the small frame home where Paddy lived.

A woman, her graying hair pulled straight back and coiled into a tight little bun on the back of her head, walked to the door and watched Paddy and Kate. They opened the picket gate, the weight on the chain pulling it closed behind them.

"Mama," Paddy said and held out the string of fish, "Miss Caitlin was up in the woods today when I went fishing. I wanted to give her these, but—"

"Hello, Mrs. O'Grady," Kate said, smiling and walking past Paddy, "I'm Caitlin Callaghan."

A slow smile spanned the woman's weathered countenance; she studied Kate's face and Kate studied her. Wiping her hands on the large apron that covered most of her dress, she walked onto the veranda. "I be a'knowin' who you are, Miss Caitlin, and I be mighty happy to welcome you to my home. Would you care for a cup of tea?''

''Yes,'' Kate said, her voice slightly husky, ''I would, Mrs. O'Grady, and I'd like to invite you and Paddy to be my guests at the hotel for dinner tonight.''

This was her great-grandmother! She wanted to take her into her arms and hug her, to tell her who she was. She wanted Brigit O'Grady to tell her stories and to sing her songs about the old country.

''That's mighty kind of you,'' the older woman said, ''but—''

''Please, Mama,'' Paddy interrupted.

Brigit O'Grady dropped an arm over her son's shoulders and smiled at him. To Kate she said, ''Come on in for that cup of tea, and we'll chat a spell. Then we'll see.''

By the time Kate had finished her cup of tea, Brigit had persuaded Kate to stay for dinner, since Brigit had already begun cooking the evening meal. Not wanting to return any too quickly to the hotel and also wanting to spend as much time as she could with her ancestors, Kate quickly agreed. In case Blaze should return to the hotel before she did, she did not want him to worry, so she penned a note to him, which she sent to the hotel by Paddy. Also she told Paddy that since she would be eating dinner with them and had no place to keep the fish, she thought he ought to sell them to the hotel as usual. Happy with the arrangements, Paddy scurried off on his task. Kate donned an apron and was soon bustling around the kitchen, helping Brigit.

SAM WAS SITTING in one of the overstuffed chairs close to the registration desk, reading the daily newspaper, when Paddy rushed into the lobby, a letter in one hand, a string of fish in the other.

"Miss Caitlin is visiting with my mother, Miss Jennifer," he announced to the young clerk, excitement adding volume to his voice and making it easy for Sam to overhear the conversation. "And she wanted me to bring this note and leave it for Mr. Blaze, in case he should arrive from Boulder while she's at my house."

Sam slowly lowered the paper and peered curiously at the clerk, who took the letter but did not immediately put it into the designated slot. His gaze settled on the piece of folded paper, and he knew an insatiable desire to have it. The message was as much for him as it was for Callaghan.

"Thank you, Paddy," the woman said, leaning her rotund form across the desk and grinning down at the child. "I'll be sure to give it to Mr. Callaghan when he arrives. I see you've been fishing again."

Paddy grinned and nodded his head. "Yep! I caught 'em at mine and Mr. Blaze's favorite place."

"I'll bet nearly everybody in Estes Park would like to know about that spot."

Paddy's grin widened. "They sure would, but I promised Mr. Blaze I wouldn't tell nobody, and I'm not!"

"Well," Jennifer asked, "do these happen to be for us or for your mama?"

"For the hotel," he announced. "I'm on my way to see Cook with them right now."

"Good thing." Jennifer pinched the tip of her nose with her fingers as Paddy scampered toward the kitchen. In a nasal twang she continued, "They're stinking up the place. If Mr. or Mrs. Stanley saw you standing there in the lobby with those things, you can imagine what they would do.''

At that moment the toe of Paddy's shoe caught on the carpet and he stumbled, the fish flying out of his hand and slithering across the floor. Jennifer gasped and rushed from behind the counter. Taking advantage of the distraction, Sam walked to the desk. Suppressing a momentary twinge of conscience, he picked up the note that Kate had written to Blaze and slipped it into his jacket pocket. Ordinarily he would not have had the resolve to do this, but dangerous times produced strong men. He had a task to carry out, and he would do so. He turned and walked up the stairs to his room.

Once there, he locked the door and headed to the window where he pulled up the shade. Time was running out. He did not have much longer to wreak his revenge on Blaze Callaghan, and Sam had determined before he left Florida that he would avenge his wife's humiliation and death. When he had made this promise to himself, he had not known that Callaghan was married to Caitlin McDonald. To be truthful, this bothered Sam. He liked and respected her. Caitlin was an innocent bystander. In fact, if Sam did not do something, she was possibly Blaze Callaghan's next victim. Sam did not intend to let this happen to her. He was unable to save his wife, but he would save Caitlin. He would go to her, tell her what Blaze had done. Once she understood what kind of man Blaze Callaghan was, she would thank him for saving her.

As he read the note, his hands began to shake. Anger rushed up in him, anger that had been controlled for too long and was now straining at the leash. Blaze Callaghan was the scourge of the earth, and truly Providence had called on him, Sam Donovan, to rid the earth of this debaucher of women, this murderer. Sam held the paper in his hand, then tossed it onto the desk. He would talk with Caitlin and tell her all about Blaze. Then she would understand.

Sitting down at his desk, he pulled out a clean sheet of stationery and wrote her a brief note, telling her that he must speak with her immediately about an urgent matter. He took it to the front desk.

"Miss Rowlins, would you please see that Mrs. Callaghan gets this?"

Jennifer Rowlins held out a plump hand and took the note, twitching her nose and sniffing several times. "Of course, Mr. Donovan." Her eyes were openly curious, but Donovan merely turned and walked away.

Again he sat down in one of the overstuffed lobby chairs and waited and watched. Hours passed, but Caitlin did not return to The Stanley. He ate dinner, then checked back at the desk to learn that his note to Caitlin was still unclaimed. He went to bed at ten o'clock, but she had not returned.

Chapter Nine

Late the next morning Kate reluctantly walked into The Stanley, her purse slung over her shoulder. She had enjoyed her evening with Brigit and Paddy so much that she had been persuaded to spend the night with them. They had talked and laughed and shared tales of the old country until the early-morning hours, and Brigit had allowed Kate to sleep late. However, Kate could not stay away from the hotel any longer. Today was July 1, her date with destiny, and come what may, she must face it—with or without any knowledge that Blaze might have of Sam Donovan or his wife.

Approaching the front desk, she smiled. "Are there any messages for me, Jennifer?"

"Yes," the clerk answered abruptly.

Kate's smile widened and she held out her hand. "I suppose it's from Blaze."

"No, ma'am, it's from Mr. Donovan," the young woman said as she waved the letter in the air, sniffing and giggling. "What have we here?"

Looking at the envelope that Jennifer laid on her open palm, Kate wondered, too. Her heart turned a somersault as she gazed at the bold, unfamiliar handwriting. His cologne, a distinctive odor that she still found sickening, assailed her nostrils. She looked up to see the clerk's curious gaze still resting on her. Kate wanted to tell her that things were not as they appeared, but did not. No matter how hard she fought, destiny was not to be thwarted. Her heart heavy, she turned and walked to the elevator. She opened the envelope and extracted the letter, surprised at the curt message.

"Going up, Miss Caitlin?" the operator asked.

"No," she answered absently, her eyes scanning the people who had begun to mingle in the lobby, "not right now."

Kate was not sure that she was making the right choice in speaking with Sam Donovan, but she also knew that her choices were greatly restricted. She moved briskly across the huge room. Standing in the door of the dining room, the letter still in her hand, she surveyed the morning crowd.

"Good morning, Mrs. Callaghan. I can only hope that you were looking for me."

Kate spun around, no doubt in her mind as to the identity of the person who had spoken to her. If she had not recognized the voice, the fragrance of his cologne would have identified him. She stared into his face but did not return the smile he displayed. She spoke coolly. "You said you wished to speak with me, Mr. Donovan?"

He nodded. "Would you join me for breakfast, Mrs. Callaghan?"

Kate held her hands together to stop their shaking. "Not this morning," she answered, striving for a politeness that her fear made almost impossible. "I have very little time, Mr. Donovan. What is it you wished to speak with me about?"

He reached out, his hand lightly touching her shoulder. Although the gesture was cordial, Kate flinched and drew away.

"Since this is a sensitive matter, Mrs. Callaghan, let's find a secluded spot where we can talk privately," he suggested.

"Over there." Not wanting to be alone with him, Kate pointed to several vacant chairs that were clustered in the lobby.

"No," Sam said, already guiding her toward the door, "that's much too public. If you don't mind, Mrs. Callaghan, let's go outside and stroll around the lawn."

More curious by the minute, Kate walked with him across the lobby and veranda and down the flight of stairs to the lawn. When they stood alone at the side of the hotel, he turned to her, his gaze somber.

"Mrs. Callaghan, I have reason to believe that your life is in danger."

Caught completely off guard by his declaration, Kate collapsed onto the bench. His statement added to her growing confusion. She could only wonder if Sam was right. Had it been Blaze who did the shooting and not Donovan? Still, her love for Blaze would not let her accept this, no matter how much evidence the other man could produce. She began to shake her head slowly. No, she absolutely would not accept that she was in danger from Blaze. She shifted her purse into her lap and clutched it tightly. Sam sat down beside her, keeping a decorous space between them. Unable to marshall her errant thoughts, Kate continued to shake her head.

"I know that you'll find this hard to understand, madam—" he spoke softly and consolingly, his tone one that encouraged belief "—but I happen to know that your husband is not all that you probably think him to be. You have been deceived."

"No," Kate finally murmured.

"Blaze Callaghan is indeed a steam jockey and an ace driver," he said with the confidence of one who knows he has the advantage. "He's traveled all over the United States racing those Steamers."

In shocked silence Kate sat on the bench and listened as Sam talked.

"He's the kind of man all women fall for, Mrs. Callaghan, and you're no exception. He's handsome, dashing and extremely gallant...on the surface. It's when you learn his true nature that you understand exactly who and what Blaze Callaghan really is."

"Mr. Donovan, if you're referring to—"

"I'm referring to my wife, Mrs. Callaghan." He paused, sniffed dramatically, then said, "When your husband was in Daytona Beach for the races last year, he stole my wife from me."

"No!" Kate cried. "You must believe me!"

Sam persisted. "She was a young, beautiful thing easily swayed by a man like Callaghan. Saying she would file for a divorce, she left me for him. For several months they had a torrid affair, then the day came that he left for another racetrack, but he did not take Bettie with him. He was through with her. She returned to me, heartbroken and pregnant. She realized in the end that I was the one who really loved her."

"No!" Kate cried again. "You don't understand!"

"It is you who do not understand," he said kindly, but his eyes were glassy, his gaze directed at a faraway point. "Bettie came back to me after he was finished with her, after he had tossed her aside like she was a piece of garbage. My poor little darling. She had no one but me to turn to."

The longer he talked, the more emotional his voice became. He paused again, then said steadily, "I took her back, giving her a home and all my love. But she...and the baby...died."

"I'm so sorry," Kate said, truly grieving with him, but despising him for what he was putting Blaze and herself through, for what he was trying to blame Blaze for doing.

"Don't be sorry for me," he snapped. "And it's too late to feel sorrow for Bettie. He beat her, Mrs. Callaghan. Blaze Callaghan beat Bettie. When she came back to me, she was black and blue. Her face was swollen. He's an extremely jealous man."

"No," Kate exclaimed yet again. "Blaze wouldn't do that."

Sam, looking at her with pity, merely shook his head, and Kate finally dropped her eyes. She thought about Blaze's confession of jealousy the night he had been playing billiards and had seen Donovan's attentions toward her.

"Do you have any evidence that it was Blaze?" Kate asked, rising to her husband's defense, determined to fight this man's accusation.

"Of course I do." Sam drew himself to his full height and glowered at her. "You don't think I would accuse him falsely, do you? I saw him and Bettie together. You don't forget a man like Blaze Callaghan."

Kate had to agree with him: one did not easily forget Blaze Callaghan. Grudgingly she admitted that Blaze was a jealous man. But that was not unusual for a man who was passionate about life in general. Most passionate people were jealous.

"He's a cruel man," Sam said. "As I just said, he's terribly jealous of his possessions, and that's all a woman is to a man like him. He's the one ultimately responsible for Bettie's death...and the death of his child."

Sam Donovan's accusations hurt Kate more deeply than she would have ever imagined. Part of her refused to believe him; another part fought for Blaze; a third part—the one that was most closely akin to her future nature—wondered why Donovan was so adamant that Blaze was guilty, adamant enough to tell the story that had persisted through the years and had cast doubt upon Blaze. Clutching her purse as if it were a lifeline, Kate rose on her unsteady legs.

Still she kept her voice even. "It's your word against his, Mr. Donovan. But even if Blaze were guilty of having an affair with your wife—and mind you, I don't believe he was—I'd say that he was not the only party involved. Your wife had to be agreeable to it. She had to want to be with him rather than with you."

Donovan flinched and his face blanched. "The devil is a beguiler, Mrs. Callaghan, and seeks the weak and unwary. I'm sorry that you can't see the truth. I'm afraid that in the end you're going to wind up like my poor little darling...dead." He stared into Kate's face, then bowed and in a melodramatic gesture brought his cane to his chest. "Thank you for listening to me, Mrs. Callaghan. All I can say is beware. Now, if you'll excuse me, I'll be on my way and won't take up any more of your time."

Kate remained where she was long after Sam Donovan had disappeared around the corner of the hotel. His accusations tumbled through her mind, churning up doubts and questions for which she had no answers; nor did she know where to find them. She was still standing there, trying to put her thoughts into some sort of order, when a bellboy approached her.

"Miss Caitlin," he called, "there's a telephone call for you from Mr. Blaze."

Kate rushed to the hotel's registration desk, leaning across so that she could talk into the mouthpiece. "Blaze!" she cried.

"Sweetheart," he answered. "Am I glad to hear your voice, but you're going to have to speak up. I can hardly hear you."

"Did you find out anything?" She spoke louder, but also cupped the mouthpiece with her hand.

"I think the puzzle is solved," he answered. "Our Mr. Donovan is right in his thinking, as far as it goes, but there's more to it than what was passed down through the years. I think once we get this mess straightened out, we'll expose him for what he really is and he'll leave us alone."

"Oh, Blaze," she exclaimed, "I'm so glad!"

"I can't hear you, honey." When she repeated her words, he said, "I'm going to hang up now. Our connection is awful, and we're having to shout back and forth. I'll tell you all about it when I get home. Wait for me either in the suite or in the lobby, and be expecting me about midafternoon."

Ecstatic, Kate rushed up to the room to bathe and to change clothes. Afterward she ordered breakfast served in her room and while she ate on the balcony in leisurely fashion, she wrote in her diary. Stretching out on the chaise longue, she thought about their future. Until today she had not allowed herself to believe they had one. But they did.

ANGRY, Sam paced back and forth in his bedroom. Caitlin Callaghan had not listened to him. Neither had Bettie, and look what had happened to her. Well, he had tried to help Caitlin; he had not wanted to hurt her, but she had refused his help. Therefore she was responsible for whatever happened—just as Bettie had been.

He crushed Kate's letter to Blaze into a small wad and tossed it onto the floor. But quickly he thought better of it and stooped to pick it up again. He walked to his desk, laid down Kate's letter, and hand-pressed the wrinkles out of it. From one of the desk drawers he also removed Blaze's note, in which he had written the gunsmith's name and given directions to his house.

Sitting down, he shed his coat and rolled up his sleeves. Then he pulled out a sheet of stationery and dipped his pen into the inkwell. Looking at Caitlin's and Blaze's handwriting, he practiced copying each of them over and over, crumpling and dropping sheet after sheet to the floor. His face contorted in anger and frustration as he tore the sheets into shreds.

Finally he leaned back in his chair with a sigh and a smile and surveyed with satisfaction the letters he had written. He would hide in Caitlin's desk the one expressing Caitlin's infatuation for Sam and accusing Blaze of seducing Sam's wife. Although he hated planting the letter—he had, after all, tried to make her see the light—it was a necessary precautionary measure, should Sam fail to kill Blaze. He would see that the other letters for Caitlin and Blaze were delivered in due time.

Picking up all the crumpled pieces of paper and the shreds strewn over the floor, he dropped them into the wastepaper basket and carried it to the window. Extracting the sheets and scraps, he laughed and burned them one by one, dropping the black ash out the window and watching them disintegrate as they fluttered to the ground. He would leave no evidence to prove that he was the man who had finally caught up with the Lothario called Blaze Callaghan, the man who had exacted payment for the shame and humiliation Callaghan had wreaked on innocent young women across the United States. Yes, indeed, Sam Donovan believed in an eye for an eye, a tooth for a tooth. He also knew that many innocents had to be sacrificed for the cause. That was the sad part about his duty.

Sam knew that there would be no accolades for him, no glory for the job he was performing, but he was a modest man, and knowing that he had done the job he was ordained to do would be enough praise for him. He did not really care what happened to him as long as he punished Blaze Callaghan. He walked to the chifforobe and opening one of the drawers, removed a black case, which he carried across the room and laid upon the bed. Opening it, he withdrew his rifle.

Yes, he was prepared to kill Blaze Callaghan. At first he had found the idea repugnant, but as time passed, he had realized that this was the only way he could heal his soul and cleanse himself from the humiliation Callaghan had heaped upon him. Even in death Bettie had wanted the steam jockey—even after Sam had taken her back and would have loved her and her child. Yes. Once Sam had accepted his responsibility, he had begun making his plans. In a few days they would be complete.

He had wanted to avoid hurting Caitlin, but was beginning to wonder if she were not made of the same faulty material as Blaze. If so, she needed to be done away with also. The world would be far better without the two of them. Sam blotted and folded the letters he had written, then slipped three of them into his inner coat pocket. He had to get Kate's original letter back to the desk, before Miss Rowlins realized that he had taken it and before Kate remembered to ask for it.

He was glad that he had been standing in the lobby when Blaze's call to Kate had come in. Because of the bad connection, she had shouted her news to the entire world, and what he had not heard from her, he had learned from the chatty little receptionist.

Locking the door behind him, he took the stairs two at a time and arrived at the registration desk to see Jennifer organizing the daily mail. Stooping in front of the counter, he pulled one of the letters he had written from his pocket, then straightened and waved it in the air.

"Miss Rowlins," he said, "I found this on the floor. I don't know if it's important or—"

"Oh, there it is! Miss Caitlin's note to Blaze!" Jennifer sighed her relief and reached for the letter with her free hand. "In the commotion over Paddy and his fish, I had forgotten all about it. It must have blown onto the floor. Good thing she didn't ask about it earlier. I'd have been in a bad fix. And if she had reported me to Mr. Stanley..." Jennifer rolled her eyes and made a face, leaving her sentence and punishment unspoken but implied.

"A corner of it was stuck under the baseboard. Naturally you wouldn't expect it to be on this side of your counter." He extracted the second letter from his pocket. The cologne he had doused upon it clearly assailed his nostrils, and he knew Jennifer would notice it, too. "Would you please put this in Miss Caitlin's box? She'll be expecting it."

Jennifer took the letter and sniffed; then she glanced at him suspiciously. "You really must like to write," she gurgled. "This is the second one in two days."

"By the way," Sam said, ignoring her comment, "could you tell me how I would go about ordering a picnic lunch for two?"

"A picnic lunch for two?" Jennifer echoed, her eyes getting bigger by the second. "You're going on a picnic with someone?" Her gaze fell to the letter she still held in her hand.

"I am," Sam answered. "Now, if you'll be so kind as to tell me what to do."

"Uh—" Jennifer cleared her throat "—you can either tell Cook directly, or I can tell him. The cost will be added to your account."

"Thank you," Sam said. "If you don't mind, please tell Cook that I'll pick up the basket about eleven o'clock in the morning."

"Yes, sir," Jennifer said. "Is there anything else you want, Mr. Donovan?"

"No, thank you, Miss Rowlins. If anyone should be looking for me right now, I'm going to the stables to arrange for a horse," he answered with a smile and took several steps toward the front door, then stopped and turned back. "By the way, has Miss Caitlin said anything about going riding this morning?"

Jennifer was obviously dumbfounded; she could only shake her head. His smile broadening, Sam saluted her and whistling, walked briskly out of the hotel, his cane keeping time with his steps. When he was on the veranda, he turned and looked back in the direction of the registration desk. Jennifer and two other young women were in a huddle, Jennifer talking nonstop, waving the letter in the air and pointing toward the door.

Yes, he thought, things were progressing quite well. He began to move again, but rather than going directly to the stables, he moved to the middle of the front lawn and looked at the second-story balcony, the one that led to the Caitlin McDonald Suite, as the group of rooms that Caitlin and Blaze shared had come to be called.

The French doors were open today—as they had been every day and every night since he had been a guest at The Stanley—and Kate was resting on the chaise longue. Getting into the room to plant the letter would require caution, but should not prove too difficult. Kate would be leaving quite soon.

Now to handle the final details.

KATE OPENED her eyes, blinked at the bright morning sun, and looked around, momentarily wondering what had awakened her. Then she heard soft raps on the door and remembered. Picking up her diary from her lap, she rose and walked into the room; then she looked at the small porcelain clock. It was nearly twelve o'clock; she had slept longer than she'd thought. Blaze would be home soon.

The knocks echoed through the room again and she opened the door. A small boy stood there, a piece of paper in his hand. "Mr. Blaze told me to give this to you," he said and was gone as soon as Kate took the note from him.

Apologizing for the hasty scrawl, Blaze explained that he had sent the message by the child, because he did not want to come directly to the hotel and risk seeing Donovan before the two of them had a chance to talk. He asked her to meet him at Paddy's fishing spot; that way no one would know where they were and they would be safe.

Kate understood Blaze's strategy at once. Only he knew what was to happen on July 1, and he was taking pains to ensure that neither of them would be near the cabin. Grabbing the large purse, she hastily stuffed her diary into it—not daring to leave it behind—and ran out of the room, pausing only to lock the door. She thought about walking up the mountain, but did not wish to take the time today. Instead she raced to the stables and had them saddle a horse for her. When she arrived at the spot where she and Paddy had spent the afternoon the day before, she dismounted and tethered her horse to a low-hanging branch of a nearby tree. She moved into the clearing and looked around.

"Blaze, are you here?" she called, then heard twigs breaking and ran in the direction of the noise. "I got here as soon—" Gazing into Sam Donovan's smiling face, the words died on her lips.

"Yes," he said smoothly, his rifle in his hands, "I rather thought you would get here as quickly as you could, if you thought your summons had come from your husband." He laughed softly. "It took me a lot of practice to get his handwriting near enough that you would think it was his."

Donovan had changed drastically, and Kate felt as if an iron band were twisted around her heart. She remembered the night when Donovan had asked Blaze to recommend a gunsmith. She had thought it strange that he had also asked Blaze to write the directions to the smith's home, but had quickly dismissed the reflection. Now she understood what he had been seeking all along: a sample of Blaze's handwriting. She licked lips suddenly gone dry. This could not be happening to her; it could not!

"What—do you want with me?"

"I don't want to hurt you," Sam said, a strange gleam in the depths of his eyes, "but I will, if I have to."

"Please don't do this," she said and backed away from him in fear.

"Don't do what?" he asked in a silky-smooth voice, moving toward her, the rifle pointed at her heart. "You have no idea what I intend to do, *Caitlin*. Now I want you to mount your horse, and both of us will head for the cabin."

So this is how it was done, Kate thought. All along she had thought she was running away from destiny, but in reality she had been running headlong into it. No matter how hard she tried to change the past, she could not. "How did you know about Paddy's fishing spot?" she asked.

"He was boasting about it yesterday, when he delivered your note to the hotel. I didn't know where it was, but it was a simple matter to follow you up here."

"Rather stupid of me," she said and untied the reins.

"Yes," he agreed, "it was. Once you've mounted, please lead the way to the cabin and don't try to get away. I'll shoot you, if I have to. Dead or alive, you'll serve the same purpose to me."

"I'm the bait that will lure Blaze to the cabin?" she said.

"That's right."

"It won't work," she said. "He won't come to the cabin, no matter what you tell him."

"He'll be there."

She mounted the horse and watched as Sam did the same. Her eyes moved to the lunch basket tied to the horse's back. She thought about escaping, but remembered his admission that he was not only a trapshooter and marksman but a hunter. And she knew that Sam

Donovan would hunt her. He was insane. She could see the maniacal gleam in his eyes. She believed him when he said he would shoot her with the least provocation, and if she were dead, she could not help Blaze.

"Why are you doing this?" she asked.

"Justice demands it," he said, and Kate listened as he recounted once again the tale that had been passed down through the years. Either he believed it, Kate thought, or he had practiced it until he had it letter-perfect. She preferred to believe the latter. "Now I must balance the scales. Blaze must pay for what he's done."

"Blaze didn't run off with your wife," Kate said.

"You don't want to believe it," he replied, "and I can understand that. After all, you're married to him and think you're in love with him. But I know the true Blaze Callaghan, ace driver and steam jockey. Everywhere he went, the women swooned over him."

And they did not swoon over you, Kate thought, saying aloud, "Perhaps your wife swooned over him, but Blaze did not return her affections. He did not and does not go out with married women," she insisted. When Sam did not acknowledge her, she added, "He's hired a private detective in Boulder to investigate this, to find out who she really did have an affair with."

"Please move along," Sam ordered her, "and let's stop this chitchat. It's getting us nowhere."

As soon as Kate and Sam entered the cabin, Sam locked the door. Then still holding the rifle, he walked through the other room, pulling the curtains aside so that he had a better view.

"Don't try anything," he told her. "As I told you earlier, it doesn't matter whether you're dead or alive, now that I've gotten you away from the hotel. Callaghan will be here, and he's the one that I'm after."

A smug smile on her face, Kate sat down at the table. "You're mistaken, Donovan. Blaze will not come to this cabin. I can guarantee that."

Walking to the front window, he pulled the curtain aside and stared out. He laughed softly, the eerie sound swelling through the cabin. "No, my dear Mrs. Callaghan, you've really guaranteed that he will come directly here. And when he walks in that door—" he pointed the barrel of the rifle "—I'll shoot him in the heart."

"You're insane," Kate whispered.

"No," he replied quietly, all humor instantly wiped from his expression, "I'm merely the instrument Providence chose to rectify a horrible mistake. I shall set the record straight with Callaghan's death."

"What makes you think Blaze will come here?" she asked, fear binding itself around her heart. Donovan kept repeating things with such conviction and regularity that she was beginning to believe him.

"Do you think I stole your note because I needed reading material?" he asked sarcastically. "Well, I'm sorry to disappoint you, but I did not. I needed a sample of your handwriting, so that I could learn to write like you." He laughed, the identical maniacal sound that Kate had heard in her dream. "Handwriting also was my best subject in school."

"You wrote him a note."

"No," he corrected arrogantly, "you wrote him a note and sent it by a messenger boy, so that he won't even go by the hotel, but will come directly here. You, my dear, explained that Donovan left on the morning train, and that you were waiting for him in the cabin."

"Even if he doesn't go by the hotel and check first, he'll surely check at the train station to see if you really did leave," Kate said.

"I bought a ticket," he said, "and since this is the busiest season, no one is going to have checked to see if I left or not. By the time anyone finds out for sure, Blaze Callaghan will be dead, and the evidence I planted at the hotel will be all the world needs to believe him capable of getting both you and himself killed. You see, the Irish are famed for their hot tempers and passionate natures."

Knowing that she was running out of time, Kate took out her diary. She had to record what she knew about the events that were happening right now, events that no one would know about in the future.

"What's that?" Sam asked. When she answered, he said, "It's not going to do you much good to write in it. I'm going to have to destroy it. I can't have people believing the lies that you and Callaghan will tell about me."

"May I continue to write in it until you tell me to stop?" Kate spoke calmly, realizing that the insane Donovan had to be treated carefully if she valued Blaze's life ... and her own.

He thought for a second, then nodded his head. "I suppose so. It'll keep you quiet."

Turning her attention to the diary, Kate began hurriedly to write. Covering page after page, she explained in minute detail all that had happened. When her hand cramped so badly that she could not write another word, she stood and moved about the cabin. As Kate Norris, she knew that this cabin would someday belong to her and that she would restore it.

If she were going to secrete the diary, this would be the place to do it. But where? It had to be a spot where it would be protected through the years. Without letting Donovan know what she was doing, she walked through each room, carefully searching. Eventually she returned to the living room and moved to the fireplace. It was the only part of the cabin that would remain intact through the years.

Then she remembered the cellar. She could hide it there, where no one would ever think of looking for it. No one. She could not remember one time that it had been disturbed in the intervening years. Her diary would be protected by eighty years of erosion and neglect. Before she could hide it, though, she needed to put it in a container to preserve it. Casually she walked through the house again, quietly opening and searching through drawers, but finding nothing.

"What are you doing?" Sam called from the living room.

"I'm—hungry," she called back. "How about you?"

"I could do with something to eat," he answered.

"I'll prepare us something." She opened the pantry in the kitchen, scanning the shelves from top to bottom, then bottom to top. Then she opened the cabinet under the sink and saw a hammer and chisel. That was exactly what she'd need. Closing the cabinet door, she investigated the pantry shelves again.

"There's no need for you to," he answered with a whoop of satisfied laughter, but Kate continued to push aside the canned goods on the shelf. Then she saw the cracker tin and rocked back on her heels. "I've taken care of things, down to the minutest detail. I brought us a lunch."

The tin was perfect. Taking off the lid, she dumped the contents into a bowl and set the tin to the side of the counter. "I found some soup and crackers," she said, "that would go nicely with the picnic lunch."

She had to return to the living room to get her books without arousing Donovan's suspicion. Standing in the doorway, she said, "That is, if you don't mind."

"No," he said after a pause and shook his head, "I guess I don't mind."

"I'll need some wood for the stove," she said. "May I go get it?"

Donovan's eyes narrowed, and his gaze moved from one side of the front lawn to the other and back again. "Okay. That will make it look more like you're waiting for him," he said and unlocked the door, following her onto the porch. "While you're getting the wood, I'll get the basket off the horse. But don't try anything. I'm not going to take my eyes off you."

"I won't," Kate promised.

When she had an armful of firewood, she returned to the cabin and while Donovan was locking the door, slid the diary into her purse and carried it into the kitchen.

"What are you doing with that?" he asked and she pulled up short.

"I have matches in there," she answered.

"Oh." He paused, set the basket upon the table in the kitchen, then murmured, "All right."

Donovan returned to the living room, and she placed the wood in the stove. Once she had the fire blazing, she set her diary and the two volumes of poetry inside the tin. Her heart beating faster now, she returned the sealed can to the pantry and closed the door. It would be safe in there until she could hide it. For the next thirty minutes she concentrated on preparing their meal.

As soon as they had eaten, Donovan was on his feet again. "It's about time for him to be getting here. I'm going outside to hide in that clump of bushes across the pathway. Since that's the only way up here, I'll be sure to see him before he sees me. You get in the living room."

Kate glanced at the pantry but said nothing. She did not dare call attention to it. No matter what his emotional state of mind, Sam Donovan was an astute man. She watched him lay his rifle on the table and pick up the rope he had brought in earlier. Tying Kate to the chair, he pulled a handkerchief from his back pocket and gagged her.

"Sorry, I had to do that," he said without any sign of remorse in his voice, "but I can't have you warning him, if you should happen to see him first."

Before he left the cabin, Donovan closed the curtains on all the windows and locked the doors. She heard his footsteps as he walked across the porch; then she waited to make sure that he was not coming back.

This was her opportunity—perhaps her only one—to escape. Grabbing the seat of the chair in both hands and kicking the floor with her toes, she slowly bumped her way from the living room into the kitchen. After what seemed hours, she reached the table, where she lowered her head and used it to swat a knife to the floor. Then she rocked the chair until it toppled and she was lying on her back. Grunting and twisting, she eventually grasped the knife handle and raised it so that she could cut the ropes.

The process was slow and painful. Because of the awkward position and the thick ropes, her fingers hurt. Soon she had blisters on her hand; still the fibers defied the dull, serrated edge of the kitchen knife. Kate refused to give up. Blaze's future was at stake—and hers. Only she could save Blaze now, and she had to reach him before Donovan did. Although Donovan planned to kill her also, his main objective was Blaze, and Kate was not willing to see Blaze die before she did, while she was still living in the past.

Finally the rope gave and she slowly unraveled it. When her hands were free, she untied the gag and leaped to her feet, stumbling around a bit until the circulation returned. Moving the table and jerking away the rug, she caught the metal pull and opened the trapdoor to the cellar. She must hide her diary. Whether she could change the past or not, the diary had to be protected for posterity. She had no option but to take the time to hide it, and to do it, she needed a light. She went back into the kitchen to find the matches and a lamp. Once it was burning, she opened the cabinet under the sink and grabbed the hammer and chisel, then swung open the pantry door, reached for the cracker tin and tucked it under her arm. Holding the lamp in the same hand, she threw the hammer and chisel into the cellar, then froze as they thudded to the ground. She only hoped that Donovan hadn't heard the noise. She waited, then climbed down the ladder.

She set the box on the table and, holding out the lamp, moved around the cellar, trying to find where the hammer and chisel had landed, as well as the right place to put the box. Locating her tools, she closed her eyes and tried to imagine all the spots that had been exposed with the ravages of time and man. From the way events had taken place since she had returned to the past, she was fairly certain that everything would happen as it had done the first time around. This also assured her that if she could not change the past, no one else traveling through time could or would be able to effect change, either.

Setting the lamp on the table, looking over her shoulder all the time, she used hammer and chisel to find a rock that was loose enough for her to pry out. After several minutes of digging dirt and pebbles from behind one stone with shaking hands, she had a hole large enough in which to hide the cracker tin. Grunting and casting another fearful glance over her shoulder, she lifted the rock and slid it into place, using the hammer to press it back into line with the remainder of the wall.

Fearing Donovan's return and knowing that he would destroy her diary if he knew about it, she picked up the hammer and chisel. But before she had reached the top of the ladder, she dropped the hammer again, and it landed on the floor of the cellar with another resounding thud that resonated through the cabin. Kate laid her forehead against the ladder; it would be a miracle if Donovan had not heard the noise this time. Perhaps he had, she thought. That could explain why Caitlin's diary had never been found. Donovan had destroyed it.

After seconds had stretched into several eternities, Kate drew in a deep, steadying breath. She descended the ladder, retrieved the hammer and climbed up again. This time she held on to the equipment, her heart racing within her chest. She returned them to the cabinet under the kitchen sink, then rushed back into the living room, descending the ladder a second time to bring up the lamp. Setting it aside, she spread the rug over the trap door and returned the table to its usual position. Breathing easier, she carried the lamp to the kitchen and replaced it on the shelf.

Wiping her clammy palms down the front of her shirt, she reentered the living room and looked directly at the fireplace. Sam Donovan, in all his scheming, had overlooked one significant item. Walking across the room, Kate reached up and took the Winchester rifle off the rack. Blaze told her that he always kept it loaded, but with trembling hands she checked to make sure.

She would not let Sam Donovan kill Blaze.

Her decision made, she grew very calm. Holding the rifle in one hand, she walked into the kitchen, unlocked the door, quietly cracked it and eased out. Bracing her back against the wall and keeping behind the shrubbery as much as she could, she slipped around the cabin.

She would only have one shot, which she had to make count; so she could not shoot prematurely. She looked all around but saw no sign of Donovan. Still, she knew he was out here, hiding and lying in ambush.

Taking a deep breath and holding the rifle close to her chest, she ran in a crouch to another thick clump of bushes. Her heart beating furiously in her chest, she drew several steadying breaths. She loved Blaze so much that she had no fear of the situation, no qualms about what she must do. Again she looked around, this time spying Donovan in the heavy foliage in front of the cabin, directly in front of the path Blaze would travel.

She knelt in the bushes, her limbs cramping so badly that she wanted to scream. But could not; neither could she abandon her vigil. She would not allow Sam Donovan to get out of her sight. She was the only person standing between Blaze and death. The afternoon sun beat relentlessly upon her. Perspiration beaded on her upper lip and rolled down her face and neck, her spine, between her breasts. Still she did not move.

Then she heard a distant noise; perhaps the Runabout? Later she heard a faint sound, as if someone were whistling. Leaning forward, she listened. Yes, it was someone whistling. The sound grew louder, and she recognized the tune, "I'll Take You Home Again, Kathleen," and knew that it was Blaze.

It was obvious that Sam also thought it was Blaze. He lifted his rifle and settled the stock against his shoulder, his right index finger caressing the trigger.

The whistling grew louder, and Kate's palms grew wet. What she must do was important; so was the timing. Higher on the mountain slope than Sam, she could see better. Through the bushes and trees she saw the top of a dark-haired head.

Now! she thought.

She aimed the rifle, her finger gently touching the trigger. Pointing it into the air, she pulled the trigger and screamed, "Blaze, it's a trap!"

"Kate!"

Another shot roared through the forest and Kate was suddenly aflame. Clutching her chest with her left hand, wet, sticky blood oozing through her fingers, she reeled and fell to the ground, the impact knocking the rifle from her other hand.

"Kate!" The agonizing scream echoed through the air.

"Blaze," she gasped. But there was no one to hear her. She was all alone...and dying. She did not mind the dying, but did mind leaving him. She heard heavy footfalls and could only hope that Blaze was coming to her.

"Kate!" He was calling to her.

Her head spun at such a speed that she was dizzy and nauseated. She heard Blaze cry her name again; there were more shots, then silence. Sweet silence. Tension drained from her and the pain diminished. With a little effort, she thought hazily, she could float away from this body.

"Kate, oh, my darling Kate!" Now Blaze was kneeling beside her, cradling her in his arms.

Feeling warm and protected, she lifted her hand and pressed it against his cheek. She felt his tears on her palm. "You were right," she whispered. "We can't run away from our destiny."

"Kate, don't leave me," Blaze whispered. "Please don't leave me, darling."

"Just for a little while, darling," she promised and drew in a deep, quivering breath. She felt his cheek beneath her hand, but he was fading. "I'll be—waiting—for you."

"I'm not going to let you die," Blaze said and scooped her into his arms. She cried faintly as he jarred her wound. "I don't want to live without you. You're my *dama de suerte*, don't you remember?"

Kate smiled. "I remember the fickle lady," she murmured. "Donovan? What happened to him?"

"He pulled a revolver on me, and while we were fighting, he was shot," Blaze answered. "He's run away. I don't want to talk about Donovan. You're the only one who matters to me."

She clutched his shirt in her fist. "His wife," she whispered. "What happened to her?"

"According to what Tubman found out, she ran away with a racer, all right, but it wasn't me. This happened four years ago, Kate, in 1906, not last year, as Donovan claims. That's why it took us so long to find out what happened. We thought it was at last year's race. Once I knew which race it was, I knew who it might have been. It was a steam jockey named Swanson. Either Swanson lied to Bettie, or she lied to Donovan to protect Swanson."

"Don—" Blaze jarred her badly as he walked down the sharp incline; she drew in a deep, ragged breath "—o—van said he saw you with her."

"Swanson looks a lot like me. It would be easy for Donovan to mistake the two of us, especially if he saw us at a distance or at night. And just think about it. Most of the time when Donovan saw us we were wearing our helmets, goggles and jackets. Swanson would distribute photographs of himself in his racing outfit. If Bettie told Donovan that it was me, he probably believed her."

Kate smiled and nuzzled her cheek against his chest. I knew you couldn't have done that, darling. I wouldn't have fallen in love with a man like that. She thought the words but could not say them.

Reaching the Runabout, Blaze stepped up and laid her in the back seat, the jarring causing her to moan softly. "Sorry, sweetheart," he whispered. "I'm taking you to the doctor, and everything is going to be all right."

"The photo—graph," Kate whispered thickly. "Have one...made for—"

"I did, my darling. I had one made on my way back from Boulder. I was standing at the tree that marks the finishing line for the Fourth of July race." His voice cracked. "My last race, darling."

Kate reached up to touch his cheek with the tips of her fingers. "I love you, Blaze Callaghan. I'll be waiting for you."

A golden light began to envelop Kate, but she struggled to remain outside its glow. "Blaze," she whispered, "my—my—"

Blaze placed his ear next to her mouth. "What is it, darling?"

She felt his tears against her cheeks. He was crying again.

"My—dia—ry," she said.

"All right," he said, but she knew that he did not understand.

"In—the—in the—cel—lar," she mumbled, the words incoherent even to her own ears.

The circle of light enclosed her, and she began to float away. She was dying, yet she had no fear. Now she was grieving for Blaze.

"Don't worry," she assured him, her voice stronger, her thoughts lucid. "Everything is fine. I've set things right this time. I'm going to take you home." She stripped the topaz ring from her finger and pressed it into his right hand. "Here, take this, and don't lose it."

From a distance—a great distance—she heard Brent calling to her. Yes, she thought, her hand sliding down Blaze's chest, Brent was calling to her. He was not dead; he was waiting for her, and she must get to him. Not knowing where she was going or how she was going to reach him, she looked toward the brilliant light. This time she smiled and welcomed it. She seemed to be absorbed into the light, becoming part of its energy, wisdom and power. Every fiber of her body permeated with peace, her fears abated and she became one with time and spirit.

Chapter Ten

The brilliant white light dissipated, and Kate heard a noise in the corridor. She stirred and murmured, "Blaze, is that you?"

No one answered. She heard the noise a second time and wondered what it was. Perhaps it was a door shutting or something or someone hitting against the wall. At the moment she was too fuzzy to think about it. Her hand going to her chest, she rolled over. Her thoughts were hazy and elusive. She was not sure where she was or what time she was in. Confused, she pushed herself up on her elbows and looked around the room; the desk lamp was spreading soft light through the room. She was in her suite at The Stanley, but she was not sure what year it was. Music from below drifted through the open French doors; it sounded like the orchestra Hayley had hired for the Musicale.

For some reason Kate had thought she was at Blaze's cabin and that she had been . . . She looked down at her dress. She was at Blaze's cabin, and she had been shot. She pressed her palms against her breast. Sam Donovan had killed her. She had died in Blaze's arms, but was not dead. She slid off the bed and rushed to the cheval mirror, looking at and feeling herself to see if she were really alive or dead, wondering if she could tell or not.

She raced across the room, flung open the door and bolted down the corridor. As she skipped down the stairs, she saw the back of a man in a dark suit, his hair burnished to a high sheen. "Blaze!" she shouted. The man continued to walk toward the front door of The Stanley. "Blaze," Kate called again as the man disappeared into the night.

"Kate."

"Brent," Kate murmured, sliding back against the wall and looking wildly around. She did not know who or where she was. Totally confused, tears welled in her eyes.

Ron Townsend pushed through the crowd and stopped at the bottom of the stairs. He smiled up at her. "What's wrong?"

"Ron," she mumbled disbelievingly. First disappointment, then relief surged through her. She knew who and where she was now. She was truly back in the present. Reaching up, she brushed a hand over her forehead. Maybe she had never traveled back in time. Maybe she had been dreaming. Yes, that was it. She had been dreaming about Brent...and Blaze...but somehow they were one and the same.

"Kate," Ron said and began to walk up the stairs, "are you all right?"

Kate retreated. "I'm fine," she said and held out her hands. She did not want him to come any closer. "I'll be down in a few minutes."

"Are you sure?"

Kate nodded her head and turned to flee up the stairs, intending to closet herself in the safety of her room. She had only been dreaming, she thought. Hayley and Nicki were right. She had lived with Caitlin McDonald and Blaze Callaghan until she was obsessed with them. She had dreamed that she was Caitlin. But she was not. She was Kate Norris, and Blaze was not Brent.

Brent was in Boulder with Caleb; they were repairing his Stanley Runabout, so he could drive it in the parade tomorrow. Or were they? Her head ached, and she knew she ought to remember something—a part of her dream that was evading her.

Back in her suite, she reached up with her left hand to touch the brooch that Mrs. Engels had pinned to the velvet ribbon, her fingertips lightly caressing the oval piece of jewelry. Kate gasped and leaned forward to stare disbelievingly into the mirror. Then she dropped her trembling hand and stared. The topaz ring was gone; she had lost the ring.

She rushed to the bed, where she knelt and began to run her palms over the floor. When she could not find the ring, she hurried to the desk, removed the shade from the lamp and brought it to the floor. Frantically she moved in an ever-widening circle until she had combed the entire room, but she found no ring.

Sick with disappointment, she returned the lamp to the desk and sat down in the chair, staring blindly into space. She hated to tell Mrs. Engels that she had lost the ring. Finally she turned and began to thumb idly through her research material. When she reached the color photograph of Blaze, she picked it up and leaned back. It really did look like him, she thought, only it did not pick up the tiny spot of silver hair on his left temple. But only someone who knew him would be aware of...

Abruptly Kate sat up straight. How could she know that this photograph looked like Blaze, and how did she know he had a small spot of silver hair on his left temple? It was not a dream; she *had* gone back into the past. *She had gone back in time!* The ring had taken her back. When she was dying, she had given it to Blaze and he had told her about the photograph—the one he'd had taken especially for her. That would explain his secret smile.

Blaze, however, seemed to fuse with Brent, and she remembered bits and pieces of her dream...or vision...about him. No longer could she separate fact from fiction. Not even recalling her reason for coming to her room after the performance, she ran once more from the suite, down the stairs and into the lobby. She needed to talk with a friend—one who understood. Frantically she searched the crowd, hoping that she would not see Ron again. Finally she saw a head of shining black hair that she immediately recognized.

"Nicki," she called, waving and threading her way through the crowd.

Nicki turned from the man to whom she was talking, smiled and waved back. "Kate. Your performance tonight was exceptional. I don't think I've ever heard a Musicale to equal this one."

"I haven't seen one to compare it with," Jake Kelly said, draping his arm around Nicki and hugging her to himself, "but I have to agree with my wife. It was lovely, Kate."

"Thanks," Kate said, but her thoughts were not on the evening's music. She caught the younger woman's hand and began to tug at her. "Nicki, I need to talk to you...alone."

Her brow furrowed with concern, Nicki searched Kate's face, nodded and looked at Jake, who said, "You two go find a quiet place to talk. I'll join Mason and Ron in the MacGregor Room. You're going to join us when you get through with your conversation?''

"Yes," Kate and Nicki answered together. Jake had not taken a step before Kate said, "There's no quiet place down here. Let's go to my room."

"What's wrong, Kate?" Nicki ran to keep up with Kate's long strides. "If you don't mind my saying so...well, even if you do...you're acting *very* strange."

"You're telling me," Kate murmured dryly, leading the way down the second-floor corridor. "Just wait until you hear what I'm going to tell you. You'll probably have me committed."

Nicki grinned. "This is sounding better and better, Kate. I think senility suits you."

Kate cast Nicki a quick grin, but at that moment she did not appreciate her friend's sense of humor. Her hand curled around the doorknob to the Caitlin McDonald Suite. "I lost the ring."

"You what?" Nicki exclaimed and stopped walking to stare at her friend. Before Kate could repeat what she had said, Nicki asked, "How? When?"

"Come on in," Kate suggested, "and I'll tell you all about it. I don't want the whole world to know."

"This better be good, Kate," Nicki said, but her eyes were gleaming with interest.

"I don't know how good it is, but it is different. I was up here resting after the performance, and I must have—yes, I must have gone to sleep." Kate reached up and massaged her aching temple. Something was nagging at her, but she could not remember. "When I awakened, I was—I had gone back in time." Slowly she told Nicki all she could remember about what had happened to her.

Nicki, sitting in the large overstuffed chair beside the bed, her hands bridged in front of her, gazed at Kate in open-eyed silence, not speaking until she had finished. Finally she said, "I might have known that you'd have to outdo all of us, Kate. Hayley gets three wishes with her golden apple, I have a few dreams and solve...a murder, but you have to travel back and forth between time phases."

"You do believe me, don't you?" Kate asked. She feared she was losing her sanity. Only the loss of the ring made her believe that she had *really* gone back in time, that she had returned it to its rightful owner.

"I believe you." Nicki rose and walked to the desk. "And Hayley will believe you, but that doesn't mean anyone else will."

"I've thought about that," Kate said. "My book will end with an opinion that cannot be substantiated by any new primary ev...i...dence...." Her voice trailed into silence and she snapped her finger. "The diary. I hid the diary in the cellar." She grabbed Nicki's hand. "Come on, let's go to the cabin and see if it's there. If it is, I'll know I'm not crazy."

"At this time of night?" Nicki exclaimed. "Let's wait until morning, Kate, when we can see."

Across the room by now, her hand twisting the doorknob, Kate shook her head. "No, I want to go tonight. Just think what this will mean, Nicki. I'll have new evidence, proof that Blaze did not kill Caitlin."

"I'm not going to that cabin tonight, and that's final."

"If only Brent were not in Denver," Kate grumbled. "He'd go with me."

"I wonder," Nicki said. "Kate, I'm sick and tired of that book and those people. I'll be so glad when you get them out of your system."

"Come with me to the cabin. That's a sure way to get your wish," Kate said and walked out of the room. Nicki followed closely behind.

Nicki argued with Kate as they hurried into the lobby, but Kate would not be deterred. Stopping at the registration desk, she drummed her hands on the desk and asked the clerk, "Do you have a large flashlight I could have?"

"I'm not sure," the woman said. "I'll have to look back here," she added and disappeared into another room.

"I'll have to tell Jake where we're going," Nicki said. "He's not going to be too pleased to have me hike up the mountain in the dark to search through a cabin cellar."

"That's all right," Kate said. "You can stay here. I'll go by myself."

Nicki sighed. "No, I'm not going to let you do that, either. Wait for me here. If I'd tie all those little bows on my buggy for you, why wouldn't I crawl into a snake-infested cellar in my new evening dress, to dig for a diary hidden in a cracker tin that may or may not be there?"

As Nicki walked in the direction of the MacGregor Room, the clerk reappeared with a small purse flashlight. "This is all I could find," she said. "You'll have to ask Hayley. She'll probably know where one is."

"I suppose I'd have to ask her about a hammer and chisel, too," Kate mused.

"Uh, yes, ma'am," the clerk said, and Kate had to laugh at her expression.

"I know my request sounds strange, but it's not."

"Kate!" Hayley's voice sounded through the lobby. "What's this I hear about Caitlin's diary?"

"Nicki told you?"

"A little bit," Hayley said, "but not nearly enough."

"Enough to whet my appetite," Mason said, pushing his tall, lanky frame around his fiancée. "Can I go with you, Kate?"

Kate grinned. "I would love to have your company, Mr. Wilder, but I must warn you that Nicki has already predicted that the cellar we're going to be working in is snake-infested."

"We might as well do this right," another male voice said with a sound of authority that brooked no argument, and Kate turned to see Jake. "Let's all go home and change clothes. Then on our way up to the cabin, Nicki and I will get a spotlight from the station. Mason, what are we going to need to dig for this?"

"Not having seen the cellar, I'm taking a guess," he said, then went on to enumerate certain standard excavation tools.

When he was through, Jake caught Nicki's hand and said, "We're going to be on our way. We'll meet you up at the cabin in say—" he looked at his watch "—an hour."

"An hour," the others agreed.

"Kate," Mason asked, "what are you going to do with the diary?"

Kate grinned at him. "I'm going to keep it myself for a long while, but I think eventually it belongs in a museum, don't you?"

Mason grinned back at her. "I do, Professor. I really do."

"Come on, Mason." Hayley tugged his sleeve. "Let's go change and start gathering the stuff we're going to need. We don't have much time." She looked at Kate. "I'm so excited. I haven't had this much fun since Harry appeared with the golden apple. Where are we going to meet?"

"Here in the lobby. In about thirty minutes," Kate said, stopping at the front desk to leave word where she was, in case Brent returned while she was gone.

"Are all of you really going on this wild-goose chase?" Ron asked. "Can't you see how ridiculously you're behaving?"

Mason grinned at his friend and slapped him playfully on the shoulder. "That's what makes life interesting, Ron. You can come along if you like, but with or without you, we're going."

Ron cast them a scathing glance and moved away, saying over his shoulder, "Definitely without."

THE MEN WORKED for an hour getting the lights set up, so that the spotlight faced the front door. Then, large flashlights in hand, Mason carefully examined the interior of the cabin.

"How's it going in there?" Jake called out.

"Slow," Mason answered. "The planks have pulled loose through the years, and there's a lot of rotten spots. Billions of cobwebs."

Cupping her hands as the wind flapped over her slacks, Hayley called out, "Be careful!"

Nicki and Jake stood side by side, their arms around each other. Kate, dressed in black slacks with a tailored white blouse, her arms crossed over her chest, paced back and forth in front of the cabin. She heard every creak of the floor as Mason slowly moved toward the cellar door. An ugly, abrasive squall filled the air; rusted metal moved for the first time in years.

"It's open," Mason called out, his voice lively with excitement. After another pause, he said, "The ladder is gone. We're going to have to bring one in, or we'll have to lower someone into the cellar by rope. We could jump," he added. "It's not that deep, but we don't know what the floor down there is like. It's hard to determine with the flashlight."

By the time Mason exited the cabin, Jake, Nicki and Hayley were moving the ladder from the bed of the pickup truck. "Since we don't know what condition the cellar floor is in," Mason said, "I'll be the first to go down."

"No," Kate said quietly, "I'm going to be first."

All of them turned to look at her.

"That's not a good idea," Jake began, but Kate held up a silencing hand.

"But the way it's going to be. I'm still fuzzy about what happened, and the cabin has changed so much." She turned. "In fact everything has changed. The road has been bulldozed so that cars can come up to the top now, and they couldn't then. Blaze had to park the Runabout down there." She pointed, then realized what she was saying and felt like an idiot. "Anyway, it's my cabin and my diary, so I'm going in."

"It's too dangerous—" Mason began.

"She's right," Hayley said and added teasingly, "I've seen enough movies to know that you can tie ropes around her, and if she finds something wrong down there, all she has to do is tug, and we'll swing her to safety."

"Okay." Mason acquiesced. He pulled an extra pair of leather gloves from his equipment box and handed them to Kate. "Put these on. You go down."

Batting away cobwebs, Kate was nervous; carefully she followed Mason across the aged timber to the cellar opening. After they had lowered the ladder and tied ropes around her, she began the slow descent into the darkened hole, flashing the light all around as she went.

"What's it look like, Kate?" Mason called, leaning over the opening.

"Dusty, humid, and full of cobwebs," she called back.

"Move out of the way," he said. "I'm on my way down."

"Jake," Kate called, "is there any way you could bring the spotlight into the cabin? All of these rocks look alike, and I'm not sure which one it is anymore."

From the distance Kate heard Nicki's laughter. "I shouldn't wonder. After all, it's been eighty years since you last looked at it."

"Will the floor hold the weight of the light?" Jake asked.

"I think so," Hayley answered, "if we're careful."

While the two of them worked at moving the big light, Kate and Mason moved around the cellar. "The table was sitting here," she said, "in the middle of the room. The ladder hung suspended from that wall. I remember as I climbed out, I was facing the kitchen. So it would have to be on that wall."

She and Mason moved to the spot she indicated, and she began to run her hand over the surface.

"Somewhere in here," she said, drawing a large circle with the beam of light.

"Well, I guess we better get started digging." He grinned and removed equipment from his belt. "Do you want to hold the light or dig, madam?"

Kate laughed softly. "I'll hold the light, but I give you fair warning. When you find the cracker box, I want to be the one who takes it out."

Mason worked for half an hour, digging out the stones one by one. By now Jake had rigged the light in the cabin, so that Kate could put down her flashlight and join in the search.

"Kate—" Mason stopped to lift his arm and wipe the perspiration from his forehead. "I hate to say this, but I think maybe you were having a dream. I don't think we're going to find a cracker tin filled with books."

"Yes, we are." Kate jabbed across a large stone with a small chisel. "I put it here, and I'm going to find it."

"Well, you better find something quick." Jake stuck his head into the door opening. "I'm going to have to turn in this equipment soon."

"And I'm pooped. I'm going to have to turn this body in to bed," Hayley added. "It would be more fun if all of us could be down there digging."

"Not enough room," Mason said with a grunt as he displaced another stone. Using his hand, he began to shovel loose dirt and gravel. Then he yelled, "Kate, I found it! I found the stone!"

Kate rushed to where he stood. Taking the flashlight, she beamed it into the deep hole. Her hand was shaking inside the leather glove she wore, but she extended it into the hollow until her fingers curled around the can.

"Did you find it?" Hayley yelled.

The can grated against the rocks as Kate dragged it out, loose pebbles splattering on the floor. Standing in the middle of the cellar, holding it in her hands, she felt tears prick her eyes. Completely enveloped in silence, she looked at Mason, who was grinning from ear to ear; then she glanced up, to see three faces peering down at her.

"This is it," she whispered.

"Open it, Kate," Nicki said, her voice low.

Holding the can against her body with her arm, Kate tried to pull off the lid, but it would not budge. "It's rusted with age," she said.

"Here, I'll help you." Mason moved closer and taking one of the smaller chisels, pressed it under the lid and pried it off.

Kate stripped off the gloves and reached into the box. Her fingers closed over her diary. "This is it," she murmured as she brought it out. "This is Caitlin's diary. I always knew that she had one."

"Oh, Kate," Nicki exclaimed, "this is marvelous!"

Mason dug into the tin and pulled out two smaller books. "What are these?" he asked.

Eyes only for the diary, Kate said, "Books of poetry. They belonged to Blaze."

Tears coursing down her cheeks, she opened the book to her last entry and began reading aloud. Everyone listened in rapt silence. Then Kate closed the book and clasped it to her chest with one hand. Using the other to pull herself up, she began to climb out of the cellar. How proud of her Grandpapa and Martin would have been; how proud Brent was going to be.

"May I see it?" Hayley asked as soon as Kate stepped onto the cabin floor.

Smiling at her favorite student, Kate handed it to her.

"Let me see," Nicki said, pushing between them, her hands reaching for the diary.

But Hayley swung the book away from Nicki, and Kate had to grin. It reminded her so much of the way they had acted toward each other as children. "Be careful," she admonished. "It's old."

"Look at the title page," Hayley said, and all of them clustered around her. She read, "This diary belongs to Caitlin McDonald." She flipped over several more pages, reading bits and pieces throughout the book. "What day was it when you started writing in the book, Kate?"

"June 25," she answered.

Only the gentle rustle of turning pages could be heard in the room.

Finally Hayley said, "I don't believe it, Kate. The handwriting is identical. I can't tell the difference."

"Of course there wouldn't be any difference," Nicki said. "She was Caitlin."

"Well," Jake said, breaking away from the group, "all of this is quite interesting, but I have to get this equipment back to the station. I don't think I want to be the one who has to explain why we were up here at the Blaze Callaghan cabin, digging in a cellar at midnight."

Mason laughed. "You don't think people will believe you?"

Jake ran a hand through his hair and shook his head. "They have a hard time accepting that Nicki had those psychic dreams. This is absolutely too bizarre for them."

"Well, Kate," Hayley said, returning the diary, "you finally have the material you've been looking for. Your book on Caitlin and Blaze will be the most definitive one that's ever been written."

"I would never have dreamed that our macho race car driver loved poetry," Mason said, gently handling the two volumes. "And two books of it. Kate, this discovery is remarkable. You don't know what these items will do for the reputation of our museum."

"If people believe they're that old," Nicki said. "Some may claim that they were planted. You know, Jake is right. All of this is rather bizarre."

"People won't doubt the authenticity of these babies," Mason said. "We'll have them carbon-dated."

"Now we know for sure that Blaze did not kill Caitlin and that old Sam was the villain," Kate murmured. "And on this pleasant note, I think it's time to dismiss class, students, and go home."

Carefully they made their way out of the building. Hayley and Nicki stayed close to Kate, the three of them using the flashlight to read in the diary, while the men loaded the gear into Jake's pickup.

"Since we missed dinner and none of us are that sleepy, why don't we go to McDonald's and have a bite to eat?" Mason suggested, grinning. "Don't you think it would be fitting, as we've just unearthed Caitlin McDonald's diary?"

"What time is it?" Kate asked.

"Why?" Hayley asked.

"I was wondering about Brent."

"He's a big boy," Jake said, "and can take care of himself. Don't be worried."

But she was and did not know why.

HAVING EATEN her hamburger and fries, Kate now sipped her cold drink and listened with half an ear to the story that Mason was telling. She found her gaze returning time and again to the main road as she strained to see the familiar Bronco pulling the trailer with the Runabout. She could hardly wait to share her good news with Brent. Having found Caitlin's diaries and Blaze's books—now locked in her car—she ought to be one of the happiest women on earth, yet she was not. She was unable to rejoice in her discovery.

Something nagged at her and she could not remember what it was. She reached down and caressed her ring finger—the finger on which she had worn the topaz ring, until she had taken it off to give it to Blaze. Leaning back against the padded booth, she glanced out the window—and saw an ambulance race down the street, its light spinning, the siren piercing the night.

"Well, good people," Jake said and rose, "I hate to part from such good company, but I'm a working man, and morning comes early."

"I need to be going, too," Kate added.

"Only you're not going to bed, are you?" Hayley teased as she and Mason stood and moved out of the booth. "You'll be up all night, reading those books and writing the final chapter to your book."

"And she'll be waiting for Brent," Nicki added, her eyes glowing. "She told me earlier that he's taking her to a sunrise breakfast."

"Hey," Mason interrupted and pointed. "Look out there! I'll bet that's one of your antique cars, Hayley."

Five heads turned simultaneously to look through the large plate-glass window at the strange sight. A wrecker was towing a crushed Bronco that was pulling a trailer. Its cargo had apparently at one time been covered with a tarpaulin, which now was loose and flapping in the wind. Exposed was what remained of an antique automobile.

"Oh, my God! It's Brent!" Kate screamed and rose to her feet, the back of her hand against her mouth. Now she remembered the dream she had had about Brent. She knew what had happened to him. Had Brent been killed in his Stanley Steamer like Blaze? *Dear God, no! Don't let it be true!* she prayed.

"It is Brent," she said in a deathly quiet tone. Her hand tightened around her purse, her dream about Brent returning with full force. She felt as if her heart had stopped beating...and might never beat again. "It can't be." But it was, and she knew it. She might be too late to save him. "Jake," she asked, "is there any way you can find out about the wreck?"

"Sure thing," he said and walked to one of the pay phones, dropped several coins into the slot and dialed. After a short conversation, he hung up the receiver and returned to them.

"Carlton, all right. One of them is in ICU, and they don't know if he'll live or not. The other is in critical condition, but he'll pull through."

"No!" Kate cried. "No, this can't be happening! I can't lose him again." If she did, her journey back to the past meant nothing.

"Kate," Jake said, gently clasping her shoulders, "get a grip on yourself. You're not going to be good to anyone if you're hysterical."

"I want to go see him," Kate said, tears flowing down her cheeks.

"Not tonight," Jake said. "You've been through too much tonight already. I'll go check on him and let you know."

Kate shook her head furiously, the coil coming loose, her hair falling down her back. "I'm going."

"I'll take her," Hayley said and draped an arm around Kate's shoulders. "She has a right to be with him. She's not going to rest until she knows he's all right."

"And I'll be there for his family," Kate said quietly. "They're going to need someone."

"Get in the pickup," Jake said with a sigh. "Nicki and I will drive you over there."

"Thanks, Jake," Kate said, reaching into her purse and extracting a tissue with which she wiped her eyes, "but you don't have to be my keeper. I'm perfectly capable of driving myself. You and Nicki go on home and go to bed. You have to get up in the morning. I don't."

"I don't want you to go by yourself," Hayley said. "Mason and I—"

"No," Jake said to Kate, "Nicki and I will take you. I'm the one who may be able to let you do more than sit in the waiting room. With a little luck you may be able to see your friend." Kate opened her mouth to protest, but Jake shook his head. "Being an officer of the law does have some rewards. Let's see what I can do to help you."

THE ANTISEPTIC ODOR assailing their nostrils, Kate and Nicki followed Jake and the briskly moving nurse down the corridor that seemed to be ten miles long.

"Thank you, Glenda," he said softly. "I really appreciate your doing this for me."

"Think nothing of it, Jake," the woman answered and reached up to adjust her white cap on equally white hair. "You've done so much for me. This is the least I could do for you. You say the fellow was going to drive his Stanley Steamer in the parade tomorrow?"

"Mmm-hmm," he answered. "It's one of the few Stanley Steamers left."

"Well, it's gone the way of the world. These young people just aren't careful enough."

When they reached the nurse's station, Jake asked about Brent and Caleb, and she nodded, moving to her files and flipping through them. She lifted the white receiver, laid it against her ear and talked in such low tones that although Kate could hear the sound of her voice, she could not make out the words.

"Brent Carlton is in ICU," the nurse said and replaced the receiver in the cradle. "His brother is in Room 125."

Tentacles of fear circled Kate's heart and contracted, robbing her of precious blood and oxygen. "I must see him," she said.

Glenda smiled and said, "I've done all I can to help you. You'll have to check up at ICU."

"Where is that?"

She pointed. "Down the hall, through the swinging double doors."

Kate looked first at Jake, then at Nicki. "I'm going to ICU to see him."

"Well," Nicki answered, "I guess we'll go with you. We've come this far, and might as well go the rest of the way."

The three of them were moving toward ICU when a huge man, wearing a short-sleeved, navy-blue cotton uniform and carrying a plastic bag in his right hand, walked into the waiting area.

"Jake!" he exclaimed. "What are you doing here?"

"Bill!" Jake looked at the paramedic and grinned. Walking over to him, he shook hands. "We're on our way to ICU to see Carlton. How did the accident happen?''

Bill shrugged his shoulders. "We're not sure, but we don't think another automobile was involved. They were hurt so badly, neither one could tell us anything. Since you're headed in that direction, would you mind taking this? It's their personal belongings. We were in such a hurry to get them into the hospital, we left this in the ambulance.''

By the time Jake had taken the bag and said, "Sure, why not?" Kate was already rushing down the corridor. She could not reach ICU quickly enough. Nicki and Jake followed at a more leisurely pace, but neither Jake nor Kate had any success in getting the nurse at the duty station to let them see Brent. She adamantly refused since neither was family, and the patient was in a coma and unable to talk with the police.

"What are you going to do?" Jake asked.

"I'm going to stay here," Kate replied. "You and Nicki can go on home.''

"I'll stay," Nicki said, her gaze straying over the deserted waiting area that was just being cleaned. "I don't want you here by yourself.''

"I don't mind," Kate replied, crossing her hands over her chest and rubbing her arms. "You have to get up early in the morning.''

"Kate," Nicki began and reached out to lay a hand on Kate's shoulder.

"I want to stay, and I don't mind being alone," Kate said and smiled weakly. "Besides, I have the diary and Blaze's books to read.''

Nicki nodded and dropped her hand. "You're determined to stay.''

"Yes.''

"Kate." Now Jake picked up the threads of his wife's argument, but Nicki caught his arm and hushed him with a shake of her head. He sighed and said, "Since you're staying, then, will you keep this and give it to the family?"

Nodding her head, Kate took the plastic bag from him. She saw them to the lobby, then returned to the waiting area. Every few minutes she walked to the swinging double doors that led to ICU and peeped through the small glass window. When Kate saw that the room was empty of nurses, she looked up and down the corridor. She saw no one. Gathering all her courage, she pushed on the door and entered the large room that seemed to have more life-support machines in it than lives to support. Moving from one cubicle to the other and peering through the glass window, she recognized none of the patients. Finally she came to the last one and knew it was Brent.

His face was turned away from her, but monitors, beeping and flashing, flanked both sides of his bed, and tubes ran from his body. She moved in order to see him better, her breath caught in her throat, and she fell back against the window. Although his face was swollen, cut and bruised, she recognized her love and knew that he, too, had traveled through time to be with her. If only she was not too late.

She opened the door and moved into the room. Standing next to the bed, she reached out and gently touched his cheek. "Hello, love." Tears burned her eyes. He didn't move; his lashes lay perfectly still against his cheeks. Bending, she brushed the lightest of kisses upon his lips. She straightened, and when she saw a tear on his cheek, she wondered whose it was—hers or his. She touched the tip of her fingers to it and wiped it away.

"Please don't leave me again," she begged, feeling loneliness as she had never felt it before. "Remember, darling, I'm your *dama de suerte*."

Did his lashes flutter? she wondered or had she just imagined it?

"Ma'am," a feminine voice said softly from the doorway, "are you related to the patient?"

Kate turned and looked at the young nurse, a different one than had been on duty earlier.

"If you're not, ma'am, you can't be in here with him. Visiting rights are restricted to immediate family only."

"I'm related," Kate said quietly. "I'm his—I'm his wife." The words were not a lie; Brent was her husband. That explained her having fallen in love with him the first time she saw him. They were indeed soul mates. She had been separated from him in one life, only to find him in another, and this time she would not let Brent go. She would not lose her love a second time. Blaze Callaghan had been the only love for Caitlin McDonald; Brent Carlton was the only love for Kate Norris. Closing her eyes, Kate silently thanked Caitlin and Blaze for giving her a second chance.

She slipped quietly out of the ICU unit and walked down the corridor to Caleb's room, marking her progress by the room numbers painted in large white letters on each door. 123. 124. 125. Her palm flattened against the sterile green panel and she pushed, the door gently whooshing open. Kate walked to the bed.

Caleb's head was turned to the side, his golden hair spread across the white pillowcase. His dark lashes were in direct contrast to the pasty-white skin of his cheeks. His face was cut, his forehead bandaged. Monitors stood on either side of the bed, graphs flashing with each breath he took. Oxygen hoses were fastened to his nostrils, and he was hooked up to intravenous tubing.

"Hello, Caleb," Kate said, swallowing the lump in her throat as she gazed at Brent's little brother.

Caleb's lids flickered open, and he stared at her a long time. Then his swollen lips curled into what Kate thought might have been a smile. He mumbled something and she bent closer, putting her ear to his mouth to hear him better. He spoke again, but was still too incoherent for her to understand.

A nurse walked into the room and set a tray of medicine on the night table. "Please don't stay long," she said. "He needs his rest."

"I won't," Kate promised.

She saw fear in Caleb's eyes; he reached out and caught her arm with his hands, his fingers biting into her flesh. She pressed her hand reassuringly over his. "Do you know who I am, Caleb?"

He moved his head in a slight nod.

"The nurse told me that your family had already been notified. They should be here any minute now." Again the almost imperceptible movement of his head. "I must go now, but I'll be back in the morning."

His fingers tightened on her arm and he pulled her closer. When her face was again close to his lips, he spoke, and this time she understood.

"Your brother?"

Caleb nodded and tears misted in his eyes.

"He's—he's sleeping now," she said. "I'll stay here at the hospital until your family arrives."

Caleb's expression was one of desperation, and this time he shook his head, groaning from the pain of moving. "My fault," he mumbled, his words slow and tortured. "He . . . can't . . . Don't let . . . him . . . die."

"I won't," Kate promised. "He's going to be fine."

Caleb stared into her face for a long time, then his grip loosened and his hand dropped to the bed. His swollen lips twitched again, he breathed deeply and closed his eyes.

Kate eased out of the room, hoping that she could keep her promise, praying that she could be true to her prophecy.

The only noise in the waiting room was the soft crunch of Kate's loafers on the highly polished linoleum tile. A cup of hot coffee in her hand, she paced a beaten path from the vending machine to the window, putting coins into the slot and reaching for the foam cup, then standing in front of the window and looking down on the asphalt parking lot, illuminated by huge streetlights.

Daylight should be here soon, she thought, glancing at the huge, round clock on the wall. Ten or eleven hours since the accident, since Brent had gone into the coma.

"Mrs. Carlton," a man called.

Kate spun around, the coffee sloshing out of the cup. Not bothering to correct the erroneous assumption, she hastily set down the coffee and reached into her pocket for a tissue with which to dab her hands.

The man, a large clipboard in hand, walked up to her. His thinning white hair was cut short and parted on the side; glasses covered his chocolate-brown eyes. "I'm Dr. Henry, a neurosurgeon. I'm taking care of your husband."

"How is he?" she asked. "Is he going to regain consciousness?"

He caught Kate's hands in his and guided her to one of the chairs. "Let's sit down, shall we?"

"Is he going to regain consciousness?" Kate asked again.

In a low, soothing voice, the doctor began to talk. His prognosis was dim, and the thought of Brent spending the remainder of his life in a coma devastated Kate. She slowly slipped into a state of deep depression. Phrases like "Brain-dead," "Life-support systems are keeping him alive," and "He cannot breathe on his own," kept running through her mind.

"When can I see him again?" she asked dully.

"Not until visiting hours in the morning," he said. "Now, I would advise you to go home and get some rest. You're not going to be good for anybody, not even yourself, like you are now. But I do want you to think about what I've just told you."

"Thank you," Kate murmured, reaching to pick up her purse and the plastic bag. Numbly she walked down the corridor toward Caleb's room. Easing by the nurse's station, she entered the room and he turned his head. His eyes brightened when he saw her.

"I've been with Brent," she said when she stood beside his bed. "He's—he's still sleeping, but the doctor has assured me that he's . . . he's going to be all right." She could not force herself to say that Brent was going to live. She was still exaggerating Brent's condition and the doctor's report, but she did so out of concern for Caleb. If she could not save Brent, perhaps she could save his younger brother. He sighed deeply, and she saw the tension ease out of his body.

"Your family still hasn't arrived, but I'll be coming back periodically to give you any news. Okay?"

He blinked, and she knew that he understood. His lids closed, and his dark lashes lay against his swollen, discolored cheeks. She laid her hand over his.

"Sweet dreams, Caleb. I'll be back shortly."

Before she left his room, she called for a taxi that was waiting by the time she exited the building. Tossing in the plastic bag, she told the driver to take her to The Stanley and slid onto the smooth plastic seat. Throughout the ride she sat there, staring at the hospital, a huge, redbrick building that spired into the air. Full of doctors with the best educations in the world, she thought, full of the latest technology, yet they could not save Brent.

Her left hand curled around the door handle, and she gazed longingly at her ringless finger. She had no right to condemn the doctors of this medical institution. She had traveled back in time with the knowledge to save Blaze and herself, but had not done so. In fact, because of her own stupidity she had been killed a second time...if that were possible.

Now the doctor, assuming she was Mrs. Brent Carlton, wanted her to kill Brent. One word, and the life-support systems would be taken away. A hot tear scalded a path down her cheek. She had lost both of the men whom she loved: Blaze and Brent.

Her entire life seemed to be predicated on abandonment. Just when she thought she had found the love and companionship that she so desired, it was snatched from her hand. Providence had allowed her to return to the past, but she was unable to figure out why. She had done nothing differently; she had not changed one shred of history, other than learning where the diary had been hidden.

Sure, she would be able to write a history book based on the information in the diary, but she had failed in her mission. Caitlin had died, and three days later so had Blaze. Now Brent, by some quirk of fate, on his way to the Stanley with his Runabout, had been in a car wreck and was now in a coma.

As the sun first showed its head in the eastern sky, the taxi pulled into the parking slot at The Stanley. When Kate reached for her purse, she realized that she had brought home Brent's and Caleb's personal belongings.

Oh, well, she thought, she would have to take them back, but not before she took a bath and changed clothes. Grabbing her purse, the books, and the plastic bag, she entered the hotel, going straight to her room. After a shower, a change of clothes and breakfast, Kate was behind the wheel of her car, heading for the hospital. Plastic bag in hand, she slipped unnoticed by the nurse's station, first going to ICU to check on Brent—whose condition had not changed—then on to Caleb's room.

In the shadow-filled room, she saw that Caleb was asleep. In a chair beside the bed huddled a small form. Pushing the door all the way open, she walked in. "Evelyn Carlton?" she called softly.

The woman sat up and stared at her through swollen eyelids. "Yes?"

"I'm Kate Norris. I was Kate Douglass, you know, the one who posed for the photographs of Caitlin McDonald—"

"Oh, yes," the little woman said, a smile flitting across her face, "I remember. The doctor thought you were Brent's wife."

Kate nodded. "I allowed them to think that, so I could visit with Brent. I wanted him to know that he wasn't alone."

"Thank you." Tears ran down her wrinkled cheeks. "I appreciate your doing that for my son."

Blinking back her own tears, Kate said, "I was here last night when they brought in Caleb and Brent. My friend is a policeman who was investigating the accident." She did not bother to relate the incidents in chronological order; the order was not significant. She held out the garment bag. "Somehow I ended up with their personal belongings."

"Thank you." Evelyn leaned forward to take the sack and laid it across her lap. "I'm glad you came back today. I'm sitting with Caleb. The boys are down in the ICU waiting room. I'll be going down there later for the visiting hour, but I find it more restful to stay here until then. Won't you sit down and stay awhile?"

Kate dragged up a chair and the two of them talked, first of all about Caleb. Caleb, having sustained only cuts and bruises, was recuperating beautifully and would be out of the hospital in a few weeks, at most. The doctors were not optimistic about Brent at all, but Evelyn could not accept their suggestion that she pull the plug. Kate, sharing Evelyn's pain, changed the topic so that Evelyn would be distracted. They caught each other up on all the major events in their lives for the past seventeen years.

Talking again about Brent, Evelyn said, "I never understood why he and Alyce married. Not that I didn't like her. I did. She was a sweet girl. But they just weren't suited for each other, and when he told her he was returning to the States, she asked for a divorce. She wanted to remain in Europe with her family. I'm just glad they had no children. Think what it would be like to have your grandchildren so far away from you." She moved and the bag slithered to the floor, the contents spilling out. "Oh, gracious!" she exclaimed and pushed herself out of the chair. "Look at me!"

"Don't worry," Kate said, immediately kneeling beside Evelyn to pick up shoes, socks, watches and rings.

"This is odd," Evelyn said, straightening up, holding something between her fingers. "I don't think I've ever seen it before." She walked over to the entrance and flipped on the switch. Light filled the room. She held the object to the light.

By this time Kate had returned all the brothers' personal effects to the bag and had placed it on the dresser. She turned to find Evelyn scrutinizing the object that she had found. "What is it?" she asked.

"A ring," Evelyn answered wonderingly. "A topaz ring."

The word was hardly out of the woman's mouth before Kate was standing in front of her, staring at the ring...her ring...the topaz ring that Blaze had given her. It was all she could do to keep from snatching it from Brent's mother.

"That's my ring," Kate said quietly, amazed at how calm she sounded. "It must have dropped into the bag. My—my husband gave it to me before he died. It's my birthstone."

"It's really a lovely ring," Evelyn said and handed it to her, but Kate did not put it on.

Knowing now what she had to do, Kate picked up her purse. "Evelyn, I must go, but I'll be back to check on you later. Make a list of anything you need, and I'll be glad to get it for you."

Kate was so excited that she was trembling. As soon as she left Caleb's room, she headed for the ICU unit. Peeking into the waiting area, she saw two men, who she supposed were Brent's brothers, evidently waiting for the visiting hour. But Kate did not have time to wait; she must return the ring to Brent. If her trip in time meant anything, it meant that she should save him. His life was not in the past but now, here in the present, and she *could* save him.

She opened the door, marched into his room and picked up his hand, pushing the ring onto his little finger; the fit was too tight for it to be easily removed. "There, darling, I've done all I can. The rest is up to you." Holding his hand in her own and running her fingers over the brilliant stone, she looked down at him and whispered:

I have been here before,
But when or how I cannot tell:

She was too choked up to continue. Closing her eyes, she sniffed back the tears. Then she felt his fingers curl around hers. Her eyes flew open and she gazed down—into the most beautiful blue eyes that she had ever seen. He spoke.

You have been mine before,—
How long ago I may not know:

"Oh, Brent!" Tears of joy coursed down her cheeks.
"Hello, my Lady Luck," he said. "I heard you calling me and I returned."
"From where?" she asked.

He wrinkled his brow. "I'm—not sure. Everything is so fuzzy. My Steamer, it's wrecked, isn't it?"

Kate nodded. "It's ruined, darling." *In fact, both of them are wrecked.*

"If I can find another one, would you like to help me restore it?"

"Yes."

He looked at his hand, in particular at the ring that fitted snugly on his little finger. "I thought I had lost it," he said.

"No," she said, thanking both Blaze and Caitlin for having given her a second chance.

"Kate, I don't understand—"

She smiled. "I'll explain it to you when you're stronger. Right now we're going to concentrate on getting you all better."

His hand tightened on hers. "Don't leave me, Kate."

She laughed softly. "Never, my darling."

Epilogue

Estes Park, Colorado
1990

Six months later Kate stood on the mountain bridge that overlooked The Stanley Hotel and awaited Brent's return from Elk Ridge Resort. As she listened to the song of the aspen in the autumn breeze, she gazed at the rushing brook, then at the white cliff that rose behind the river to spear into the sky. The mountainside was splashed golden with sunshine. The mountains gave life; they promised life. Kate would be forever grateful to Blaze Callaghan and Caitlin McDonald, because they had given her a second chance to find happiness and love. She would always love them, but each day they were becoming more and more a pleasant memory; they no longer held a place of priority in her thoughts. She had said goodbye to them and was now embarking on her journey in this life.

Holding out her left hand, she gazed at the topaz ring on the fourth finger—her wedding ring, given to her first by Blaze and now by Brent. Three months ago she and Brent had been married in a morning ceremony held on the front lawn of The Stanley. Hayley and Nicki had jokingly accused her of having a whirlwind courtship, but Kate knew differently. She and Brent had loved each other through the ages; they were soul mates who were so determined to be together in this life to fulfill their destiny that they had traveled the universe together and had crossed the barriers of time.

Kate felt Brent's presence behind her, seconds before his hands clasped her shoulders and he brought her to rest against his chest. "I always know where to find you, love," he murmured; Kate smiled to herself. How many times had she heard him call her that? Yet it thrilled her anew each time. "How was your trip to Denver?"

"Marvelous," she answered and turned in his arms. Sliding her palms up his chest, she gazed into the eyes that were as soft as sapphire pools. Her hair, hanging in deep waves about her face and shoulders, brushed her cheeks as she lifted her face for his kiss, and after a long, breathless moment, she murmured against his lips, "How was your day at the office?"

He grinned. "I'll bet I didn't spend nearly as much money working as you did shopping."

She returned the grin. "And I'll bet you didn't enjoy your day nearly as much as I did mine. Come into the house and I'll show you what I bought."

Slowly they broke the embrace, caught hands, and walked toward the log cabin. Then Brent stopped and turned to look at her. "Would you rather we live somewhere else?" he asked, and Kate could hear the concern in his tone.

She smiled reassuringly and shook her head. "No, darling, this is what I want right now." Her gaze strayed to the cabin nestled against the side of the mountain. "I think this is one of the most beautiful places in the whole world, and right now I want its peace."

Brent laughed and caught her left hand, lifting it and looking at her ring. "It takes so little to make you happy, my darling—a cabin in the wilds of the Colorado mountains and an antique topaz ring." He brushed the pad of his thumb over the gem. "I was quite surprised when Mrs. Engels insisted that you keep the ring."

Tears misted in Kate's eyes, and she lifted her hands to cradle his face. "She understood what the ring means to me."

"To us," Brent said and caught her tightly in his arms as if he feared losing her. "When I first met you, Kate, I couldn't understand your preoccupation with Caitlin McDonald and Blaze Callaghan. I'm thrilled that you found the books and diary that are going to enable you to write a definitive work on Caitlin and Blaze."

"But you still don't believe I traveled back in time," Kate teased her husband.

Brent shrugged. "It's difficult for me to believe, love, but I don't discount your story. Whatever happened was real to you, and that's all that matters to me."

Kate laughed softly into his shoulder. "I know this is a hard admission for you, Brent Carlton, but it proves that you're not the cynic you were when I first met you."

"No." He pulled away to look deeply into her eyes. "I'm not. I can't disallow what happened, Kate. I know for a fact that you came to me in that wreck. Had it not been for you, I wouldn't be alive today. You, my precious *dama de suerte*, saved my life."

"Love knows no barriers, not even time. If there is such a thing as reincarnation—" and Kate truly believed there was "—love is the ultimate reincarnation. It's forever." *We're fortunate that we were able to re-*

turn as the lovers we were before, Kate thought, promising herself that she would take full advantage of this chance she had at love.

"Remember that day so long ago, when you told me that you would only love once?" Brent asked.

Kate nodded and searched his face for a clue to his urgency.

"I have to know, Kate. Do you love me, or are you in love with the memory of Blaze?"

Kate smiled and pressed her palm against his beard-stubbled cheek. "You are my first and only love, my darling."

Brent sighed and moved his head to kiss the palm of her hand. "I think I've loved you from the very beginning, but you were so young."

Kate nodded her head. "I know."

Brent caught her hand and guided it from his mouth. Bending his head, his mouth gently touched hers in a breath of a kiss. Kate's arms slipped about his shoulders, and she drew him nearer, surrounding him with her love. Moments later he raised his lips from hers, swept her into his arms and began to walk toward the cabin, his boots crunching on the rocky ground.

"Are you ready to see what I bought today?" she asked on a trill of laughter and wondered what her two lovely protégées would think if they could see their staid college professor now.

"I am, but not in that order," Brent replied, his eyes twinkling. "I'm taking my bride across the threshold and into the house, so I can make love to her first."

"Do you think we have time before our guests arrive?" Kate asked, her gaze going to the smoking barbecue grill on the back deck. "You do remember that

Hayley and Mason and Nicki and Jake are coming over for dinner.''

"I remember, and we'll make time," Brent said and without setting her down, opened the door and carried her into the cabin. "Besides, they'll just have to understand."

As he laid her on the bed and bent over her, Kate stared into his face, her arms looped around his neck. "Lady Luck has been good to Hayley, Nicki and me," she said. "Each of us has found true love and happiness, and we didn't have to leave our valley to do it. Thank you, darling, for allowing Nicki to open stables at Elk Ridge."

"Mmm-hmm," he murmured as he stretched out beside her and began to unbutton her blouse.

"And just think Hayley and Mason are going to spend their honeymoon in Brazil with Mom and Dad, tromping around those Mayan ruins. Mason's bound to return with something nice for his museum. But nothing quite as distinctive as the Caitlin McDonald diary," she added.

"Mmm."

"But I dare say," Kate continued as if she had his full attention, "we'll be the first of the three couples to have a baby."

"Mmm-hmm," he murmured again, his mouth moving in slow provocative motions across her collarbone. "If we don't, it won't be for lack of trying, love."

Kate chuckled. "Dr. Haversham assures me that by summer's end we'll have at least one baby."

"What—" Brent bolted upright "—are you telling me?"

Kate's chuckle turned into rich laughter. "I'm telling you that I'm pregnant, and our baby is due next August."

"Oh, Kate," he murmured, embracing her, "I don't know what I would do without your love. You've made me the happiest man in this world."

"Keep up the sweet nothings, darling," Kate said. "In about nine months I think you're going to change the words of that song."

"Never, love," he whispered. "As surely as you and I were destined to be together, we were destined to have this baby." He flopped over and pushed himself up on the pillows, still cradling her in his arms. "If it's a girl, what do you think about naming her—?"

Laying her head on her husband's chest and listening to the rhythmic beat of his heart, Kate stared out the window at the autumn loveliness of the mountains and listened to her beloved. The sun, sinking low in the western sky, cast the Colorado mountains in gentle colors. Grandpapa had always contended that the mountains were magical, and Kate believed him. The mountains had saved the topaz ring and given it to Constance Engels, who had kept and protected it for so many years. Here on this mountain, high above The Stanley, Kate had given the topaz ring to Brent before she left the present for her journey into the past; and it was here that she had given the ring to Blaze when she returned to the present.

"If it's a boy," Brent said, breaking into her ruminations, "I'd like us to name him Patrick."

"I'd like that," Kate murmured, "and so would Grandpapa."

HARLEQUIN
American Romance®

COMING NEXT MONTH

#341 IMAGINE by Anne McAllister

Frances Moon was a woman of the '90s. The 1890s, that is. At least she was convinced she'd have been more comfortable back then. She had everything she needed in the wilds of Vermont. And if she'd wanted a man, she could create one. Then Jack Neillands showed up. Inch-for-masculine-inch he embodied her perfect man. But fantasy heroes were safe and predictable . . . and Jack was anything but!

#342 LUCKY PENNY by Judith Arnold

Syndicated columnist Jodie Posniak got all sorts of household hints, recipes and questions from her readers. Until now she'd never gotten a love letter. Into Tom Barrett's missive, Jodie read an aching over lost love. Though his words were simple, she envisioned a man who would charm her with his tenderness . . . and ignite her with his passion.

#343 SPIRITS WILLING by Leigh Ann Williams

New Yorker Angie Sullivan flew off to the Coast to collaborate with a Hollywood living legend on her autobiography and found her employer distracted by a New Age mystic who'd spellbound Tinseltown. Angie suspected she was being hoodwinked California-style. Angie's own mental energy was being diverted by guru biographer Lance Wright, who definitely enhanced Angie's aura—on a purely sensual plane.

#344 BEST BEHAVIOR by Jackie Weger

Willa Manning longed to give her beloved adopted daughter the grandparents she dreamed of, but not at the risk of losing her forever. Nicholas Cavenaugh understood Willa's reservations, but he'd promised to bring his friends the child their lost daughter had borne so far from home. Fate, which had brought Nicholas and Willa together, had put them on opposite sides in the only struggle that could tear them apart.

In April, Harlequin brings you the
world's most popular romance author

JANET DAILEY

No Quarter Asked

Out of print since 1974!

After the tragic death of her father, Stacy's world is shattered. She needs to get away by herself to sort things out. She leaves behind her boyfriend, Carter Price, who wants to marry her. However, as soon as she arrives at her rented cabin in Texas, Cord Harris, owner of a large ranch, seems determined to get her to leave. When Stacy has a fall and is injured, Cord reluctantly takes her to his own ranch. Unknown to Stacy, Carter's father has written to Cord and asked him to keep an eye on Stacy and try to convince her to return home. After a few weeks there, in spite of Cord's hateful treatment that involves her working as a ranch hand and the return of Lydia, his ex-fiancée, by the time Carter comes to escort her back, Stacy knows that she is in love with Cord and doesn't want to go.

Watch for *Fiesta San Antonio* in July and
***For Bitter or Worse* in September.**

JDA-1

HARLEQUIN
American Romance®

Live the

Rocky Mountain Magic

Become a part of the magical events at The Stanley Hotel in the Colorado Rockies, and be sure to catch its final act in April 1990 with #337 RETURN TO SUMMER by Emma Merritt.

Three women friends touched by magic find love in a very special way, the way of enchantment. Hayley Austin was gifted with a magic apple that gave her three wishes in BEST WISHES (#329). Nicki Chandler was visited by psychic visions in SIGHT UNSEEN (#333). Now travel into the past with Kate Douglas as she meets her soul mate in RETURN TO SUMMER #337.

ROCKY MOUNTAIN MAGIC—All it takes is an open heart.